SONGS

FOR THE
NEW DEPRESSION

SONGS
FOR THE
NEW DEPRESSION

A NOVEL
KERGAN EDWARDS-STOUT

C

circumspect press

circumspect press

Library of Congress Control Number: 2011915793
ISBN: 978-0-9839837-1-2 (hc)
ISBN: 978-0-9839837-0-5 (pbk)
ISBN: 978-0-9839837-2-9 (ebk)
10 9 8 7 6 5 4 3 2 1

Book Jacket Design by Russell Noe
Author Photograph by Scott Council

Printed in the United States of America

For

Shane Michael Sawick,
who introduced me to
Bette Midler,
Paris,
and Bobby Short,

and for

my family,
Russ, Mason, and Marcus,
who introduced me to
myself

SONGS
FOR THE
NEW DEPRESSION

PROLOGUE

JAMES BALDWIN ONCE WROTE that Americans lack a sense of doom, yet here I stand. Although I am not entirely certain that doom is indeed what brought me here, except most literally, that yin-yang, sturm und drang, heaven and hell push-pull has guided me, nay—ruled, since I saw my first hairy chest. Though others have struggled mightily in their quest for self-acceptance, for me, being gay has never been an issue. And in all of my hours spent contemplating the propriety of acting on such desire, I have encountered no downside. For if all roads lead to that same dreary destination of death, why not take the more enjoyably scenic?

Opposite, on the Right Bank, Sacré Coeur perches on the horizon, the late afternoon sun turning its pure white travertine a rich shade of gold. Without bitterness, I offer it a nod, acknowledging its divine providence in leading me to this place.

Wind, bracing here as always, whips through the crowd, prompting a herd of elderly tourists to warily step back from the edge. Watching, I wonder why they bother. For if, by some strange twist, one *had* been swept up by the prevailing thrusts of the invisible and flung to their death, would it truly have been tragic? Perhaps they would have had an hour, a day, or even twenty years more, but eventually they would have died just the same, albeit in far more perfunctory fashion. But to plunge from la Tour d'Eiffel? Can there even *be* a more spectacularly impressive departure?

This is a trip I have made many times, but never alone, and never to stay. Now that I am a denizen, my appreciation of Paris is bound to be different; in fact, ordained to be. How I pray, though, that the old pleasures will still taste as sweet. Please, let my former haunts retain their familiar allure! If there is any justice, permit my memories to register as before, unaltered by time or circumstance. For if I am here, and yet everything changed, how will I ever find peace?

The elevator doors send a rush of Japanese out onto the platform, forcing me back inside the vestibule. Turning to view the glassed tableau of a mannequined Monsieur Eiffel visiting with Thomas Edison, I consider my finger-smudged reflection. Not quite as forced as the figures before me, nor as dusty, but not altogether normal, either. My skin retains its ashen tint and the brown of my eyes is somewhat hazy. Still, given the road I have traveled, I could look worse.

It seems impossible that my choices have led me here, to this spot, drained of every ounce of life. Despite my long-held belief that one's journey—or ride, if you will—holds more importance than one's destination, I am no longer so cocksure. For if I, at age 17, had been handed a snapshot of myself as I am right here and now, providing the gift of foresight, isn't there a chance I might have chosen a different path?

Monsieur Eiffel gives no hint as to his view, appropriately leaving Thomas Edison to pop the requisite light bulb above my head. I linger, but none appears.

Perhaps I would have ended up here, regardless of choice. Perhaps it was destiny. Fate. An unlucky draw of the straw. Whichever, it is much too late to ponder, for no amount of wishing can change who I am or what I have done.

Were my life a play, it could easily be broken into three acts: before, after, and redemption. But while living, I never was able to step back, untangle myself, peel back the layers, and see things for what they were. Aside from Jon, life seemed confusing, filled with uncertainty. Now though, I can see that had I just made one single decision differently, all that came aft could have been forever altered.

While the tourists just beyond "ooh" and "ahh" at the surrounding sights, I stare into the masks of Eiffel and Edison, pondering the need for such a display. What could its creators have hoped to achieve? No matter how lifelike, these poses cannot possibly compete with the city below, teeming with the laughter and terror collectively known as "life."

I am about to journey on, shaking my head at their folly, when a thought occurs.

Perhaps these figures serve not to compete, but to remind. Remind us that, in spite of our vision of an omnipotent God, pulling our strings and jangling our nerves, it is the human who debates, chooses, and acts. It is the human who regrets. It is the human who remembers. And it was a human who envisioned a skyline commanded by a metal sculpture of grace, stature, and beauty—and built it.

But for that conscious decision, Monsieur Eiffel's vision would have remained purely spectral. He would have died, just the same, and none would have been the wiser. Wandering along the Seine, tearing chunks from our baguettes, we would have been blissfully unaware of the gigantic hole gaping high above our heads. But, happily, Monsieur Eiffel resolved to act, and this marker upon which I now stand, etched on so many souls, remains as proof of his ride.

PART I
GABE: 1995

"Shiver Me Timbers" by Tom Wait
Track 1A, Side B of Bette Midler's album,
Songs for the New Depression

GABE: 1995

WITH MORE THAN 200 holiday CD's alone, it is impossible to choose. The music must be subtle, bittersweet, emotional—but not weepy. Dance music and rock are out, so skip ABBA, the B-52's, and Blondie. Karen Akers, although I love her, is much too wobbly. Kathleen Battle and Sarah Brightman at their most ethereal could work. But nothing overtly classical. Whenever I hear that at some queen's funeral, I think, "Jeez, she never listened to that! Put on some Jerry Herman."

If I was doing this my way, as I truly wanted, all that would be played upon my demise would be Midler. As in Bette. The Divine Miss M, herself. But I don't need the backlash that would cause. Perhaps, if I'd died in the 80's, I could have pulled it off. But not now. No, little Miss M ruined everything when she cashed that first tainted check from Disney. She may have gained a billion more followers by selling out for celluloid stardom, but not fans who really understood her. What the masses got was an airbrushed Canter's waitress; a Celine Dion who tells fart jokes.

In any event, Miss M need not worry about saving a date for the festivities. Exactly when my demise will be, I can't really say, as not even I am desperate enough to commit suicide merely to guarantee a clear date on my friends' calendars.

The choice of music, though, is extremely important. You want people to feel comfortable enough to grieve, or laugh, or flirt, but not so comfortable that they have a really, really good time. ("We had *such* fun, we're coming back tomorrow!") Cunt-ree western is out, as is techno, rap, bluegrass, jazz (too disorienting), children's songs, and fado. About the only thing left is cabaret, which I simply will not put my guests through.

Anyway, it's too late now for any grand decisions. Jon went to sleep hours ago. Although how he can sleep at a time such as this is beyond me. Has he no compassion? No soul? That I should be up at this dark hour, unable to rest, and yet he slumbers peacefully... It's unfair, to say the least.

Well, perhaps I'm the one being unfair, overstating my case. To clarify, my T-cells are currently at "acceptable" levels, I haven't had any major infections since '93, and the drugs seem to be working. Currently, my viral load reads as undetectable, sending my doctors into giddily optimistic spasms. But I'm not convinced. I know that, somewhere, deep inside where it counts, this virus is gaining ground, gnawing through me quickly and voraciously. Despite the doctors' proclamations to the contrary, I know that I will not survive the year. It is not a lack of willpower or strength that will do me in, it is the virus itself. I've always known it would get me, and am at peace with that knowledge. In fact, there's something empowering in giving myself over to the disease. Now, *I* can control *it*, instead of the fear controlling me. Not that I can lessen its affect or stop the disease—or that I want to—but that I can ride this kayak down the river and over the falls, without being thrown out along the way.

"For Christ's sake," Jon cries out down the hallway. "Will you turn out the light and come to bed? You can die tomorrow."

My always-sympathetic husband. But he's right, in a way. Tomorrow, I just might die.

Upon reflection, I realize that your image of me right now might be a bit skewed. Actually, kind of fucked. I am neither a nihilist, inordinately depressed, nor jaded. Though I can be and have been all of the above, and fully expect to be again.

But I have been battling this monster since 1987 and have learned that, for me, going along for the ride is easier and less taxing than fighting. Giving myself over to HIV is actually an act of self-preservation.

And despite, or maybe because of, the advances in treatment, my body is now on the decline. The doctors can quote any outstanding test result they want, but one quick glance in the mirror tells me all I need to know. For example, I now have AZT butt, defined as a loss of muscle and visible sag. (My ass, once talked about all over town, now looks suspiciously like a Shar-Pei, prompting even more talk around town.) And my face... My face, alas, has changed, too. Inflamed lymph nodes have given me a jaw line resembling a boomerang. And the combustible combination of pills, gel caps, tablets, capsules, shots, powders, and Satan's sperm, which I devour daily, has ignited a flame that eats at my face still, leaving harsh lines and cavernous skin. The only noticeable physical improvement has been the unexpected emergence of cheekbones. Jon jokes that I'm just like Jodie Foster. But it is a hollow laugh I give in return, for I know that it is not age which bears such features, but death.

Awwwwwww! Jesus Christ—Morbidity 101. Again. Gotta change that fuckin' channel. Find me some happy talk.

Jon has been a godsend in so many ways. And yet, he's also the biggest pain I've ever met. To say that I was initially attracted to him would be a lie. Taken individually, Jon's physical assets are quite remarkable: full, eager lips, curving into a grin; small round glasses hiding dark, penetrative eyes; ears that tilt forward slightly, giving him the look of competent listener. But once put back together, Jon's looks can only be described as Geek-Meister. That I should love him so still takes me by surprise. For when we first met, I was neither searching for, nor desiring, a partner.

In 1993, having wandered for years through a world of darkened back rooms in sticky shoes, I found myself suddenly dumped into a brightly-lit fluorescent world of doctors' offices and hospital hallways. Unexpectedly, and with unnecessary irony, a fatal disease prompted me to save my life. With dramatic swiftness, I violently shattered the cockpit window and pulled my war-torn body from the self-induced wreckage.

Out of work and desperately in need of a job, I perused my resumé. With past jobs including substitute teacher, interior designer, sales (art gallery and retail), bathhouse attendant, actor, and jackhammer operator, my future was mapped out for me as clearly as the skies above: my destiny lay in AIDS education. I had all the qualifications necessary: I was cute, needed work, and possessed the ability to become histrionic over even the smallest non-issue. In short, I was the perfect candidate for the world of non-profit. (It is important to note that today I would not get that same job, unless I could also become histrionic in Spanish.)

And so it was that I arrived at the Los Angeles Department of Eat, Drink, and AIDS; otherwise known as LA-DE-DA. Given the above-mentioned qualifications, I was quickly promoted beyond my ability level to the position of Director of Volunteer Resources. As I'd never been a director before, much less a volunteer, I was somewhat nervous about the demands of the job and wondered if I had what it would take to succeed. I quickly learned, however, that my past jobs proved instrumental in my new role as Emperor of the HIV Kingdom. From my stint of substitute teaching, I'd learned how to separate unruly children, which proved invaluable in brokering peace between the warring Directors of Education and Communication. From my extensive experience of selling clothes at J. Jacobs, I had learned to guide volunteers to the programs in which they were needed, regardless of fit. And from my days picking up cum rags at Club Way-Ho, I had learned how to give expert blow jobs, which is essential for volunteer retention.

And it was in this glorious, heady time that I found myself leading our weekly Vogue (Volunteer Orientation Group), as one of my serfs had called in sick. Of course, we in the Vogue knew that the real reason Miss Thang called in was because she was down on her knees pleasuring a well-known local weatherman at his historic Los Feliz home.

But as Miss Thang was otherwise occupied, it was I who addressed our new recruits that cloudy Thursday evening. And it was I who took note of the geeky volunteer's cute cowlick.

And it is I who holds my dear, loving Jon in my arms tonight.

"Where is the research?"

"Do I look like Dr. Gottlieb?"

"So, what—you implicitly trust everything you're told? You swallow whatever your drug company-sponsored doctor tells you? That could be what's killing you!"

I took a deep breath before responding. In these new volunteer orientations, you usually get a bunch of sheep, but you never know. Sometimes people wander in off the street...

"Well, Mr. Frank—"

"Jon—"

"Jon." God, I liked them feisty. "Do I know for certain that HIV causes AIDS? No, I do not. Could it be that AZT actually causes AIDS? Probably not, but I don't know for sure. But I do know this: the odds are in my favor. You can believe in conspiracy theories, or think the doctors don't know what they're doing, or that AIDS is caused by eating blue cheese and pork rinds when the moon is full. Believe whatever you want. But within these walls—these hallowed walls of LA-DE-DA— our message is this: HIV attacks the T-cells, leading to a weakened immune system, which is susceptible to illness, which can lead to death. That is what we believe, and that is what we teach. Now." This guy had me so riled, I almost forgot there were others in the room. "Moving on..."

Jon's hand shot up into the air. "But if you're not certain—"

"Jon, I'm not certain I'll be alive to get up in the morning, but I brush my teeth at night just the same. I have a choice: do I believe all I've learned about HIV since working here, or not? And do I trust that my knowledge is correct? Do I trust that every pill I take will work its magic on me? I don't have to believe it, but I do. I believe it with every fiber of my being. I trust it, and all I'm doing, because I want to live."

In a perfect world, the volunteers would have remained silent for a moment, savoring my impassioned rhetorical skill, praising my brilliance while wiping racing tears from their cheeks. Then there was Jon.

"But—"

I exploded. "Goddamn it—what the fuck are you doing here? Why did you walk in the fucking building? You could be at ACT UP. Or on a Tina Louise Hayride. Or at a Course in Gobbledygook... Why are you here?"

For a moment, it was silent. Jon focused on his feet before looking up at me with the most pained eyes imaginable. "I'm here because I'm scared. I'm scared—and I want to help."

Being challenged isn't necessarily a bad thing, so long as the aim is to better and strengthen rather than tear down. And better is exactly what Jon did with me, on a daily basis. Although assigned to the Phone Friends program, which met in the building's windowless dungeon, Jon stopped by each day, popping his head into my office to say hello. At first, he got on my nerves. But soon I began to look forward to his daily assaults. Stupid, challenging people are annoying, but with smart people, the sparring becomes an aphrodisiac.

We began to meet after work. First, it was only coffee. Oh, how The Abbey walls burned with the fire of our discourse! Seeing our eyes locked, faces flushed, as we debated everything from politics to plays to the existence of God, others would veer quickly away from our table, fearful of being singed by the flames. Coffee soon turned into dinner, dinner into movies, movies into concerts, concerts into everything. We became inseparable. And yet...

We hadn't even kissed. The fervor from our conversations was so intense that, by the time an evening had ended, I'd often feel as if we *had* had sex, so wet was I from perspiration. Perhaps we feared that the physical could not possibly surpass the emotional. But that didn't stop me from fantasizing.

I'd lay awake for hours, stroking myself lightly as I imagined his fingers brushing mine. The images were never salacious. I dreamt of his face, impassioned by rhetoric. His arms, tense with meaning. And that lopsided grin, warily admitting that I might have a point—one that he would thoughtfully consider.

Luckily for Jon, though his opinions were often misguided, he did not suffer from a lack of intelligence. He knew when he was wrong and was open to learning more. Emotional and psychological growth were stimulants, inspiring him to further his experiences and delve more deeply into the unknown.

I, on the other hand, was usually correct in my views. Spurring him on, I often felt as if I were his personal 'Enry 'Iggins, preparing him for the ball. I never voiced such thoughts, certain that he would disagree, but I did find pleasure in knowing that I wielded that power.

Being infinitely generous, I would gently prod him toward important books, music—anything that he might have overlooked in his studies. Plus, my varied life experiences aided immensely in Jon's search for self-discovery. Indeed, much can be learned about life by cleaning rooms littered with used condoms.

"You're so fucking irritating," Jon exploded, shaking the walls of my office. "No matter what the topic, you think you're right."

"Moi?"

"It's more important for you to be correct than fair."

"What's wrong with honesty? Just because I have a wide range of interests—"

"Can't we talk about things without taking sides? It's the struggle to expand oneself that's important. Not just choosing—or *guessing*—correctly."

I paused, letting his anger subside, as I knew it would. "What, exactly, are we arguing about?"

Jon reached into his backpack, pulling out the match that would ignite our first full-blown fight.

"This." In his hand he held a CD. The original cast recording of *Cabaret*.

"Where—?" I stammered. "How did you get that?"

"I had it at home." He handed it to me. "Read it."

"But—"

"Read the credits."

"Look," I said, trying to slip the CD onto the desk unnoticed. "Let's talk at lunch. There's a great Thai place—"

"Read it!" Jon shoved the CD back into my hands. "Out loud."

"Can't we just...?"

With a force I didn't know he had, Jon spun me about, marching me into the outer office. Cupping his hands, Jon beckoned my busy volunteers. "Come on, everyone! Gather round! Witness a sight unseen in 30-some very-odd years. Your tireless leader—for the first time ever—will publicly *eat crow!*"

As a crowd quickly gathered, I tried to make a break, but the encroaching swarm pushed me back to Jon's side.

A blonde bimbo intern, unfamiliar with our strange tribal ways, bopped into the office, "Hey, gang, what's going on?"

One volunteer answered, "I think they're raffling off a prize. Some kind of bird."

"No," said another, crusty nose ring swinging. "It's a lover's quarrel."

"Those two are *lovers*?" gasped the intern.

"Not yet," said Mucus. "But just watch."

The crowd assembled to witness my humiliation now surpassed that of our most recent fundraiser. Jon stepped onto a chair. "Ladies, gentlemen, and girls, thank you for being here today to witness the unbelievable, the unfathomable. A most incredible act will occur," he paused. "Gabriel will be proven wrong."

A gasp ripped through the assembled, for they knew that such a moment was not likely to be repeated in their lifetimes.

"That's right, my friends. Our own Gabe Travers will own up to a mistake, publicly and humbly."

The volunteers eyed each other worriedly. Even if I had been wrong in the past, I'd never admitted it. I am a firm believer in stating what you have to say with conviction, especially when uncertain of the truth. Would I, these volunteers' diligent leader, their moral compass, submit?

Jon stepped down, gently pushing me toward the chair. I made a whispered plea. "I'll give you anything... The keys to my kingdom!"

He pushed me from behind, more forcefully. "Read."

Shakily, I stepped onto the chair. The room was silent, breathless with anticipation.

I gave it one last desperate shot, yelling, "Quick! Janet

Jackson is over in the food bank!"

The bleary-eyed queens eyed me savagely. I should have known better than to try that with a breed able to sniff out celebrities at 300 yards.

And so, in an unnatural voice, audible only to animals and gossip-loving queers, I began to read.

"Uh, *Cabaret*. The new musical starring Jill Haworth, Jack Gilford, Bert Convy, and Lotte Lenya." I coughed, clearing my quickly gathering phlegm. "Boy—look at that! Joel Grey gets billed below Bert Convy. What does *that* do to your self-esteem, huh? And speaking of Joel—did anyone else catch him on *Brooklyn Bridge?* Not bad, huh? Or how about in *Kafka?* Wow, is he an entertainer or what?!? But that daughter—Jennifer— whoever told her she was an ingénue? If only she'd stuck to character parts..." Sensing the lack of responsiveness, my patter slowed to a trickle.

"We're waiting," Jon persisted, arms crossed adamantly. I looked again at the credits.

"Book by Joe Masterhoff. Based on the play by John Van Druton and the stories of Christopher Isherwood." I stopped, unable to continue. "This is really hard for me."

One volunteer reached up, taking my hand in his, "It's okay, honey. We're here for you."

The bubble-headed intern turned on her heels. "I don't get this. You guys are way too faggoty for me." The nearest queen viciously shoved her to the door, kicking it closed behind.

"Continue," said Jon.

I hesitated. "I—. Uh, music... music by John Kander. Lyrics, Fred Ebb."

"Who?" queried Jon.

"Ebb. Fred Ebb. Music and lyrics by Kander and Ebb."

"Not Kurt Weill?" Jon pushed. "Not music and lyrics by Kurt Weill?"

"No," I admitted, the CD hanging limply in my hands. "Kander and Ebb. Kander and Ebb did *Cabaret.*"

"Well, what did you think, honey?" gasped one nearby queen. "Everyone knows that!"

As the room burst into a swell of gleeful satisfaction, so

happy to see me taken down a notch, Jon took my hand, pulling me down from the chair and into my office. Shutting the door, I could still hear the excited voices beyond, replaying my humiliation for latecomers.

"It had to be done," Jon stated, not as excuse, but as fact. Unable to respond, I sank silently into my chair.

For the next hour, Jon tried to talk with me. To get me to see the wisdom of what he had done. But it was futile. He had embarrassed me in front of my colleagues. He had orchestrated my public humiliation and expected gratitude. Rather he, Jon said, than someone who didn't care about me.

When, after getting no more from me than a shrug, he finally left, I pondered his definition of caring. Whereas our past tangos had been harmless, stimulating even, this felt like betrayal. Maybe I had it coming. In fact, I'm certain that I did. But that knowledge did not mitigate my pain.

For the next two weeks, I screened all calls, took my lunches early and out, and generally did everything possible to avoid contact with Jon. It was not only anger that kept me in flux, but the fear that, in planning my downfall, Jon knew more about me and my anxieties than anyone. And if he could know such demons and be unafraid, maybe he was someone I could truly love. But if his invasive act had, in fact, been a maliciously lucky strike, aiming entirely to wound, then—frankly—Jon Frank spelled trouble.

"You only hurt the ones you love." This astute assessment of the human condition arrived courtesy of my best friend, Clare. Friends since high school, Clare is the one person I can count on for empty wisdom drenched in meaning. Perhaps it is because her name is an anagram for *clear*, leading one to assume that her very being is focused and stable. Or that her similarity in name to *clairvoyant* imbues her with special powers. Regardless, somehow Clare is able to utter incredibly vacuous sayings which, upon passing her larynx, become instilled with such dignity and significance they can stand up to Gandhi.

"Wow. You know, Clare, I think you're right? We *do* only

hurt the ones we love. Why didn't I see that before?"

Clare shrugs, shoveling another fork full of Chinese Chicken Salad ("Dressing on the side, please") into her already overflowing mouth. Although painfully, paper-cut thin, Clare was cursed by delusions of chunky cellulite, viewing herself as one big box of Velveeta. As such, she continually alternated between the latest fad diet and intimate encounters with Hostess snack products.

"You know, Jon may have hurt you, but maybe there's a reason for that. Maybe you can turn that pain into a positive."

"Yes, that's it!" I nodded enthusiastically before becoming lost in her continuing platitudes.

As she talked, I studied her, taking in every movement. Her jaw muscles, tensing and straining as if they were the legs of a quarter horse trying desperately to reach the finish line, never did. Instead, her jaw flapped on and on, veins pulsing, as her invisible horse raced endlessly onward, furiously circling the track, as if on some unaired episode of *The Twilight Zone*. And it seems that I am the jockey, screaming in terror the faster she runs, the stadium swirling maddeningly as I search for some means of halting the sickening ride.

The image blurs as my thoughts somehow land on Clare at age 16, hiding her slender arms beneath a frayed fisherman's sweater, two sizes too large. She had reached out to me, become my friend. One of the few. And yet I wondered why.

Was she so enjoyable that I couldn't bear to be away from her? Sadly, no. Did her emotional nurturing offer me solace, sufficient to endure her less-endearing traits? Hardly. I viewed Clare as a handball wall. I could bounce things off her, knowing that she would return the lob, however inefficiently, somewhere in my general direction. But the things I needed now, such as depth and nuance, were beyond her grasp.

Why do I keep such people as Clare in my life, I wondered, when I get so little from them? True, she has always been there for me... But is loyalty enough?

As I observed her mouth, continuing its gallop, my eyes began to glaze like the limp piece of ham on the plate in front of me, before veering over to the nearby waiter's perfectly rounded ass. God, why are there so many cute waiters in the world? Why can't they be accountants? Stockbrokers? To waste such beauty on food service...

"So what does Jon say about this?"

With Clare finally back on planet earth, I returned as well. "I don't know."

"What? You mean you haven't talked to him?"

"What is there to say?" I stared at my barely picked-over meal. "I didn't do anything wrong. I mean, I *was* wrong. Factually. But motivationally? No. My motive, my drive, was simple human discourse. A talk about musicals. Every queen's fallback discussion. That I would confuse my composers is excusable."

"This, from the very person who picketed Dan Quayle?" God, Clare could be annoyingly accurate. I decided to ignore her.

"But to throw it in my face! To make a mockery in front of everyone." I lapsed into silence, pained by the memory.

Clare, just for a moment, put down her fork. "You know, dear, that you are my favorite person with a penis in the entire world. You are funny, sporadically caring, and smart. Perhaps too smart. That you are wrong, even occasionally, isn't the end of the world. But just look at what the past few weeks have done to you. You're a mess! Give up the ghost, honey. It's not worth it."

"If my dignity, my sense of self, isn't worth the fuss, what is?"

Clare eyed me steadily before picking up her fork. "Your health?"

I paused, looking again to the beautiful waiter, gracefully pouring water from a pitcher. Clare was right. To have HIV is one thing. Almost any gay man can deal with that these days. But to be a diseased, down-trodden, worn-out victim of AIDS, spending my days wrapped in a fringed shawl... Better to be like a waiter after all, who, despite the fire in the kitchen, greets each customer with a carefree and welcoming smile.

Upon returning home that evening, I entered from the garage, as usual. I wouldn't have discovered the enormous package if Maxie hadn't slumped against the front door, emitting little yips. I didn't even have to look at the card to know it was from Jon. Setting it on the coffee table, I stared intently at the cardboard box, wondering what on earth could be inside, before quickly ripping it open. In it were close to 20 CD's and albums: every Kander and Ebb recording ever made. *70 Girls 70, The Happy Time, Chicago, The Rink, Flora the Red Menace,* and more. Everything in existence, from A *(The Act)* to Z *(Zorba.)* I was astounded.

Then I noticed another package, wrapped separately, at the bottom of the larger box. Opening it, I broke into a huge grin. *Cabaret.* And not just the original cast recording we'd fought over. There were also CD's of the film soundtrack starring Liza (never better), the 1966 London version (with Judi Dench as Sally Bowles—wouldn't you have loved to have seen *that?*), a symphonic version by the Royal Philharmonic, vocal highlight albums, and original cast versions from Italy, Austria, Greece, Hungary, and Israel.

Unable to stop myself, I began to cry. For someone to care that much, despite all, was more than I'd ever dreamed possible. Pushing aside the jewel cases (a truer name there never was), I picked up the card:

Just as you have taught me, so I shall teach you.
Musical Theatre 101.   Class begins tonight at eight.
My place. - J.

The ringing of the phone broke my revelry.

"Yes, yes, yes! I'll be there!" I shouted joyously, almost tonguing the receiver.

"You'll be where? Did we have plans?" my mother asked, confused as always. "Are you coming here or something? I didn't make dinner. But we could go out..."

In my life, I long ago learned that my mother alone had the ability to destroy even the teensiest bit of happiness by simply saying "hello." She never calls or drops by at an opportune moment. It's almost as if she is being cued by some unseen stage manager, timing her entrance for maximum devastation.

And so it was that, instead of responding to her garbled thoughts, I hung up the phone. I knew that there would be hell to pay later, but I simply could not—would not—let her ruin my moment of bliss. Instead, I celebrated the package's arrival with a shower and douche, then called Jon.

So cautiously did he answer that I knew he was as uncertain of the next move as I. I thought seriously of punishing him by giving sullen, uninspired responses, but instead rushed giddily into an overblown declaration of my affection and desire. My words tumbled forth unguarded, so grateful was I to finally release my thoughts, until I finished, and was met by a moment of stunned silence.

It was only later, at his apartment, that words were replaced by actions. Although nervous, I happily let the moment carry me into sexual oblivion, where loving kisses and forceful gropes gave voice to our promised coupling.

Screeching, endless and unvarying, rang in my ear for a full fifteen minutes before I finally jumped in.

"Mom, I'm sorry! I had a problem with my phone—"

"For a week? You're telling me your phone was down that long?"

"It's fixed now."

"And during that time, your voicemail miraculously survived, recording each message? Including mine? And still, you didn't call? You're telling me that for the entire week you haven't made one single call. Not even from work."

"It wasn't intentional," I lied. "I just, you know, forgot."

"Forgot your own mother. That's a fine how-do-you-do."

"Can't we drop it? I'm calling now."

"You know I spent eighteen hours in active labor. Eighteen."

(Now seems to be a good time to note that I often feel that those who believe that homosexuality is caused by genetics are barking up the wrong tree. Though many may protest, every gay man I have ever met has a mother who is, in some manner, domineering. That they would have passive husbands who retreat to the den to escape their wives is understandable. In fact, it is a tribute to the gay man's sensitivity that, despite our mothers' ability to harangue, we still love them so. It is in this vein that I relent.)

"Of course, Mom. You're right. I'm sorry. I should have called. Can I take you to dinner tonight to make it up?" (I've also found that domineering mothers love free food.)

"Oh, so now my son who does not care enough to pick up the phone actually wants to pick up the tab?"

"Yes. Definitely. Your choice."

Without hesitating, she jumped in.   "Café La Boheme. Cocktails first, at the bar, then dinner. Maybe dessert afterward at Sweet Lady Jane's, if they're open. Make the reservation. Pick me up at 7." Click.

Moms. Gotta love them.

Arriving at her house, I am stunned by what greets me. Given, it has been two months since my last visit, but never the less I am at a loss. My mother has shed approximately 30 pounds, had her hair cut and lightened, wears a fashionable red jacket with oriental detailing, and seems to have had a facial peel. For some reason, she just glows. Forget for a moment that this sixty-some suburban housewife is my mother—she looks hot!

Trying to brush aside such thoughts, I stammer.

"You look—Wow! Amazing."

"I do, don't I?" This is said neither rudely, nor without a small measure of pride. Though she has always been attractive, recent years have seen her as if through a haze. Never quite of the times, yet not entirely out either. Although my father died many years ago, it is as if only now has Gloria emerged from her cloud of depression.

"So—what?" I ask pointedly.

"What what?"

I look at her closely, trying to find any trace of the woman who raised me. "How do you explain this? Are you dating someone? On the hunt?"

"Would you believe I've found God?" she asks, double-checking for her house key before pulling the door closed.

"Where was he hiding?"

"You think I'm joking? Open the car door for your mother. No wonder you don't date."

"I do date, for your information. But tell me more about God. Have I met him?"

"Is it so hard to believe that I've found solace in the word of our Lord, Jesus Christ?" She holds my stare, daring me.

"Oh fuck. Mom, I have enough worries in my life without you going off the deep end."

"Far from it," she says, as we pull up to the valet. "I feel better than I have in years. I've let go of old issues... Resentments. And I'm happy. Truly happy. What could possibly be wrong with that?"

Honestly, I have no reply. I wish I could be as happy as she sounds right now. As the valet opens her door, she steps out.

"Thank you." She leans back to me with a wink. "Now... How about some martinis?"

As she sashayed up the restaurant steps, I took some comfort in the notion that, even if my mother had indeed found herself a new house of worship, she was still driving there on the same old fumes.

Against the richly-textured velvet backdrop that is La Boheme, my mother set herself off like a pearl. The sheen to her hair, the bright red jacket, the becoming smile she offered to all—together conspired to turn this former housewife from Northridge into a dazzling beauty of indeterminate age. This woman whom I have loved-hated-loved-hated with every ounce of my being has suddenly turned into Cinderella. Which begs the question, am I, then, an ugly stepsister?

"I feel the need for a little drinkie," Gloria purred, leading me by the arm toward the crowded bar. "How about you?"

Quickly I ordered myself a stiff Long Island. It would clearly be that kind of evening. Just as quickly, Mom ordered two rounds of her usual and began sucking an olive with youthful abandon.

"Did they teach you that in Sunday school?"

My mother ignored me, concentrating instead on her olive. The hunky bartender reluctantly tore his eyes away from her, shifting his growing betrayal out of sight.

"You can drink, being religious and all?"

"Of course, darling. What kind of simpleton do you take me for? Do I look Mormon?" Given that, as she said this, her lip-gloss reflected the dancing light from the votives, she looked more starlet than anything. "We Episcopalians know how to party."

"So that's what you are now?" I couldn't take it all in. "How did this happen? Did I miss some lunar eclipse?"

As she began to tell her tale of woe, leading me slowly through the familiar trauma known as her life, I began to fade. After a while, though, a recurrent name began popping up, one I'd never heard before.

"Mom, who is Sally?"

"Why, my pastor. She's so sweet. And the biggest bundle of whoop-de-doo you'd ever hope to meet."

"And so Sally introduced you to the church?"

"Yes, and I am so glad she did! I never knew self-enrichment and devotion to a higher power could be so much fun!"

Dubious though I was, I continued. "How did you meet her? Pastor Sally?"

On this, my mother paused, unusual for her, and became somewhat evasive. "Oh, you know, through friends."

"Friends?" I prodded.

"At a dance, really. A kind of—square dance."

Clearly, I would need another drink.

"We meet weekly," she informed me, swirling her martini about in a do-si-do. "The group's been around forever. Some of those old things can barely push their walkers, but they show up every Friday night, just the same."

"Why didn't I know any of this?" I shifted in my seat, surprised at how unsettled I felt.

"Since when have you taken an interest in my life? Or anyone else's? Face it, Gabey, your favorite topic is you." She had a point. But in this world of such rampantly low self-esteem, is that so wrong?

"I can't believe I didn't know this. Fill me in. Is there anything else I should be aware of?"

"Well, I'm engaged. We're getting married next month."

As I paused, absorbing this new information, my mother grabbed the waiter and ordered another round.

"Jeez, you work fast. Congratulations, I guess," I sputtered. "Anyone I know?"

"Why, Pastor Sally, of course."

Huh. The Lord indeed works in mysterious ways.

While the revelation that one's own mother may in fact be a lesbian might be shocking to some, to me it was not altogether surprising. Looking back, I can remember how, as a child, I would watch her run for the mail every day, smoothing her hair as she did. Of course, it was not the mail itself that excited her. After all, how stimulating could bills and circulars be? It was the messenger, our faithful carrier Pauline, who prompted my mother to smile and duck her head, as if a schoolgirl. Though nothing sexual ever occurred, the chat and attention Mom received must have provided some inner satisfaction. She certainly never got that from my father. And I distinctly recall how saddened my mother was once Pauline was transferred. Getting the mail never seemed quite so important again.

That my mother should, at this stage of her life, find love would seem cause for celebration. But my well-wishes, though given enthusiastically, were somewhat empty. She couldn't tell the difference, so sauced was she by the time we were seated, but try as I might, I could not summon up sufficient feelings of happiness for her.

I am embarrassed by this, and am appalled to admit that my lack of enthusiasm comes from a genuine dislike of vaginas. While I have compassion for my Sapphic sisters involved in the struggle, I find the idea of munching grass personally repugnant. I've heard that some lesbians get off on watching gay male porn, turned on by the men's power and seemingly equal stature. I wish the reverse were true for me. But I've always found the vagina to be a very scary cavity, and have done my best to avoid close proximity. That it should inspire adequate fervor to prompt some to drink from the well is unfathomable, and the thought of such has induced nausea. Again, I own that this is my issue and not an indictment of others. But I know that is little consolation for those who like to graze.

"So you are now officially a dyke?" I couldn't help but ask.

"Well, no—not officially. But after our wedding night..." She let her little nugget sink in.

"You mean, you and Sally haven't—?"

"Oh, no!" she gasped. "Premarital sex is a sin!"

Tactfully, I refrained from questioning how sinful post-ceremonial muff munching will be.

"Mom, have you—I mean, I feel strange even asking this—but have you ever slept with women?"

"God, no! Would I look good in work boots and plaid?"

"So how do you know it will work with Sally? I mean, you may have an emotional connection, but if you don't like the sex...?"

"I never liked the sex with your father, and we were together over twenty years. Probably still would be if it hadn't been for that semi." She paused, lost in thought, before promptly wiping her mouth and pushing her plate aside. "Honey, we never know if love will work. But we have to believe that it will somehow. All joy in life comes from love, in one form or another. It's up to us to grab it."

As I stared at my mother, it was hard to believe that she had changed so much from the image in my head. Not that she was suddenly incapable of driving me insane, but she seemed to finally and comfortably inhabit her own skin. I wondered if I would ever find that kind of peace before the HIV semi bears down on me.

It was at this moment that Jon made his entrance, appearing abruptly at our table.

"No dessert for me, thanks," my mom said, not looking up.

"Sure you don't want something sweet?" he offered, before leaning down to give me a kiss.

"Hmm," Mom averted her eyes. "This restaurant has just about everything, doesn't it?"

Sliding in beside me, Jon extended his hand to my mother, completing the introductions.

"My mom is getting married next month—", I offered, eyeing her to see if I got the desired rise.

"How wonderful!" Jon raised his glass in toast.

"To a woman," I chimed, filling in the blank.

"Wow... Gabe, you never told me your mom was a lesbian."

"I'm not!" my mom pouted. "Well, not yet..."

"Can we stand outside your window and bang pots and pans?" Jon implored, his head filled with visions of *Oklahoma*.

"Oh—let's!" I clapped, happy with any opportunity to make my mother squirm.

"I don't think Pastor Sally would like that," Gloria demurred. "She's kind of traditional."

"Not Sally Porter? Of the Round Circle Squares?"

"Why, yes," my mother said, questions swirling in her eyes. "But how—?"

"I used to be her square dance partner! Well, I'll be! Boy, can that dyke lead..." Jon smiled fondly. "You've got a great one there. I hope you'll be very happy."

"Yes, I'm sure we will," Gloria smiled tightly. "Now, who are you again?"

Once adjusted to the other's rhythm, Jon and Gloria got along famously. As much as I wanted these two dear people to like each other, even I was dismayed by how easily each complemented the other. Not only was I the third wheel, but I was quickly deflating.

To their credit, though the potential was there, neither appeared interested in ganging up on me. In fact, their conversation flew so fleetly that I don't recall ever being mentioned. With the common bond of Pastor Sally, there was little room for anyone else. They talked about music, movies, restaurants, societal ills, their inexplicable love of country western, and debated why Bobby Short had not yet been elevated to national icon. I sat silently, screaming inside, *How can you be having this conversation?!? I was the one who introduced both of you to him in the first place! You'd never even heard of him! Jon, I lent you his CD's. And Gloria, who took you to see him at the Carlyle?*

But instead, I kept my mouth shut and sulked. For at least

one and one half hours, I pouted, sighed dramatically, sourly pursed my lips (until I caught a cute guy eyeing me strangely), drummed a rat-a-tat-tat with my fingers, and kicked the table. And remained irritatingly unnoticed.

It was only after the valet had retrieved my car and Gloria was safely seated inside that Jon began to get the hint.

He pulled me close for a goodbye hug. "Will I see you tonight?"

"Don't you have other plans?" I queried.

"What are you talking about?"

"Oh, I'm sorry," I smiled tightly. "I thought tonight you'd be fucking my mother."

Jon looked at me, aghast. "Gabe, you know premarital sex is against her religion."

I glared, flouncing to the driver's door as only a wounded diva can.

"Ah," Jon nodded, finally getting it. "I see—you felt excluded. And now you're pouting. Very appealing."

"Not at all. I'm perfectly fine."

"Can I come over later?" Jon entreated, his lower lip parting seductively. "See if I can, uh, find a way to make it up to you?"

I hesitated, weighing the options. Though the power of withholding could be wicked fun, I wasn't up to game-playing tonight. I went for the blowjob instead. "I'll be at your place in an hour."

My mother is quiet as we navigate Laurel Canyon. I adjust the stereo, letting Mary Chapin Carpenter's evocative "Come On, Come On" fill the air.

"That's nice," Gloria says, tilting her seat back slightly and soaking in the music. "So is your friend."

"Thanks, on both counts."

"This Jon...? It's serious?"

"I don't think you need to worry about switching to a double wedding. But—yeah, it's serious. For me, anyway." I grinned, despite myself.

"This is the first of your boyfriends, aside from Keith, that I've really liked. Not that the others weren't nice—."

"But—?"

"Jon seems very kind. You don't see too much of that in this town."

"That's true."

"Plus, if you got sick..."

"Mom, I'm not auditioning nurses."

"I know that. But after all you went through..." She's silent for a moment, and I can tell she's thinking about Keith. "I just mean, Jon doesn't seem like the type to scare easily. He seems stable. I guess what I'm saying is that I don't want you to be alone."

"I have you, don't I?"

"Of course, honey. Always." She reached over and grasped my hand, her intimacy surprising us both. "But there is only so much support a mother can give. I think Jon can give you the other kind."

Kissing her on the cheek as she hopped out, I then turned the car back toward my support, which tonight would come in much-needed oral form.

As we entered Oil Can Harry's, I searched the crowd for a familiar face. Who were all these people? And why on earth were they fascinated by something as anachronistic as country music? These were the hills of Studio City, for God's sake, not the Appalachians.

As the sea of cowboy hats parted, I spotted an impeccably dressed woman holding the hand of Paul Williams, star of all three *Smokey and the Bandits* and composer of Bab's "Evergreen". Upon seeing us, Gloria dropped Paul's hand and rushed to our side, offering her cheek for kisses before dragging us back to Paul.

"Jon, I believe you know Pastor Sally," tittered my mother, happy to have us in her realm. "And Gabey—"

Still startled that Paul Williams was actually a woman, my mother's fiancée yet, I was barely able to extend my hand in greeting. Pastor Sally squeezed it firmly, and then pulled me to her for a gigantic bear hug.

"Howdy-ho, there, Gabey! It sure is nice to finally meet

you!" Pastor Sally chortled, her wad of grape Bubble Yum tucked in her cheek.

"You too, uh, Pastor," I wheezed, still caught in her vise-like squeeze.

"Call me Sally. Or, a lot of folks just call me P.S. Kinda like the sound of that, so long as I don't become an after-thought!"

"Not you!" Gloria laughed affectionately. "No one could possibly forget you."

You can say that again, I thought, finally pulling free from her sugarlicious breath. Close-up, with her denim vest and patchwork skirt, P.S. did not resemble Paul Williams so much as Kathy Bates playing *Calamity Jane*. You could easily picture this woman twirling pistols on both index fingers, saying things like "rootin' tootin'."

As P.S. pulled Gloria onto the dance floor and Jon went in search of sustenance, I wondered why I felt so adversely toward Pastor Sally. Was it her outfit, which would have looked great on old Homeless Annie? Was I resentful that she had so quickly captured my mother's heart, whereas I was still a suitor? Or was it perhaps because the things in which she reveled (religion, square dancing, my mother) I viewed with some degree of disdain?

The ice cold beer felt good in my hands, and even better going down my throat. I hardly had time for another sip before I felt a firm grip on my arm, swiveling me toward the dance floor. With a hearty "Here we go!" P.S. and I twirled about like music-box ballerinas, dancing past my mother and a laughing Jon.

"Pastor Sally, I—"

"I know, you've never done this before," she grinned. "Probably say that to all the boys."

Gritting my teeth, determined not to be out-danced by a soup can wearing knee highs, I threw myself into the dance, only to step on her toes.

"Hey-ho there, Fred Astaire—you're a-*scare*-n me! Get it? A-scare? A-*staire*?"

Du-par's is an L.A. institution renowned for its reliably awful food and even worse service, which, at three in the morning, makes it even more appealing. Joined by Pastor Sally's friends Bethany and Clod—er, Claude—the six of us wedged ourselves into a four-top booth, herded by our slit-eyed waitress bearing food-caked menus. I was struck by how closely her white ensemble resembled that of a hospital nurse, and could easily imagine her delight in using large needles.

As Nurse Ratchet walked away, our group broke into titters.

"Go ahead and laugh," said P.S. "But I dated that woman."

We laughed even more. I'm not certain why, but at that exact moment, I began to warm up to Pastor Sally. I liked her undemanding sense of humor, her ability to reach out to all, and her attentiveness toward my mother. Without effort, Pastor Sally always seemed to have her hand on my mother's knee, or be patting her shoulder at just the right moment. The message: "You matter to me." Something Gloria had never gotten from Lenny.

Throughout the meal, Clod sat mutely, without expression. I wondered if something was wrong with him.

Bethany, her dreadlocks swept elegantly behind her ears, laughed gaily as she recounted her first square dance and how she had been imprisoned by P.S. until she had mastered the basics.

"Hon, you don't know it, but she won't let you go until you can dance like Savion Glover."

I smiled. "I'd settle for Danny."

"But you've always been a wonderful dancer!" Gloria protested, leaning forward. "When he was little, Gabey loved Ginger Rogers. He'd dance around the living room, twirling about in his bathrobe ball gown..."

I smiled thinly, "Thanks, Mom!"

"Now there's a visual!" Jon laughed with a wink. "Wish I could get you back in that ball gown."

"Hey—no more talk about ballin', y'all," giggled P.S. "This here is a church-goin' crowd."

Bethany leaned toward me with a whisper, "You can tell me the details later. Gay men get me so hot!"

After Bethany and her monosyllabic friend departed for an after-hours club, leaving just the four of us, Pastor Sally turned to me.

"So, Twinkle-toes, how long is it gonna take for me to convert you?"

"Oh, Pastor Sally," I hedged. "I'm really not much of a—. The church just doesn't do much for me."

"Couldn't agree more," she snorted. "Whole lot of hogwash, if you ask me. I don't believe it matters much to the Lord where you go to church, or even if. What's mighty important, though, is what's in your soul. What kind of person you are." She smiled. "Besides, the conversion I'm talkin' about is much more important. When am I gonna get another chance to spin you around the dance floor? You got mighty nimble feet, for a size 13."

I laughed my first really good laugh all day. "Sally, I am liking you more and more."

"That's good," she winked. "That's what I've been praying for."

Later that night, at home and exhausted, I looked into the bathroom mirror. "Do I look hardened to you?"

"I don't know," Jon grinned. "Take off your pants and I'll check."

I peered back into the mirror, pulling my wrinkled brow apart in hopes of achieving smoothness. "Sometimes I look at people, folks I don't even know, and immediately think the most awful thoughts about them. Like tonight, with Pastor Sally."

"What do you mean?" Jon pulled off his socks and glanced my way.

"Well," I sighed, "My first reaction was that my mom was marrying Ma Kettle."

"And she is!" he laughed. "So your observation was correct."

"Yeah, but P.S. is more than that. Much more. And yet I had already trivialized her. Taken her down a notch."

"Only to you. We didn't know what you were thinking. And you can always boost her right back up."

"But I do this all the time! More often than not, I am right in my assumptions, but sometimes—. What about all the people I'm not right about? I never even give them a chance."

"To do what? Prove themselves to the great and powerful Oz?" Jon faced me now, speaking with gentle force. "Hate to break it to you, Gabey, but most folks don't live for your approval."

"I know. But how many have I let pass by, based on some false impression? Being judgmental comes second nature to me. I'm not even aware I'm doing it until it's too late."

Staring back into the glass, I wondered how transparent I really was. Jon perched on the edge of the bed, watching me.

"You asked me, Gabe, if I thought you were hardened. And perhaps there is a side of you that is. Given what you've told me about growing up, what happened that night, and with Keith, and Lenny—I can understand that. But only you choose whether to share that side with the world. Maybe the next time you meet someone, try keeping your mouth shut and your brain in neutral. Ask questions. Find out everything you can about the other person. The more rounded they become, the less easy it will be to dismiss them."

It was at times like this that I hated Jon. Although what he said made perfect sense, I knew that the chances of me making such a change were slight, if not altogether impossible. But even more irritating was that Jon had been able to quickly decipher and prescribe solutions for issues with which I had struggled my entire life. Shouldn't God, if there is one, have given us all the code to our own locks, instead of merely handing them off to others? And if you never find the person who holds your card, does that mean you lose the game?

Jon slipped off the rest of his clothes and into bed. "So what about me?"

"I don't think you're hardened at all. Just the opposite."

"But, when you first saw me, what was your impression? Was it accurate?"

"Definitely," I said, repressing a smile. "I knew, from the moment we first met, that you would be a total pain in the ass."

Only a few days later came a phone call that would prove this very point.   Ric, a producer of TV game shows created specifically for those with little or no intellect, and his lover Tim had been together almost 20 years. Longer than anyone I knew. He was calling with an invitation to dinner. Now, I should explain that dining with Ric and Tim would be like dining with the Kennedys or Vanderbilts. Memories of an evening spent in their realm linger dreamily for eons, blanketing you in warm subtle layers long after the meal itself concluded. I knew it would be unforgettable. Still, I hesitated.

You see, Jon and I, though completely enraptured, were still in the first phases of young love. It was tender, passionate, and focused solely on each other. The swift entrance of friends, I feared, no matter how charming, might shatter our fragile coupledom.

Sensing my hesitation, Jon looked to me and nodded as Ric prattled on about the other guests. After writing down the details, I expressed my thanks and hung up the phone, turning silently to Jon.

"It sounds like fun."

"It will be. Their dinners always are..." I pulled a soap opera moment, looking off into the distance, with a sigh attached. Jon wasn't buying it.

"Pregnant pause equals—?"

"Well—you and I, right now, we're enchanted. A fairytale."

"Exactly. How else should fairies be?"

"But my friends... They're kind of—"

"What? Alien beings? Monkeys with mohawks?" Despite myself, I smiled. Jon walked over, taking my hand. "Hey—we made it through a meal with your mom. We can handle anything."

Although I knew he was right, part of me wanted to continue living in our own plastic bubble. I wanted to seal up my apartment in Saran Wrap and Super Glue, with our only visitor Glinis O'Connor.   She would bring us hermetically sealed oatmeal chocolate chip cookies and send them sliding through the feeding portal and into our waiting mouths. Between Jon's love and Glinis' cookies, there was nothing else I'd ever need.

Jon pulled me close, kissing me just behind my ear. As I

relaxed into him, grateful for his protective arms, he whispered softly. "I don't own any rose-colored glasses, you know. I see more than you show, Gabe." He offered another sweet kiss, and then retreated into the bathroom.

I stood motionless, staring at the now-closed door. How was it possible that he could know me so well? My every thought and fear? My insecurities? And, knowing all this, how could he even *like* me, let alone love?

The steps to Ric and Tim's home were adorned with glass votives, sprinkling the walk with stardust. It was the kind of evening evoked in countless Hollywood romances, but which rarely occur in Hollywood proper. Smoothing my hair, I wished that I had the confidence of a Hollywood starlet at a media-packed premiere. Instead, I continued to question my attire, wishing I'd gone for something less flashy. No matter how many times Jon has assured me of my attractiveness, I knew that true beauty comes from confidence, and in that I am sorely lacking. Plus, it is difficult to feel truly at ease in fuchsia.

As we waited at the door, I glanced at the host basket Jon held, happy we had gone for the simple spring fruits instead of something more lavish. The plaid bow had been just the right touch.

Eventually, Ric appeared, greeting us warmly and ushering us into the sunken living room, where the other guests had already assembled. One couple, Henry and Christophe, I knew and liked. Another, Gene and Rod, I knew and loathed.

With a shriek, Rod launched from his seat, kissing me and offering his hand seductively to Jon. Then, grabbing the fruit basket from Jon's hands, Rod squealed, "Oh, I hate it when queens don't know how to bow!" With that, he shepherded the basket into another room to perform an emergency bow makeover. Jon looked at me, cautiously, knowing that the bow faux pas had come from my fingers. I glued a smile onto my face, sinking my nails into his arm.

Luckily, Tim made his entrance with a tray of smoked salmon canapés, chèvre pastry puffs, and tiny pillars of caviar stacked onto homemade crackers. As we "oohed" and "aahed" appropriately, Tim demurred, "It's nothing. Just some things I threw together." No longer famished and a cosmopolitan plastered in hand, I finally managed to relax.

It was amusing to watch Jon interact with my friends—and enemies. He had that easy way with people which I've always envied. Jon knew when to tell a joke, when to sit back and listen, when to interject. Every movement was natural, no pretense.

As dinner was announced, we were lead into the dining area, where the panoramic view of the city was but a backdrop for Ric and Tim's exquisite country table, discovered at some "little forgotten shop in Mexico". In its center, a low glass pool held a mix of floating candles and flowers. Tim entered, producing plates of braised lamb with pomegranate sauce, accompanied by grape leaves stuffed with prosciutto, dried fruit, and herbed rice. As the accolades piled up, Tim predictably demurred, "Oh, it's nothing." Knowing that our local supermarket does not normally make a habit of carrying grape leaves, as few of us have the urge to whip up a quick batch of dolmades, Tim's protestations, unlike his grape leaves, were difficult to swallow. But I smiled, knowing that I would have said exactly the same.

Most of the meal was spent discussing Ric and Tim's latest adventures abroad. Escapades freshly engraved, their stories poured forth, each more charming and humorous than the last. So perfect was the recitation that it almost seemed scripted, but like everything else Tim and Ric do, their narration was without guile.

"So," asked Ric, turning toward Jon, "what's your favorite country?"

Jon paused, perhaps anticipating the reaction to his response. "Uh, Canada."

As everyone chuckled, Ric pursued it. "Seriously—"

Jon smiled, somewhat tightly, "Well Ric, seriously, the only places I've been outside the U.S. are Mexico and Canada. I haven't been to Europe. Yet."

Though honesty is usually a welcome respite at parties such as this, every gay man knows that in certain situations, it is far better to flat-out lie. This was one such discussion.

"You've never been?" gasped Rod. "Oh, you poor dear."
Rod attempted to pat Jon's arm, which Jon swiftly retracted.

"That I haven't traveled to Europe isn't an occasion for
consolation, Rod," Jon stated benignly. "I do want to go,
someday, but it hasn't been my priority. Instead, I've gone
rafting in Colorado, fly-fishing in Wyoming, and last summer I
hiked the Sierra for three weeks straight."

"Did you march with the abolitionists in Selma, too?" Rod
parried. "You don't have to justify yourself to us."

"Apparently, Rod, I do. Just because we're all gay men
doesn't mean that we have to have the same goals, hobbies, or
ideals. We're not cookie-cutter cut-outs," Jon implored. "Take
dinner tonight."

I shot him a look, instantly afraid of where this was headed.

"This meal has been fantastic. Tim and Ric did an amazing
job, creating culinary art I've seen only in magazines. And yet, as
good as it was, I would've been just as satisfied with a bucket of
KFC."

No one dared speak. Jon's words swirled over the table, an
apparition none quite knew how to exorcise. Everyone suddenly
took inordinate interest in what few scraps remained on their
plates.

Rod's eyes rolled, looking like a seasick sailor. "Next you're
going to tell us you voted for George Bush."

"No. I vote Independent. Libertarian, usually—this time for
Andre Marrou," Jon muttered, dashing any hopes of salvaging
the evening. "I knew he wouldn't win, but I just feel like we will
never break free from this two-party stranglehold if we don't act
upon our convictions."

Rod smiled evilly, pleased at unmasking what was clearly an
inferior being. "Wow! How avant-garde! You've certainly got
yourself a winner, Gabe."

"I think so," I said, as assuredly as possible.

Tim stood, still uncertain whether Jon had insulted his
cooking. "I don't—uh—would anyone like dessert?"

Everyone nodded, dutifully, as attempts were made to
recapture the spark of conversation. Luckily, Tim quickly
produced dessert, quelling the need for further forced chat.

Again, and for the final time that evening, we "oohed" and "aahed" at the offering.

"Oh, thanks," Tim smiled, dipping into his fresh fruit pavlova with hand-spun sugar bark. "It was nothing."

While Rod's attack on Jon bothered me, it bothered me more to watch Jon on the ride home. He was detached, which was unusual, and left the radio off. As he maneuvered his way back down through the hills, I placed my hand on his knee. Whereas this normally would result in his hand on mine, my hand remained alone.

"You know that Rod is an ass, right?"

Jon kept his eyes on the road. "If I didn't before, I do now."

"And you understand that I love you, ill-considered vote and all?"

He glanced to me. "You love me?"

I averted my eyes to the passing Angelyne billboard. "Did I just say that out loud?"

Jon didn't respond, instead turning left onto Sunset, a slight smile on his face, and reached for the radio dial, filling the car with "Love Songs on the KOST."

The next weeks flew by as I wholeheartedly dove into my mother's wedding preparations, attacking it with a level of zeal usually reserved for my own self-interests. Given that we had less than a month to plan and execute it, the day itself came quickly, so busy were we arranging caterers, outfits, and entertainment. At least Pastor Sally had the church, as well as her pick of supportive pastors. Recognizing my aesthetic flair, I was put in charge of decorations, though I quickly found that my counsel was needed in other areas as well.

Making my task difficult was the fact that neither Gloria or P.S. would reveal any details about their attire. Would they don traditional white dresses? Matching tuxedos? Master and slave leather harnesses? Whenever asked, P.S. would chortle "Hot pink!", to which Gloria would cackle hysterically. I could never determine whether hot pink was in fact an element of their ceremonial dress, or some thinly-veiled reference to the tint of their imminent wedding night buffet.

Given the lack of information, I decided to pick flowers of varying hues in the hopes that one would match their outfits accordingly. Tables were given white skirts, with cloths atop in yellow, green, blue, purple, orange, and red. Somehow we managed to pull off the rainbow flag motif, while still allowing those who wished to see it as a celebration of spring that option as well.

As the wedding hour approached, Gloria came up to me, still dressed in sweats.

"What?" I probed, eyeing her attire with ill-disguised derision. "You're not backing out?!?"

"Heavens, no. This is the best thing that's ever happened to me." She pushed a folded note into my hands. "We want you to read this."

"I'm kind of busy. I still have to get the place cards—"

"Not now. As part of the ceremony."

I looked down at the paper in my hands. "Mom, I really hadn't planned—"

"That's the thing about life. It rarely does come as planned." Giving me a quick peck, she hurried off. "Gotta go squeeze into my dress."

"Well," I thought reassuringly, "at least it *is* a dress."

Guests began to trickle into the church, accompanied by what sounded like a tipsy organist. Few had ever been to a gay wedding, let alone a pastor's. Even the gay men, usually adept at adapting, seemed uncertain of protocol. Jon and I did our best to help the guests relax as we escorted them to their pews.

I was glad to see that my mother had not restricted her guest list, as various friends and acquaintances filled the church. Though even by her own admission not yet a lesbian, Gloria managed a feat of cohesion between past and present lives that I had sought, fruitlessly, throughout mine. Her worlds integrated naturally, with elegant ease.

"Some turnout, huh?" Jon said, managing to pause during his escorting duties.

"They seem to have a lot of friends," I noted.

"Good people usually do," he agreed, moving to greet a new arrival.

Is it just that I myself am not a good enough person to be worthy of such friendships?   Or can people not see my goodness, so covered is it by layers of defense?

At a signal from the female-to-male transgendered preacher, Dick Novagina, the organist began the familiar strains of the processional.   Heads craned toward the back for a peek at the bridal party as the double doors opened, revealing a fiddler. With a screech, the organ music came to an abrupt halt as the fiddler shouted, "And a one, and a two, and a—" From god-knows-where, a band began playing an upbeat jig as the Round Circle Squares paraded through the doors, hands clapping and feet clogging.

I laughed as they tromped down the aisle, hootin' and a hollerin'.   Despite their combined age of 783 years, these toe-tappers reveled in their abandon.   Glancing about, I caught a quick glimpse of the face of my mother's bridge partner.   Far from the frown I was expecting, she was clapping along, throwing out what sounded like a hearty "Yippee-I-O!"

On that, Pastor Sally danced in, promenading a beaming Gloria down the aisle.   My mother had never looked happier, and, despite my issues with her, I hoped that the feeling would last.

Once the jolly group reached the pulpit, the music stopped. Though Pastor Dick attempted a smooth transition to a more solemn, familiar tone, it was difficult to view the leather vests, bolo ties, and frilly skirts without smiling.   I felt in my pocket for the reading, wishing that I'd had time in advance to prepare.   On Dick's nod, I rose from the congregation, stepping anxiously to the podium.

Although I do a great deal of public speaking in my position at LA-DE-DA, this was profoundly different.   I was not reciting a well-rehearsed litany of volunteer opportunities.   I was not an actor, lines committed to memory.   I was Gabriel Charles Travers, supporting my mother as she took this important step in life.

Glancing to Jon, I hoped that someday we'd find ourselves here as well, without the twangy band or glitzy colors. Perhaps this ceremony might inspire similar thoughts in him. Thoughts that, though I'd had them repeatedly and increasingly, I'd chosen not to share.

Jon smiled softly, knowing how nervous I was, as I unfolded the paper, placing the poem on the stand in front of me. It was new to me, and I wondered how they had chosen it. Looking down at my mother's familiar cursive, I began to read.

"This poem, by Adrienne Rich, written with something entirely different in mind, somehow seems quite appropriate in describing the joining of two lives." Inhaling, softly and steadily I continued to read.

"Final Notations" spoke of a commitment so epic, it could be seared into one's soul, occupying an entity entirely. The verse warned that the all-encompassing journey would not, however, be simple. Success would demand both effort and dedication, but the very act of joining would eventually morph, becoming one's will.

When finished, I stepped quickly to Jon's side. That such a commitment could be made, seared into one's soul so that it becomes the will, seems entirely possible with Jon. But, although I know he loves me, whether he is desirous of such a vow is something I have been too afraid to ask. If he is not, what does that then say about us? Would I be content for things to merely remain, unchanged, as pleasurable as they are, or do I, at my core, desire more?

Squeezing my hand, he looked at me fondly, but in a way he never had before.

"That was wonderful," he whispered. "As are you."

I smiled back, wondering if those were tears gathering at the corners of Jon's eyes.

Holding Jon's hand as Pastor Dick continued with the service, I knew that a life committed to Jon was that for which I had yearned. A union, strong and fortified. A haven, perhaps, for solace, when the world appears too much.

Not that it would be easy. Or rather, simple. But that it would *be*.

Clare would not shut up. "Gabey, you're so lucky! He's perfect! The best one yet!"

As the guests swirled by, their happy faces blurred in a champagne-induced haze, I wondered how many glasses I'd had. Five? Twelve? Regardless, it was not nearly enough to mute the corny western band, nor Clare's utterances. And we were only on the second course. I propped my elbows on the table for support.

"Hopefully, Jon's the best one—period," I said, smiling tightly.

"Oh, you know what they say," Clare leaned toward me, "That which is for us will not pass us by."

"Clare," I rolled my eyes, unable to stop myself. "When you talk like this, it sounds like everything has been preordained."

"It is. It's fate," she nodded.

"So, fate has planned everything for us? We play no role in charting our own future?"

"Well, you should never *tempt* fate, you know? Look before you leap, and all that." As she picked up her fork and blindly bit into her quasi-chicken, not taking her pre-leap look, I pondered the wisdom of leaving all to fate, who clearly spelled his name G-A-B-E. "But otherwise," she continued, "the universe will provide. In abundance."

"Jeez, Clare!" I slammed my champagne flute down. "Do you ever listen to yourself? You're more hokey than that Hee-Haw band over there! I feel like I'm chatting with Stuart-fucking-Smalley."

Frowning, Clare finally shut up. Sitting in silence as the party continued on around us, I knew that I had pushed over the line, but had no idea how to salvage the awkward moment. I glanced about, seeking deliverance, when I spotted Jon. Chatting with a euphoric Gloria, Jon caught my glance, then his brow furrowed in concern.

I shrugged, uncomprehending, then followed his eyes over to Clare. Silent tears streamed down her face, which she made no attempt to conceal. Leave it up to her to be dramatic.

"Okay, Clare—show's over. Your Oscar's in the mail." She looked at me with such revulsion, I immediately understood and wanted to swallow my words, forcing them back down my throat.

"Jeez, I am such a schmuck." I reached for her hand, which she instinctively withdrew. "Clare, I—that was a really shitty thing to say. I am so—"

"Don't, Gabey."

"But you don't even know what I—"

"You're going to say something you don't really mean, and don't really understand. For you to say the word 'sorry' is easy. But to truly ask for forgiveness, to beg for it, requires humility. And that, my dear, is something you're not remotely capable of."

"Aren't empty gestures better than none?" I stumbled. "You know I love you—"

"You're such a fucking prick!" Clare cried. "You think that, because you care about someone, you can say whatever you want to them, without repercussion. But the rest of us aren't as thick-skinned, Gabey. Words hurt—you of all people should know that! You've turned into *them*, Gabe—Joey and Kid. You purposely hurt, whether to test us, or simply for fun, or—I don't know—revenge at what they did to you. You're still fighting that same fight, all these years later."

"So, I'm a shit, Clare. This is not news."

"You're right, of course. As always," Clare sighed, petulantly. "But it used to be, underneath it all, there was something more—. Some decency. Some human emotion. But it's like you've locked that all away."

I fired up. "You hate me? Is that what you're saying?"

"I don't hate you, Gabe, because I know you," she sighed, resigned. "I know your story—I know why you can be an absolute asshole. You've said the meanest things to me, and, up until now, I've stayed."

"What are you saying?"

"Venomous attacks trigger consequences, as you—more than anyone—know. You can't expect to hurl a spear and not draw blood."

Nervously, I glanced at the packed dance floor, wishing that I knew the latest dance, the Macarena.

"Clare, I should circulate..."

"Made you uncomfortable?" Clare was almost smiling, and I hated her. I wanted to take that wedding cake and shove it into her mouth, making her engulf it in one gulp. And I wanted to see that cake take root, turning her miniscule waist into the hoola-hoop she imagined it to be. "Well, honey, the truth hurts."

"You don't make me uncomfortable, Clare, so much as nauseated." I stood, unable to remain in her smugness any longer. "You want the truth? You cling to your safety net of strung together proverbs, but ignore the fact that they don't make a cohesive whole. You are so pathetically oblivious."

"You don't know me at all, do you?" Clare eyed me with what looked like pity. "Do you realize what I've put up with over the years, just in being your friend? Do you know how much therapy, how much time I've spent, trying to better myself? To understand why, despite all you've done both to me and to others, I've continued to support you?"

"I'll write you a check."

"Mock all you want, but at least I believe in something," Clare held my eye, composed but firm. "I try to be optimistic. To make each day better than the last. It's time for you to grow up, Gabey. To be held accountable. You have to stop, or you'll lose everyone around you. Just like you lost me."

On that, she stood before I could summon an appropriate parting line.

"Please give your mother my best."

As she walked away, I couldn't stop myself, calling out, "Going to spend some quality time with a carton of Twinkies?"

Clare stopped in her tracks, then turned back. She looked at me sadly before offering a bit of a smile. "You take care."

Just then, as Gloria and P.S. took to the floor to the strains of Anne Murray's "Could I Have This Dance?", Clare walked out of the Fellowship Hall, and out of my life.

For the next few weeks, I refrained from calling her. Not only was I pissed that Clare had ruined any good feelings I had from my mother's wedding, but I knew that she was right. I do play dirty, as if by quickly drawing my dagger and mortally wounding my foe, I will be the one to walk away unscathed.

Unfortunately, such insensitivity on my part is nothing new. It has been my nature, in the beginning of each relationship, to push everyone else aside, in order to focus more fully on my beloved. Then, six months later, when I am left brokenhearted and alone, save for the parting gift of crabs, I stare at the phone and wonder why my friends have deserted me. Much like Dr. Doolittle's famous Push-Me, Pull-You, I am a llama who will wrap you in the tightest of hugs, and then not return your calls for two months.

That this is a part of me is embarrassing. I wish I could give myself more fully to both friends and lovers, but I have only so much energy to give, and so juggle according to need.

But, when all is said and done, at the end of the day, excuses are for losers. Once again, I fucked up, and it was time to face the music. As Clare's phone rang, I pondered what to say. Although honesty is *always* the best policy, there are times when it clearly is not. So I chose levity as my distracter of choice. Upon her answer:

"Hello?"

"Sweetie, darling! Are we still friends?"

"Friends?" Clare muttered numbly.

"Of course, darling!" I charged on, "You and I, we're like Stoli and O.J. Better yet, O.J. and Nicole."

My repartee was met by silence. I tried another joke, but she wasn't budging. In fact, every attempt seemed to float out into the void, forever lost in space with Dr. Smith and the irritating Robinsons.

"Listen—maybe I should call back. I truly am sorry, but maybe now isn't such a good—." Pausing, I contemplated when a good time would actually be, and couldn't find an answer. Softening, I continued, "You're my best friend. My conscience. You keep me from getting too full of myself."

"Is that possible?"

Now it was my turn for silence. Where, exactly, was my misstep with Clare? This wasn't the first time I'd crossed the line, and we'd always managed to find our way back, somehow. But perhaps this was not so much a single wrong move as a gradual veering, ever so slowly, off course.

"Look, I deserve that. I truly do. I'm a total shit sometimes."

"Sometimes?"

"Jesus, give me a break, Clare. I'm trying to apologize."

"Do you know what you're apologizing for?"

"Well, I mean—not exactly. I know I'm not always as nice as I should be..."

"Try real, Gabey. You're not always as real as you should be. You try too hard. Always witty, or laughing, or showing how smart you are."

"So?"

"Sometimes, you need to take a break. Let down your pre-programmed walls and show other sides of yourself. Otherwise you're just one more flake in the land of Giant LA-LA Flakes. What you're living isn't a life, Gabey. It's a movie script."

"Well, thanks. Glad I called to straighten this out and apologize. Clearly you forgot your happy pill today. And I think this conversation could have used just a bit more of your endless goodness and light. Goodbye." As I went to hang up—

"Oh Gabe? One more thing—"

I sighed, "Yeah, sweetie?"

"My dad died this morning. I, uh, thought you'd want to know."

As the line clicked and the receiver began its banal death-knell tone, I slowly hung up. For a moment, I couldn't quite process that her father had died, still dwelling on what she'd said about me. I could not simply dismiss her ranting as that of a grief-stricken daughter, for I knew, intrinsically, that she had spoken the truth. I have long been haunted by my inability to emotionally connect, and I wanted to change. Have *tried* to change. But nothing—no therapy, support group, empowerment workshop, self-help book, or high colonic—has ever pointed the way toward true enlightenment.

And the really scary thing is, I used to be even worse. While my tongue can still be pointed at times, I used to spend each day in attack mode. My twenties were filled with haughty sneers and thinly-barbed assaults, cloaked with the perfectly practiced smile of a true artiste. But my years of therapy with Roberta helped, and when she retired, it felt as if my work was done. I had improved, after all, and put on my armor not as often. Still, it seems my spear is always at the ready, and the urge to pick it up—at times—too compelling.

I am haunted by this because I fear the results of my actions. I do not want to push people away, as I have done with Clare. I do not want to die, like Clare's father, alone. Whether I die this year, or inexplicably live to be 90, I want to be surrounded by loving, supportive friends and family. And yet I've found no pathway that leads to actual and permanent growth. All roads lead somewhere, clearly, but where they will take me and what I will learn is murky at best. Is any path better than no path? Will a wanderer ever find a happy ending, or are those reserved solely for the journeymen?

The funeral for Henry, Clare's dad, was short and flat. No one who knew him spoke, for none truly knew him. Even his wife and daughters sat silently, listening to an unknown pastor wax eloquently, if obliquely; a balm to their muted pain. I knew that Clare was hurting, not so much for the loss of her father as much as for the lost opportunity to know him. She had always sought his attention, hoping that one day he would take notice and allow her entrance into his quiet and uninteresting world. A man of few words, who soaked himself in nature shows and bird-watching, he could train his eyes on a previously unseen species for hours, but apparently could not focus on the eager faces peering at him from across the breakfast table.

Clare had so much to say, but would never get the chance. Perhaps, I thought, this was for the best. For if her father had it within to give, he would have given long ago. Thus, if she had confronted him, the pain of his silence could have been equated with rejection. Surely that would be worse than not knowing at all.

As I sat, several pews behind, staring at her back, I realized that while Clare may have chosen to end our friendship, it was at my prompting. She'd been nothing but supportive throughout the years, cheerfully putting herself at my disposal whenever I felt the need for comfort. But what comfort had I provided her?

What good, if any, had she received from me, besides a free drink and a laugh or two? If, as I've said, I want better relationships, the first step begins with Clare.

I glanced to Jon, and saw that he was crying. Usually so stable, I wondered what had triggered such a reaction, given the hollow staleness of the memorial. As he'd never even met Mr. Peer, his emotional state was puzzling, and a bit off-putting. Was his grief triggered by Mr. Peer or something else entirely?

Clare caught my eye as Jon and I filed past the casket, Mr. Peer's bird-watching binoculars at his side. I stared at her, trying to transmit my message of sorrow and regret, but Clare disconnected, centering instead on her younger sister's hand, held tightly in hers.

"That I could fall—have fallen—so quickly, it just scares me." As he said this, Jon tried to smile but couldn't quite conjure his cheek muscles into adherence.

"You're scared? Great—then I'm not the only one," I shot back. "But you know what? All love is scary. Only when we're really scared do we have a chance at real happiness."

"It's different for you, Gabe. You're older. You've done more."

"And you want to—what?—sow your wild oats?"

"No. That's not it at all. It's just—moving in together? It's a huge step."

"Agreed."

"Part of it feels too soon."

"We've been dating for months now. And it's not like I have time to waste."

"Exactly! If you were to—." Jon stopped himself before the words had completely tumbled forth, but it was too late. His true fear had finally materialized, revealed to us both.

It was not the commitment to love that scared him. It was the commitment, the promise, to be caregiver. Talking about death in the abstract is quite easy, but seeing it up close with Mr. Peer, in all its ashen glory, was a different matter altogether.

In truth, I'd never fully considered what I was asking of Jon. I wanted a lover, housekeeper, friend, driver, and nurse practitioner who could whip up a mean chocolate soufflé, all in one hunky package, complete with nipple ring. At 29 years old, the age when it all starts to go downhill for gay men, how could I possibly ask that Jon give up these last years of youth, knowing that ultimately he would walk away with little more than a crossed-out Day Runner?

My gaze dropped to the table, veering away from the *Cabaret* CD, trying to find a neutral place on which to settle. Futilely, there was no place left to look except into his aching eyes. I took a moment before I replied.

"I understand, Jon."

"No, you don't! I love you," he implored. "I do. It's just—"

"I know. I love you too," I said, my compassion giving way to steely nerve. "That's why you have to leave."

"Leave?"

"Yes. Now."

"But—? Can't we talk about this? I mean—this is working, right?"

"Basically living together here at my place, while you pay rent on an apartment 'just in case?' Pretending we're in domestic wedded bliss when we're really sitting on a powder keg? Is that working for you?"

Jon stammered, unable to form a sentence. He had no idea where we were headed, but I did. There was only one way for this conversation to go. Clare had accused me of living my life as a script, but in some moments, that seemed the only path forward.

I waited, giving him time, but it was clear that he had no response. Finally, I continued. "What I need, Jon, what I want from you, is a commitment."

"You know I love you."

I nodded. "But I need something I can count on."

"You've told me a million times, you can't count on anything or anyone but yourself," Jon implored, exasperated.

"And, apparently, I was correct." From the kitchen came the steady click of my black Kit Cat clock, and I could easily picture the cat eyes swiveling as its tail swung happily, left to right, then back again. I could always count on my kitty clock. As long as I had batteries, at least that.

"Jon, I'm sorry you've wasted these last few months. But you have the luxury of time." He stared at me, unable to fathom that I'd actually played the death card. "Maybe you can't count on anything in life, not even yourself. All I know is that I don't want to die alone. I thought—hoped—maybe you'd be the one to hold my hand along the way. But obviously I was mistaken."

Jon stared at me, unable to move. From somewhere within, drawing on my acting days, I summoned a tired grin, then crossed to him, arms outstretched. He fell into them, sobbing, and remained for what seemed like eternity. How easy for our roles to be reversed, if only temporarily. In that moment, Kit Cat must've blinked 300 times.

When his tears had subsided, I pulled back, wiping his eyes and kissing his cheeks.

"Gabey, I—"

"Go," I smiled wanly. "Just go."

"Really?"

I nodded, as confidently as I could.

"You—you want me to just—leave?" Jon sniffed, uncomprehending.

Part of me wanted to be honest. To wrap my arms around him and cover him in kisses. But I knew that "this" was not enough. Not anymore. I kept reminding myself that meaningful growth only comes from sacrifice. "Yes," I lied, for the first, but not last, time that evening. "I want you to leave."

His eyes implored. "But, I just—"

"Get out!" I exploded, anger storming through me like the onslaught of a hurricane.

Startled, Jon bolted for the door, grabbing his jacket. I watched as he tore down the path. Reaching the street, he stopped, turning back to me to reveal his aching eyes. Though I saw his hurt and the tide of emotion manifesting within, I stepped back, resolutely shutting the door and locking out his pain.

I leaned back against the door, ignoring Maxie and her quiet whine.

Had I been too harsh? After all, Jon is young. But where

did he think this relationship was headed, if not the graveyard? Did he actually think he could play house, but then run away when his pile of blocks had been knocked over?

Maxie pulled herself from her bed, crossing to me as I sunk into a chair. Rubbing against me, I knew Maxie intended to comfort, but hers were not the haunches I needed. I patted Maxie's head, giving it the kisses I'd meant for Jon. I tried to relax, blocking everything out, but the steady tick of the kitty clock grew louder and louder. My bookcases seemed to grow rapidly toward the ceiling, making the room smaller and smaller. A neighbor's kitchen chair scraped against worn linoleum.

With one last kiss to Maxie, I left.

It had been ages since I'd been to a bar. And even though I used to regularly patronize this particular one, it felt as if it were my first time passing through its door. Not only was the décor different and the videos unfamiliar, but the crowd seemed strange too. Almost unreal. At 36, I was well older than even the closest husband-shopper. Studying their animated, clean-scrubbed faces, I searched for any sign of zits or wrinkles or a stray grey hair, but came up frustratingly empty.

One of the blonds materialized at my side. "Buy you a beer?"

"Sure," I said, letting him lead the way to the bar.

"Name's Rory," he purred, offering a well-rehearsed smile. "What's yours?"

"Gary," I lied, for the second time that night.

We stood for a moment, gazing about the room. I hate trying to talk in bars. Luckily, we were saved as the person ahead of us in line turned away, cocktails in hand. As the bartender cocked his head expectantly, Rory turned back to me. "Lite okay? Or Corona?"

"Lite's great," I smiled, relieved at not having to spend my own money.

"You, uh, live around here?" Rory asked, clearly thinking ahead.

"Just up the street. You?"

"Phoenix. I'm just here for the weekend." Perfect. A song played, indistinguishable from the previous, as Rory and I stood smiling, searching for conversation.

"So, Gary," he leaned in. "What do you like to do?"

"Me?" I grabbed him in a virtual headlock, cementing his lips to mine. Thrown, he started to pull away, but then thought better of it and gave himself over to my tongue.

After a few minutes, we broke apart, needing beer and air. He smiled, "Well, that answers that!"

Later, as my new friend Rory bounced up and down on my dick, screaming his delight like a contestant on *The Price Is Right,* the phone rang. I didn't have to answer it to know that it was Jon, calling to make peace. Instead of picking up, I let it go to voicemail and tried to summon up any image other than enthusiastically-bouncy Rory.

I tried to fantasize about engorged schlongs spewing in my face, or gaping assholes, ready to be eaten. But all I saw was Rory.

"Oh yes, oh yes, oh yes!" I should've known better when he said he was from Phoenix. Folks there don't get out much.

Finally, he came, frothing at the mouth. "Oh yeah. Gary, you are so hot! God, I've never been so—. Uh, did you cum?"

"Oh yeah," I lied, yet again, quickly tossing the condom into the trash. "Gobs. You are one hot fuck, Rory."

Rory attempted a sweet smile, and I let him.

"Hey," he tempted. "Do you mind if I stay—? I mean, it is kind of late and all."

"Sorry, Rory," I smiled, offering my fourth and final lie of the night. "That would be nice, but I've gotta get up early for a doctor's appointment. Get my T cells checked, you know?"

I have no doubt he made it back to Phoenix in record time.

The apartment was empty and quiet, save for Maxie's soft snoring. I couldn't believe what I'd just done. Well, I *could,* as destructive acts come naturally to me, but I didn't want to believe that even I could be capable of such a swift and thorough betrayal.

While technically we had just "broken up," I knew that emotionally I was Jon's, and would be forever. My actions were merciless, as if through blindly fucking another I could somehow exorcise Jon entirely. But his imprint was on my soul, and I knew, even as I pummeled Rory's exceptionally fine ass, that this act of obliteration would end in futility.

Why would one knowingly bring devastation to a person whom they loved?

I've asked that question a million times before, whenever my father would appear in my dreams. I used to hold such hatred for Lenny, and still do, to some degree. While I wish that I could say I loved him, his act of betrayal demolished any memory that might have been warm or joyful; all affirmatives were destroyed, in the time it took him to turn around the car.

And yet I know, on some level, that my father loved me. Thinking back, I recall his awkward attempts at amends, and how at the very sight of him, my walls would shoot up, making me impenetrable. He went to his death thinking I hated him. And at the time, I did. For in that brief flash, which hangs with me even now, he took me to the lowest point of my life. I wanted to scream. To rip out his eyes, battering him to a bloody pulp. And despite all of my efforts, that feeling hasn't changed much, despite the passage of 20 years.

But tonight I was not acting with any heed to the past. With no forethought or analytics, I created a situation from which there would be no escape. No apology or pleading can erase my treachery. I have just done to Jon what my father did to me. But Jon, unlike my father, is a good man; he deserves better.

The next morning, Jon appeared in my office doorway just as I was leaving for lunch. "Mind if I join you?"

I tried to think of a quick excuse, but Rory had thoroughly taxed me. "Sure. Chan Dara okay?"

"Great."

Though we drove together, not a single word was uttered until we had been seated, menus in hand.

"Sorry about last night," Jon offered. I looked intently at my menu. "I just, taking a step like that, talking about moving in, so soon. I don't know why that scares me. Lesbians do it all the time," he laughed. "But after that funeral, I—"

"Do you know what you want?" I interrupted, cautious of the approaching waitress.

"Uh, yeah. Pad Thai and a Thai beer."

"Garlic Chicken, and a Singha as well. Fuck work!" One beer at lunch would hardly be noticed. Besides, I had a feeling I would need it.

Jon reached over and grasped my hand, oblivious to the sanctimonious sneer of the waitress. "Gabe, you may not know this, but I love you. More than anyone or anything."

I jumped in, trying to derail him. "Don't you want to eat first?"

"These feelings I have—they scare me. Not just because you may get sick, though that's part of it. But it's—these feelings—they scare me because they're *new*. I've never experienced anything remotely like this. Ever. And not only am I scared of what these feelings mean, but I'm scared of what happens if I hit these emotional highs with you, and then you die..."

This was not where I had expected our conversation to go. Where was his anger? His bitterness? It was all I could do to focus as he continued.

"You think I'm afraid of death, of all the messiness that comes with it—but that is not it. It's more—how can I love so deeply, lose that love, and ever hope to move on? Where can you go if you've already hit the top?"

I peered into my water glass, willing myself not to cry. That I could care so deeply for Jon and still have sought out Rory shames me. As much as I want to rationalize last night's actions, today they looked pathetic in every light.

"Jon," I began. "Stop for a moment, okay? You're—. You're too good. But—. Last night, I have to tell you, after you left—I was so angry. And terrified. All my life, I've envisioned someone like you. And there I stood, pushing you out the door. Watching you walk away."

"I shouldn't have."

"I didn't give you a choice," I noted dolefully, taking a needed sip of the Singha. "You left because I made you. That was my decision—fucked up though it was. That was me being terrified of being ditched, striking first. But afterwards, after you left—I went out. To a bar. And—"

"Brought someone home," he nodded. "I know."

"You—. How?"

"I never left. I mean, I got into my car, waited for the tears to stop, but they never did. Then I saw you leave." I stared, not believing that he had witnessed my horrendous betrayal. Something in my eyes must have scared him, as he immediately insisted, "I didn't follow you or anything. I'm not that masochistic. But I was still in my car when you came back home."

Try as I might, I could not hold his gaze. "Jon, I—"

"Look, it doesn't matter," he insisted. "I mean, it hurt, but I understand. I let you down. Sometimes a comfort fuck is the only thing you think will help."

"If it's any consolation, it didn't," I admitted. "Once it began, all I could think was that I couldn't wait for it to end."

"I hope you don't feel that way about us," he said, softly.

"Us?"

He nodded, gently smiling.

I stared at him, trying to make sense of all I was hearing. "I don't get you," I sighed, shaking my head. "I kick you to the curb, shit all over you..."

"It takes two to tango, Gabe."

I sat, staring into my beer. Finally, I looked up. "Why do you like me?"

Jon looked surprised. "What do you mean, 'like'?"

"I'm serious. I just—you are so good, and I'm—"

"You need to stop right there," Jon ordered. "You put yourself down all the time, Gabe, focusing on what you think you're not, and completely ignoring all the great things you actually are."

I looked away, unable to accept what he was saying.

"If you could only see yourself the way I do—"

"Yeah, but you're different," I countered. "Everyone else—"

"—Sees the same exact thing," he finished. "Trust me. You are, by far, your own worst critic."

I took another sip of Singha. "I guess."

"Besides," he said, so quietly I had to lean forward to hear him. "If you were all that bad, do you think I'd really be asking you to marry me?"

"What?" My heart stopped, and it seemed that my ears were not working either.

Grinning, Jon pulled a small box from his pocket, placing it in front of me. "For you."

I shrieked, my inner girl bursting out and scaring the restaurant. Gasping, I stared uncomprehendingly, trying to make sense of what was happening. I was being forgiven and rewarded, and was forgiving in turn.

"Go on," he encouraged. "Open it!"

Lifting the lid, the gold band inside gleamed with promise. I stared at the luminescent halo, contemplating all that it signified, and tried to reconcile that this gift was actually intended for me.

"I—I can't accept this."

"You can't? But I thought you—"

"No!" I stopped him, shaking my head. "If we're going to do this—if you're serious about getting married, I need a ring for you, too."

He laughed, pulling another box from his pocket. "I'm one step ahead of you."

As our waitress glided by, sneer still plastered on her face, Jon slid the ring onto my waiting finger.

"One step ahead," I agreed. "Sounds good to me."

Weeks passed and pleasurable routine was established, with Jon officially moving into my place, at last. We'd wake, turn on Katie Couric, shower, play with the dog, and eat. Besides a quick run home at lunch to walk Maxie, my days were spent at LA-DE-DA, diffusing ticking time bombs and sticking my fingers into very angry dykes. Evenings consisted of simple meals cooked together, an occasional movie, and the most spectacular sex I'd ever had.

Jon, far from falling into a sexual routine, worked to ensure that roles and acts shifted; were rearranged. Together, we both loosened, making sex much like a trip, as we commenced with carefully detailed exploration of each uncharted region.

Life was suddenly easy. Much of my anger gone, evaporated,

replaced by a state of unfamiliar, but welcome, contentedness. Was Jon my long-sought balance?

Jon squatted over me, arching back, as my fingers pulsed in and out of his ass. He rocked slowly to my rhythm, ignoring the ringing telephone. I glanced at it.

"Don't even think it!" he moaned. "That's why we pay for voicemail."

That I should even remotely be intrigued by an unknown caller is rather odd. I've never let anything disrupt sex before, let alone for a call that is most likely an offer for "an absolutely free weekend in Las Vegas—for only $59.95!" But lately I've felt as if I'm about to receive a reprieve from my death sentence, and I definitely want to hear it from the governor himself.

Exactly why I am feeling optimistic is less clear. In fact, my T cells have dropped slightly, which is not good. Work has been exasperatingly awful, which could be a factor in my T cell drop. And my checkbook is overdrawn for the first time since I was 26 and living the Visa-MasterCard-Macy's life. The only thing that is really, truly great is Jon.

I am in love. And not just with Jon, either. I am in love with living.

With well over 35 years on the planet, I can't believe that I'm only now experiencing life to the fullest. Little things that have occurred countless times prior suddenly carry new, important meaning.

This morning, instead of drinking my coffee in the kitchen, standing up, I took it into the backyard. Sitting with the *Times*, I slowly nursed my mug, letting its warmth seep into my marrow. I noticed a bee nearby, extracting pollen from the daylilies. Following its haphazard though purposeful journey across the garden, I was surprised to look into the kitchen and realize that an hour had passed and I now had only 10 minutes to shower and dress for work.

Heeding my promise to reverse my checkbook, I trotted off to shower. But I could have stayed in that garden until nightfall, so enraptured was I by the bee's sense of duty. How is it that such creatures take seeming pleasure in their tasks, while I greet the slightest demand with a resigned sigh? Is everyone else the same as me? I do know many who would tell you that they LOVE their work and that it fills them with esteem, but, in my view, they have just not yet found effective therapists.

In all honesty, no one *likes* to work. It is simply a means to an end, nothing more, no matter what modicum of pleasure it may offer. We clock in, charting a path borne from obligation or expectation or need, not from love for the task. If everyone were brutally honest about their desires, we would all be in the South of France, basking in the warmth of the sun, wondering where all the worker bees had gone and why they hadn't yet replenished our drinks.

For far too long I have been a worker bee without the zing. And it is ironic that in love, long resisted for all its messiness, I am finally experiencing life at its fullest.

"Shove your fingers in further. Yeah, another," Jon begs. "Oh god—fill me. Fill me!"

I am actually *in* the South of France now, lounging at Les Roches Blanches' pool, overlooking the sea. Having just ordered a kir, in honor of our arrival in Cassis, I am feeling quite smug. Jonathan, bless him, is napping and thus unable to witness my embarrassing conceit. It is a good thing, too, as he just about throttled me on the road from Marseilles. Is it my fault that, with maps, I am utterly doomed? I can barely read the signposts in this foreign country and should be spared maps as well. But, after all, as I was too tired to drive, I suppose deciphering the map was a fair trade. Still, I was so stressed and exhausted by the time we found the hotel that I could not drag myself off the mattress, and instead sent Jon in search of nuts and berries.

He returned soon after, arms laden with baguette, cheese, paté, and the most wondrous grapes, which smelled of flowers. Yet it was all I could do to prop my arm up and tear off a chunk of bread.

So blissful to be exploring new locales, Jon seems not to have noticed how completely the fatigue has taken over my body, and I haven't the heart to tell him that something is wrong. We have a week and a half remaining on our journey, and I'm hoping I can conceal it until our return. Disappointing Jon is something I loathe to do. He, after all, has given so much, and I so little.

Well, that's not true. That this trip could be afforded at all is due to the generosity of my life insurance and the viatical of such, which I'd learned from Keith. Cashing in on a life that will soon be ending seemed a bit unfair, until I rationalized that this was, in actuality, my money. Why not utilize it to make some wishes come true?

Jon, more hesitant than I, felt that selling the policy was a signal to my body that I had given up, granting permission, if you will, to proceed with demolition. Now, lying here on this chaise, barely able to lift my glass, I am not at all certain he wasn't right.

Once our Ed McMahon-like check was in the mail, full with the promise of putting my bank account into unfamiliar positive territory and us into unfamiliar geographical territory, Jon gave himself over to the trip. As he had never been to Europe, the journey became as much about him as me. I wanted him to have the trip of a lifetime and looked forward to introducing him to the places I had treasured.

We were quickly inundated with travel suggestions covering all corners of the globe. At work, my desk overflowed with copies of *Gourmet*, touting the epicurean delights of Paris, books uncannily revealing the secrets of the "unexplored" hill towns of Umbria, and list upon list of such things as "Bargain Hotels in Rome for Less than $300." From Ric and Tim alone, a 15-page typed list of recommendations, single-spaced, complete with phone and fax.

Every time I turned a corner, I would be stopped and regaled with tales of hidden cafés and out-of-the-way auberges. France and Italy, it would seem, were not cohesive territories but disjointed segments in search of a unifier. Having been, I knew differently, but Jon's eyes sparked at the thought of being the first to savor the risotto fumé at that "little trattoria, just off the beaten path."

These paths, new only to those who have never been, have proved too much for this fragile vessel. I look askance at each set of rock-hewn stairs, as if they had been chiseled purely for my punishment. That I have mastered them is more than enough to absolve me of all past, present, and future sins, granting me unfettered access to the great beyond.

In some respects, this trip has echoed others, as it began in Paris. Whether by choice or design, each of my continental journeys has begun in that sumptuous city. Despite having spent a cumulative total of 23 calendar days there, Paris feels like home in a way that Los Angeles, my city of origin, never could. All I enjoy in life can be found in Paris, simply by turning a corner. Even the streets are pretty, bathed clean every morning by the men bearing green brooms. It is as if the entire city takes pride in its grooming, throwing open the windows to greet each day with an energetic "Bonjour!"

Our little hotel on Rue Monsieur le Prince proved just the spot to begin our Parisian adventure. After a wild taxi ride through the confusing array of streets, we checked in, squeezing ourselves and assorted luggage into an elevator seemingly designed to hold only Billy Barty, on a day in which he was dieting. Following our half-hour ride up to our 4th floor room, I removed the duffle bag from my head, putting the key into the door.

The door swung open, introducing us to the most charming 8-by-8-foot room in all of Paris. I began to curse the Parisian Gods for their skewed view of human anatomy when Jon unlatched the shutters and all was forgiven. It wasn't as if we had a postcard view, with the Eiffel tower peeking over the rooftops. Rather, we looked out directly into the apartments opposite, where a woman, hair wrapped in a red scarf, provided water to her geranium-filled window boxes. Seeing us gawk, she nodded, offering a slight smile to today's tourists. Below, we could see the top of a man's head, prematurely balding, as he sauntered around the corner, disappearing from sight. Only his cheerful whistle hung in the air as reminder of his passage.

"It's more beautiful than I ever imagined," Jon whispered, taking my hand.

I knew just what he meant. For me, Europe is more than the sum of parts tourists shower you with upon their return. A postcard, trinket, or recollection can only share so much. Only through actual experience can the totality be understood. And Jon and I were more than ready to grab hold and hang on for the ride.

Prior to our departure, Jon and I had assiduously poured over possibilities for our itinerary, dissecting each option. Our list included places I'd already experienced that begged sharing, as well as new venues to be explored together. Once tallied, it became clear that to attempt even half would be folly. The decision was made to keep our list accessible, and to pick and choose at will, given desires and time limitations.

After unpacking, we checked two items off our list for exploration, and then explored our armoire for the needed attire. As it was 2:30 Paris time, we decided on a leisurely walk along the Seine to the Jardin des Tuileries, then back to the Café de Flore for drinks, with dinner at the Restaurant Cremerie-Polidor. Though Camus and Sartre were long gone, we decided that etiquette demanded that we honor the era and dress appropriately. Accordingly, Jon wore a crisp white button-down with a handsome plaid sport coat, while I selected a burnt orange cashmere sweater, which I jauntily threw about my shoulders. This sweater, it should be noted, bought with my death-wish windfall, was never actually *worn* during the trip, but served admirably as fashion accessory. If I have learned anything from my mother, it is not to always be forthright or kind or honest or even moral; rather, it is this: presentation counts!

Those words have echoed, deep within, throughout my life, but never more so than in Paris. Having outgrown the self-consciousness that high fashion demands, dressing to impress has instead become second nature. I couldn't change, even if I wanted to. Even for a quick jaunt to the store, Armani or Hugo Boss is imperative. Now, some may see this as silly, others as time wasted, but—to me—it is just one more element of the whole.

To underestimate the importance of style is to miss the point of beauty. It enhances an experience, creating a memory, something permanent and indelible. Imagine a romantic evening: start with mussels, a beautiful fillet au sole, and an oaky bottle of smooth chardonnay. The votives twinkle, illuminating the darting eyes of your one true love. Now, replace just the candlelight with fluorescents, and what have you got?

Once an experience has been deconstructed and aesthetics removed, the magic vanishes, leaving only the pedestrian and functional. With the magic gone, the memory alters as well. It may still have been a great meal, but it will never invoke the tender, longing sigh of "Remember that night...?"

And so it was that Jon and I approached our trip. Our experiences were not unlike the impossibly perfect photos in Condé Nast Traveler. Not only were we meticulous in appearance, but we had researched our expedition so thoroughly that we often felt as if we'd actually experienced our destinations prior to arrival. The trip flowed naturally, at an unhurried pace.

Today we began at the most incongruous place to greet the morning sun, the Pere Lachaise cemetery. Silent and subdued, we stepped humbly down the paths, stopping often to speculate about those entombed. For the famous, we challenged each other, urging forth memories and facts long forgotten. At Gertrude Stein's crypt, we paused, placing stones atop her simple resting place. And we completely forgot ourselves at Isadora Duncan's urn, pretending that our scarves too had been caught, until a humorless tour guide shushed us in an unfamiliar language.

Despite the early hour, or because of it, I could not stop thinking ahead to my own death. I've made it clear that I don't want to end up buried in a box. Cremate me quickly and scatter my ashes wherever you will. I do not believe in an afterlife. This one was hard enough, thank you. And though I need no monument or marker, I would very much like to be remembered. Not so much for ego or pride—I care not *how* I am remembered—but more that I want to be counted as having been here, even if for a short time.

I wonder though, when people *do* think of me, will they remember me as I currently am, or as I once was? The lines in my face are more pronounced now, my body more lean. And no amount of bronzer can cover the pale illness, just beneath my skin.

Perhaps they will see me as I stood ten years ago, primed with only a bottle of lite beer and an enticing smile, dancing endlessly on the lit floor, obliviously reveling in what would later become known as my "prime". Or will they envision a young, somewhat shy boy, whose future seemed to be blazing in sunlight? How sad that, apart from Gloria, no one will remember him, or even find it plausible that such a boy could lie within the man I've become.

It is he who I think of when I picture myself dead. He held the power to become all that he envisioned and, blessedly, knew nothing of the true nature of the world. I wish I could find some remnant of him, of his optimism, somewhere within. But it dawns on me that his funeral was held long ago, and his gravestone since weathered beyond recognition. There are no flowers on his grave. No teddy bear memoriam. Only a dirty glass jar, lodged next to the stone, filled with pennies, and obscured by layers of fallen leaves.

"Look at this," Jon calls quietly, pointing to a crypt. "Chopin."

Looking at Jon, so pleased with his discovery, notes from a piano float through my head. The song, though, is not that of Chopin, but Gershwin, with the vocals of Bobby Short. His buoyant tone reassures that, no matter what catastrophes may occur, and I was certain many would, love, though, is here to stay.

As if hearing the same music, Jon reaches for my hand, leading me back to a Paris that is *alive*.

Despite my fatigue, we have taken the Metro only a handful of times, as I prefer not to spend our few precious moments here underground. But, sensing that I am tired, Jon guides me back to the D'Orsay by a series of buses and trains. Far and away my favorite museum, the D'Orsay stands as a vivid contrast to this morning's crypts, and yet is linked in theme.

These paintings and sculptures serve to remind us of those who died long ago, and of the emotional promise only great art can fulfill. That Monet's simple *Rouen Cathedral* should provoke such feelings now as it did in 1894 is unfathomable. These days, such timelessness is difficult to imagine. While Mozart or Van Gogh have easily survived the ages, what of the artists of today? Does anyone even come close? Perhaps we have crossed a boundary, where all that is timeless has already been chiseled in stone, leaving today's artists only Charmin toilet paper for their canvas.

This morning I was wondering how people would remember me, but now I'm struck by the possibility that they might not think of me at all. Seeing these paintings, I realize that we are viewing the crème de la crème, and that there are countless artists in Paris alone who have since been forgotten. Multiply those by the forgotten politicians, waiters, window washers, shopkeepers, students, and others who have inhabited this 41-square-mile area and you are left with a whole heap of forgotten.

That someone should even want to remember me is wishful thinking. That they would have reason for remembering me is dubious. I have done little good to be chronicled. I have been, on my best day, mean, spiteful, callous, and cruel. That I am smart and occasionally humorous may rate highly in my own esteem, but savoir-faire is the most ephemeral of qualities.

I have asked that, in lieu of a funeral, a party be held in my honor. But now, standing in front of this artwork, I wonder if that is the best of ideas. I have left no legacy to prompt attendance, and though many will gather, my hunch is that it will be out of obligation rather than genuine affection.

Compiling a list, I can count on one hand those who truly love me: Jon, Pastor Sally, Gloria and, possibly, Clare. Four. Almost laughably pathetic. Had I been able to add those who now are deceased, my list would have been longer, but I also would have more funeral no-shows.

As dismal as "four" sounds, though, at least I do have people who have chosen to love me completely. Maybe four isn't such a bad legacy after all; I'm sure there are some who couldn't muster even that.

I wish death wasn't so all-pervading right now. It is not that I continually dwell on it, or even verbally acknowledge it. It just never seems very far from my thoughts. There have been many instances on the trip where Jon will peer at me, "Whatcha thinkin'?", and I grasp at the beautiful sunset or the freshly-made Gran Marnier crepe, never letting him in.

It is not that I am being evasive. I simply believe that there will be enough time later for such discussions; perhaps even sooner than we think.

The next day, we wandered into les Jardins du Luxembourg. A favorite since my first visit with Keith, it is the park's vast expanse that thrills me to the core. The stretch of trees, rowed neatly. The breadth of the pond with floating sailboats darting about, governed by stern little boys wearing blue caps. Green chairs, unimprisoned, scattered about to soothe the weary. The lively burst from the café, where tourists and locals alike lift cups, toasting their good fortune to be living a life such as this. And that manse. Serene yet imposing, it sits at the head of the dinner table, the patriarch, taking note of all who have come to gather in its midst.

Jon and I entered the grounds quietly, tired from our four days in the city. With so much that will remain unseen, there lingers a touch of melancholy. Across the pond, we watch a woman bundled up against the nonexistent cold, coaching her lap dog away from a soiled napkin. The dog paws at it, as if it were a living being, daring it to fight. As the napkin shrugs imperceptibly, the dog finally receives the message, journeying on toward a waiting pole. After completing its business, we watch as the dog squats, taking a crap on the walkway. Though conscious of her pet's actions, the woman makes no effort to remove the mess, ignoring the napkin skittering about. Averting her eyes, the woman turns and begins to walk away. Just as she turns again, calling out for her dog, an elderly man crosses, stepping directly into the excrement. With a cry, he wheels about, spotting the offending dog and even more offensive owner. A streak of French explodes from underneath his graying mustache. Park-goers turn, eyeing the scene with bemused detachment, as the woman veers back from her retreat, choosing instead to fight. Fists are pounded, lips fly at dizzying speed, while the mutt wanders off, forgotten.

Jon and I stare, unabashed, more interested than is warranted. Eventually, one or both contenders back off, for each now heads in the opposite direction—the woman in search of her dog, the man a napkin.

"What was fascinating," notes Jon, "is how both were so sure of their convictions. Why is that? Parisians don't seem as neurotic, as insecure, as us."

"First of all, I'm sure there are plenty of Parisians who are fucked up. They adore Jerry Lewis, right?"

"So?" He looks at me with profound doubt, as he is also a Jerry Lewis lover. But I've told you he's usually misguided...

"Also, their priorities are different," I continue. "Success to them is a great cup of coffee. An intense conversation with a friend. A bit of chèvre spread on a baguette," I offer. "In the U.S., if we don't become a superstar by the time we're 30, we've failed. Simply being good at something isn't enough. We want to be, are bred to be, the best. But we can't all be. Some have to fail. And there's no more direct path to insecurity than failure."

"That's kind of pessimistic," Jon says, stretching out his legs.

"No, it's not. It's realistic. How many times are we told, growing up, that if you try hard enough, you can be President? What kind of signal is that? During our entire lifetime, we'll see—what?—maybe 10, 12 presidents. It's impossible. We're setting goals no one can reach."

"But goals are what fuel us."

"It all depends on what we're reaching for," I countered. "If my parents had said, 'We don't care what you do, so long as you enjoy it, take pride in it,' I would've been better off. As it is—"

"As it is, you work at an agency that saves lives," Jon points out, ever the optimist.

I smile, allowing him the final word. To be that certain, that untainted... I had been that way once. No more.

The next morning, our last in Paris, we made our way to the definitive pastry experience in the city, Julien's Patisserie. I'd talked so much about it, I feared it would meet neither Jon's expectations nor my own. For every confection we'd sampled, I'd say, "This is good—but wait until you try Julien's!" And, finally, here we were, on Avenue Franklin Roosevelt, just steps away.

The sight of the familiar red awning instantly provided energy, and my step quickened. Reaching it, the glass door opened and a matronly woman stepped out but then stopped short, blocking the entrance as she fiddled with the string-tied box in her hands. It was all I could do not to forcibly push her aside. Jon laughed at my visible impatience, but smiled at her, holding the door and ushering her good-naturedly on her way.

Entering, I was instantly transported to my embodiment of heaven. The counter tops gleamed, and the scent of freshly baked pain au chocolat permeated the brightly-lit shop. While each item in the perfectly set rows had its appeal, I came for only one: the divorceé. Two large baked puffs, one filled with rich chocolate, the other coffee cream, and joined by icing. Noting the simplicity with which the outer layer unites the contrasting interiors, I was reminded of my fragmented self. If only a simple layer of icing could coalesce my varied elements, and make me just a tad bit sweeter. But as Julien's is not the place for self-analysis, I pushed my neuroses aside and selected one, along with an almond croissant for protein. Stepping back, I finally gave Jon room to choose. Watching him, wide-eyed, mouth open in awe, I am certain that I too shared his expression when making my selection. That a straightforward base of sugar, flour, and cream can inspire such reaction in grown men is proof that life's simple pleasures are indeed its best.

Now fortified, bellies full, the time had come to say goodbye. Leaving Paris is never easy, no matter how enticing one's destination. Ours was Lyon, where we journeyed via train before renting a tiny compact to transport us through the southern portion of France, along the Riviera and into Italy.

So much of the trip is a blur, caused by a combination of too much walking, too much food, and too much wine. But I do remember soup made from Jasmine flower in St. Remy de Provence; a night in a castle outside Asti; green apple sorbet in Bellagio; contorting ourselves into a slant with all the other hoards at the Leaning Tower, as if the Tower needed our physical support; and Venice, in its entirety.

Our last stop was Rome, where I discovered that I was much like the ruins surrounding us: though I had the will to remain strong, my body had succumbed to the elements and had begun its decline. Reluctantly, I told Jon all I'd been feeling, both physically and emotionally. My life would never be under my own control again.

At turns sympathetic and supportive, he withheld nothing. His anger, however, was unexpected. He could not believe that I hadn't shared these feelings as I had experienced them. If we were to have any hope of succeeding, he said, honesty was paramount.

Later, all talked out, Jon held me close, cuddling from behind like the proverbial spoons, and offered my ear sweet kisses. Pulling my t-shirt up, he let his fingers roam my belly, toying with the strands of hair and meandering up to my stiffening nipples. His touch was gentle, but never hesitant. Love and desire guided him, leading the way into my shorts. Slowly, his fingers grazed my thickening cock, fondling it gently. I reached behind, trying to grab hold of some part of Jon, but he brushed my hand back. "Shhh—tonight is all about you."

With that, he pulled my shorts to my knees, my now-hard dick slapping against my stomach. Continuing to kiss my neck and ears, Jon grasped my cock firmly, allowing his palm to rub softly over the head. I sighed, unable to move.

I could feel his foot bending up, snagging my hanging shorts and forcing them to my ankles. Twisting around, Jon's hand pushed the shorts to the floor and lifted my leg into the air. His tongue found my ass, no map needed, and slathered me in moisture. Reaching down, I took my cock in hand, feeling its weight shift in my palm.

Hearing fumbling noises, I was not surprised when Jon's tongue was replaced by warm lubed fingers, loosening my tense muscles.

"Are you ready?" He asked.

I looked for the familiar wrapper. "Where's the—?"

"I thought, maybe tonight, we wouldn't need it," he appealed, hesitantly. "The risks are low..."

"We always need it," I insisted, though wishing it wasn't so. "No matter what, we need it."

With an agreeable shrug he rolled over. I heard foil being ripped open, the bed shifting as Jon eased on the latex. That this should be my fate I had accepted long ago. But I was not willing to tempt the fate of another, no matter how pleasurable.

Jon sighed, "I just wanted——."

"Yeah," I said. "Me too."

Pushing into me slowly, giving me time to adjust, I marveled at how completely Jon had changed my life. By his caring for me, I in turn had learned how to care as well.

That thought, however, was quickly lost, pushed out of my head by the powerful thrusts Jon sent, pummeling my ravaged body. I rode him like a champ, backing off when he got too close.

Maneuvering, I rolled onto my back so that I could watch his face, pulling my legs against my chest. Nodding, I prodded Jon harder and harder, until he completely withdrew and entered me, again and again, into the night.

Sometime later, the sheet lightly over me, I felt an unexpectedly cool breeze, and found myself sitting up, pulling the window closed. The room was quiet, save for the soft hum of Jon's breathing. There was something comforting in the dark silence. It was odd, really, to be so bone-weary and yet to experience such a pure and contented a peace. But while his very breath brought comfort, its rhythm, like the quiet ticking of a clock, reminded me that my time was running out.

How strange, to find comfort in the end. To be both victor and vanquished, to have won and to have lost, both at the same time. Across the street, in the stillness, I heard the faint beeping of an alarm clock, and knew that somehow, in just a few hours, I'd have to summon my energy and soldier forth as best I could.

Though staying but a few streets from the Spanish steps, I saw them only through the window of a cab. Jon passed them countless times, ferrying food from the nearby McDonald's. As much as I wanted good pasta and pizza, trying to get takeout when you don't speak the language is frustrating at best. Plus, there was something so reassuring about my McMeals. They were the same each time, never varying, and I took a measure of comfort in knowing that some things, like their salty fries, never changed.

Each of the four days in Rome, I managed to see something, but for short durations, expending maximum effort. We spent our last day at the Trevi fountain, as it seemed I could do little now but stand or sit. Even walking a block was taxing.

We sat for hours, taking in the sculpture's myriad details. Of all of the sights and works of art we'd experienced on our travels, the fountain provided the most personal of connections. Perhaps because the two seahorses, rising from the water with Oceanus and chariot in tow, are named Agitated and Placid, reflecting the fluctuating rhythms of the vast blue sea. I felt such sympathy for these two, so diametrically opposed, struggling to integrate disparate parts into harmonic whole, working to complete their task. Gazing, I longed to reach out, to touch their majestic manes in solidarity. I wanted to tell them, though, not to bother in searching for symmetry, for it is a fruitless endeavor, as my wasted time has proven. Instead, they will attain collective strength solely by owning their unique, varied attributes.

Later, having sat in the sun, gathering strength, we wandered for a bit through the nearby souvenir shops. In one, I spotted a plastic replica of the fountain; eye-catching for all the wrong reasons. Someone—some anonymous frustrated artiste in China—had apparently decided that the travertine and marble tones of the fountain were not nearly impressive enough, and so had given the fountain an extreme makeover—in living, breathing Technicolor. Brown hair has been painted on Oceanus and the Tritons, complete with peach-colored skin and rosy cheeks. Even the beautiful seahorse now bore a tail of iridescent green.

Staring at the brightly-hued mermaid tail, I flashed on Bette Midler's Delores Delago, the toast of Chicago, zooming across the stage in motorized wheelchair, belting out some Polynesian show tune and swinging her poi balls into the heavens.

Somehow, I think that was not the impression the colorful artist had desired to inspire; now all I could think of was big tits.

As we meandered back to the fountain, Jon showed me the Pope bottle opener he'd purchased, which he intended to use as a Christmas ornament, prompting me to fall in love with him all over again.

With twilight approaching, the crowds at the fountain had subsided, and I found myself with an unobstructed view. Taking it all in, Jon at my side, I reflected on the well-known legend: if you stand with your back to the fountain, so the story tells, and throw a coin into the water, you shall return to Rome again. And despite my inherent cynicism, the majesty of the fountain and my love for symbolism overrode my doubts.

Optimistically I turned, said a quick prayer (though I am uncertain as to *whom*), and tossed a 1,000 lire coin over my shoulder. With a splash, I heard it drop in. Oh, happy day! The thought that I would somehow survive this journey, and indeed be fit enough to make another, fueled my return to the states, giving me hope that all was not yet lost.

Jon never had the heart to tell me that my coin first hit the rim of the fountain before ricocheting into the water. And, for that, I am grateful.

"You're just exhausted, that's all!" cried my mother, squeezing me tight.

"It's more than that, Mom," I sighed, stuffing another bag into the trunk.

"A long trip—five weeks—and so much to see," Gloria rationalized, "it's no wonder!"

"Hon," Pastor Sally threw in, "I'm sure Gabe knows his body better than we do."

"Still—," Gloria smiled.

"Besides," interjected Jon, "the LAX loading zone may not be the best place for this conversation."

Acknowledging the sense in this, everyone piled into the car, with Jon skillfully turning the topic back to the sights. As Gloria peered back with interest, Jon babbled on, recounting every significant moment for our armchair tourists. Pastor Sally adjusted her rearview mirror, taking note of my unsmiling eyes, and gave a gentle grin. Our spirits connected, I knew that she understood what was happening to me, and had an understanding of what lie ahead.

Clearly, the doctors had no clue. Besides fatigue, I had no symptoms and my numbers, though lower than normal, were still within reason.

"But that's to be expected, given the energy your trip took," Doctor #32 noted.

"So the trip of my life could be the cause of my death?" I countered.

"Oh, not the trip itself. But the toll on your body—"

"Doctor, for the last 10 years, everyone has been telling me to exercise. But, now that I do—"

"You have no other symptoms?"

I shook my head. "Nope."

"Well," he shook my hand, "Keep me posted! If anything changes—"

"Don't worry. I'll call."

It's not that my doctor wasn't proactive but, to be fair, looking for a cause when the symptom is general malaise is a bit difficult. But I was angry nonetheless. I was dying. I knew it. I just couldn't prove it.

Help came a few weeks later. I'd been so tired since our return that, besides dragging myself into work each day, I did nothing. Jon shopped, took care of Maxie, and jacked himself off. I watched Katie Couric, Tom Brokaw, old movies, and slept. But other than that, things were normal.

Almost.

I'd noticed that, whether walking or even standing still, I had trouble maintaining balance. And, when driving, I found that my reflexes weren't as sharp either. Though I would see the red light ahead, by the time I applied the brake, bringing the car to a halt, I would be sticking past the walkway into traffic. Instead of telling Jon, though, I used exhaustion as an excuse, and had him chauffeur me instead.

But it was while walking from my office to the men's room one day, a direct and simple path, when I suddenly veered to the right. Trying to compensate, I tripped, falling into a heap. As no one was nearby, I remained still, trying to figure out how I had ended up on the floor, before finally pulling myself together and continuing about my business. Though it disturbed and baffled me, initially I told no one.

Despite such incidents, Jon and I continued on as normal, devoting the usual time to work, doctors, and home. The only area in which our lives had dramatically changed was sex. We hadn't had it for two months. And it is true what they say: Abstinence does make the heart grow fonder.

I had lost a tremendous amount of weight, my butt sagged, my bones poked through my skin. Not even *I* would want to fuck me. And yet, Jon tried.

It is not that I didn't want or crave sex—I did. But I craved the beauty of passion between two young and vibrant people. If I were not sick, but merely old, I would still feel the same. No matter how great you've kept your figure, at 85 few look appetizing with their toes tucked behind their ears. Years from now, when I am gone, I wanted Jon to be able to look back on our sex as something pleasurable, not obligatory. He's said that because he loves me for me, the person, the changes to my exterior don't faze him. But I don't believe it. Even a blind person running their hands over my body would cringe. The message would be the Braille-equivalent of clichéd horror movie girl alone in a spooky house: *Run! Pay no attention to that noise upstairs! You are a pre-menopausal blonde with gregarious tits in an abandoned mansion. Can any good come of this? Turn, run, with all of your might. And whatever you do, don't look back!*

Though Jon did not run, for which I am grateful, he has not accepted my abstention gracefully. Believing that I am no longer interested in him, despite my appeals and proffered kisses, Jon gripped that fallacy and hung on to it with all the resolve of an alligator wrestler. Although this gnawed at me, so far removed from my own thinking, perhaps it was easier for him to believe that it was due to some fault of his own, rather than in accepting the reality of my decline.

Indeed, my wishes and fantasies no longer revolved around sex, but of life. Whenever I visualized myself doing something romantic, like wandering along the Seine, leafing through the offerings of the vendors, or even something more mundane, such as taking my combo meal from the drive-thru girl at McDonalds, I noticed myself stiffen. Just as with sex, the unobtainable became alluring, no matter how negligible the experience had been when it occurred.

Last night Jon woke me up. Or I woke him up. He was holding me by the shoulders, shouting, "Gabe! Gabey, can you hear me?"

I looked at him strangely, the words taking time to form, before asking, "Why the fuck did you wake me?"

"You've been talking to yourself."

"So?"

"With your eyes wide open, you looked at me and said the strangest things."

"What's the big deal? Talking in your sleep is allowed, isn't it?"

"But you weren't asleep!"

"What did I say?"

"Things like, 'Check to make sure the alarm is on the cake.' You wanted me to see if the cake was set right."

"I'm sure I meant—Well, did you set the clock?"

"Cake. You said cake. And yes, I set the clock, as always. But you said cake. 'Make sure the alarm is on the cake.' I asked what kind, and you said white angel food with strawberry frosting."

"The kind my grandmother made."

Jon ran his hands through his hair, completely freaked. "God, Gabey—the things you—you were talking about rabbits, and god knows what..."

"People talk in their sleep."

"You were awake. Our eyes locked. And we talked for over 15 minutes like that." He sighed, "Gabey, what is happening?"

I rolled onto my side, pulling the covers around snugly. What was happening? What could have caused such strange behavior? And why couldn't I remember any of it?

Flipping through the CD's, none seemed quite right. Choosing music for my funeral required that I first choose music to *listen to* while choosing music for my funeral. Though not as important as the real thing, the proper establishment of mood was still consequential.

I have no idea how I acquired so many CD's. Far from rich, whenever I peruse my stacks, I contemplate how much money I have actually spent. Periodically, I prune my collection, selling back those CD'S that have lost their appeal, at a substantial loss. What had prompted their purchase in the first place? Had I even listened to the music prior, or had I just liked the cover?

I don't feel like choosing death marches right now. Opening a drawer labeled "MAN-MOY" (translation: "Melissa Manchester through Alison Moyet"), I reach instinctively to the middle, extracting Bette Midler's latest. While not yet released, one of my fellow fanatics nabbed me an unfinished demo of what will become *Bette of Roses*. Carefully, I eject the original cast recording of *On the Town* and place this new Bette into her familiar place in the holder. Pushing in/out, I sit back and listen.

Maxie paddles over, begging, almost silently. Reaching down, I acquiesce, pulling her into my lap. Together, we listen. Though this album is better than most, I listen intently, hoping to hear some remnant of her former brilliance. But the vocals verge on calculating, and while any Bette is better than none, I am left disappointed. Had I been mistaken all these years? Could you always see her working?

At the time I first discovered her, all seemed possible. I was 17 and in love, for the first time in my life. I had found Keith and Bette Midler all in the same month, with the former introducing me to the latter. Could this buoyant outlook have colored my rationale?

While possible, it's highly unlikely. Critical astuteness has been a badge of honor with me. And Bette's early albums exceeded expectations, leaping past all others into the starry pantheon of the immortals. She could turn from a campy jaunt to bittersweet to nostalgic boogie without batting an eye, and with a rawness which, somewhere along the way, regrettably disappeared.

I like to believe that Bette, when young, was a lot like me. No great beauty, but not altogether ugly. Never part of the in-crowd, though desperately wanting to be. Each of us with only one remarkable physical characteristic (her: big tits, me: big dick.) We both funneled our frustrations into scathingly sarcastic humor, though neither of us was smart enough to know when to stop. But such similarities came to a screeching halt when it came to talent. Unlike her, while good at a great many things, I had no singular gift on which to focus.

Was it laziness that brought her down? Were the demands of craftsmanship too much? Or did Bette merely decide to live a comfy life, free from financial strain? I mean, what else could explain the amazingly raw, frayed performance in *The Rose*, juxtaposed with her mugging performances ever since?

Somewhere along the way, it appears that Bette gave up. Once she attained fame, perhaps, desire was quenched, without another dream to replace it. Let's face it—anyone whose first job was in a pineapple factory would long for something better. But once you've "made it", what then?

I won't let such complacency happen to me. My problem is the reverse. Instead of one dream to achieve, a single task to conquer, I have many, mainly around amends. But as the holidays approach, I fear I do not have nearly enough time to make things right with those I've wronged. Even so, I will not give up! No matter how difficult or painful, I know that wholeness and success is within my grasp. It will not escape me.

My only question: Where do I begin?

I started with a letter to Clare. Simple, direct, and to the point. I got no reply.

I followed with a voicemail. No frivolity or humor. No demands. Nothing needed from her. Just a message of apology, and hope for a better friendship.

She didn't respond.

I considered flowers or a gift, but I knew that friendship

couldn't be bought, no matter how many times I've tried. Instead, I persisted, leaving periodic messages and notes, inquiring about her and her family, her job, and always with an offer to meet.

In the past, when I'd attempted to remedy similar such situations, I'd leave only one message, and if that person doesn't return the call within 24 hours, they would be crossed off my list in black Sharpie. But I've realized, slowly, through loving Jon, how gentle our hearts can be. How even a slight ache can persist, follow us, when resolution is not at hand. And so my messages continued. Even if in vain.

I so want to live until Christmas, if only to play each and every CD in my holiday collection one last time. While this may not be the loftiest of goals, I've learned that baby steps count. And it is, after all, the season of the newborn's birth.

The crazy thing about this enormous collection is that you really only hear the same 23 songs. They're just repeated over and over by different artists, so it feels like more. But I don't care. Repetition breeds familiarity and comfort, so who am I to argue?

Traditional holiday favorites of mine include Kiri Te Kawana's beautiful take on "Sweet Little Baby Child" and almost any version of "In the Bleak Midwinter." But my real favorites are the less well-known songs of the season, such as John Denver's "Aspenglow" or the Partridge Family's "My Christmas Card to You." Why none of these has yet replaced "Little Drummer Boy" as the great favorite of the populace is beyond me.

But despite this love for the unusual and unique, my holiday favorite would have to be "Have Yourself a Merry Little Christmas." I can still recall the party eight years ago at my pal Tony's house, when he sat down at the upright piano and we gathered for carols. Seven men, seven friends, seven voices raised together in harmony. Each song was magical, and the singing angelically inspired. Although I cannot recall the exact order of tunes, in my mind, "Merry Little Christmas" was sung last, capturing in snapshot that defining moment, surrounded by my loving brothers.

Looking at each of their youthful faces, smiling in song, I remember wondering where we would all be 10 years hence. The song claimed that we'd all be together through the years, if only the Fates allowed, but Fate apparently had other plans.

Tony died two Christmases later, suffering from AIDS-related blindness, dementia, and pneumonia. His lover Carlos had died even earlier, also from pneumonia. Danny Goldberg, an actor on *The Young and the Restless*, made it to 28 before succumbing to wasting syndrome. Andrew, regrettably, I lost touch with a few years back, although I have heard he is again living in Topeka, taking care of his ailing grandmother and dining alone on his HIV cocktail. Of course, I am still kicking, but sweet Francis died last year. His body finally resistant to the years of drugs, he fought until the very end. If anyone could have made it, it was he. Even more painful was that, whether from guilt, remorse, or loneliness, Francis' lover Bobby died less than a month later, hanging himself from their garage rafters from a noose made of silk ties.

Eight years; seven friends; two remaining. And one, just barely.

As Christmas morning had been promised to my mother and P.S., Jon and I claimed Christmas Eve for us. To me, it had always been more meaningful anyway. A cool night, crackling fire, lights twinkling, a good meal, and people you love. Somehow, in the light of day, despite the ripping paper and screams of delight, something is lost. The tree looks paler, the pace more hurried, and our smiles come not so easily. But the night prior, in the quiet of evening, raising a glass of Zinfandel in toast, that inner part normally dormant opens ever so slightly, filling us, reminding each that we are unique individuals, capable and worthy of love.

This year, despite my health challenges, I was determined to plow through my duties without fail. At work, in addition to my normal tasks, I was charged with supervising the creation of more than 700 client holiday baskets, as well as planning our annual volunteer "Thank You" party; a challenging scenario, even in the best of conditions. Add to this my own gifts to buy, handmade cards to send, parties to attend, popcorn balls to roll, and cookies to make, and you have chaos—and ill health—in the making.

Also, I had very little money for gifts. Most of my viatical slush fund had gone toward the trip, and the little I had left I wanted to hang on to. Happily, Jon had an idea which would help us do just that, and I immediately embraced it as my own. On the other, we would spend no more than 30 dollars apiece. We could use that $30 as creatively as we liked and, in honor of his birth, stretch the cash like Jesus with the loaves and the fishes, but we could not spend one single penny more.

As the days rushed past, however, I realized that the Gods of Christmas had landed elsewhere, unhappy that I had not shown due humility, and had therefore decided to conspire against me. Instead of gold, frankincense, and myrrh, I was gifted with Christmas Crises Numbers 1, 2, and 3.

The first crisis appeared on December 8th, three days before our client holiday baskets were due to be delivered, when I received a voicemail from our contact at the record company. While he'd promised us three CDs for each basket, as he'd just been laid off, effective immediately, he could no longer follow through. Despite umpteen calls to both the record label and one very influential board member, the best centerpiece replacement I could come up with was 700 boxes of Mrs. Cubbison's Stuffing Mix.

We filled the baskets with anything we could get our hands on, and to this day I'm certain there are many clients scratching their heads at the baskets overflowing with paperclips, manila folders, and Styrofoam cups. *Happy Holidays!*

Crisis #2 knocked on my office door one week before our volunteer party, held each year at whichever club I could strong-arm into giving it to me for free. Glenn Buhtinski, our esteemed Director of Education, who graduated high school due only to the good folks at GED, leaned casually in the door frame, peering at me expectantly.

"So, Travers..." Glenn smirked. His smirk was infamous, given that it almost looked like a smile, turning upwards, but his perpetually arched eyebrows kept him from becoming genuine. Full of cocky bravado, much like myself, I despised him.

"Yes, sweetie?" I cooed, smiling pleasantly.

"Did you hear the news?"

"You've been committed?"

"No, darling... I'm helping with the entertainment for your little holiday party."

"That's nice of you to offer, Glenny, but we've got it all under control. The band Candy Kane is set—isn't that just delicious?—I've got a beach muscle Santa in a red fur thong for the photos, and the caterer is working away as we speak."

"No, Travers, you don't understand. This isn't a request. I've already talked to Ed and presented my plan to the board."

"What plan? What are you—?"

"It just seemed to me that this large gathering is the perfect opportunity to educate. To remind people why we are here."

"I think they know why they're here. Most of these folks are either positive, or have a loved one who either is or was. This party is to thank them for their hard work, not to remind them of their loss."

"Argue all you want, Travers, but it's already approved. I'm showing my Opportunistic Infection slide show, which—as you know—was so well-received in Toronto."

I gasped. The last thing I needed was crystal-clear photos of open sores on a 50-foot screen. Lunging for the door, Glenn had already retreated to the safety of his office as I hobbled into the hallway, climbing up the stairs to the golden tower, home of our Executive Director. At the top, I was dizzy and out of breath, but found it within to march through the door, man on a mission. Storming past the duly-frightened goth assistant, I grasped the door handle firmly, and pushed. It was locked. The goth backed away as I turned toward it, nervously fingering its crucifix pendant.

"Ed's not here."

"I can see that," I replied archly. "When do you expect her majesty?"

"Well, let's see," the goth fluttered, scurrying to the computer calendar. "He's at his massage appointment, and after that he's got his facial and manicure... My guess would be that he'll be back just in time for his dinner date. They've got tickets to the tour of *Beauty and the Beast*, with Tom Bosley!"

"The king has even worse taste than I thought," I muttered, before turning to the goth. "I'll try to intercept him on his way back."

"Gabe—er—if this is about the party thing, I wouldn't push it," he offered, deliberately. As my brow furrowed, uncomprehending, his eyes arched knowingly. "It's that time of the month, you know."

Stepping back down from the tower, I knew exactly what he meant, and it all became clear. This was about numbers.

As a non-profit, dependent on government grants, we were required to fill out monthly status reports in order to justify our very existence. Both Ed and Glenn appreciated the value of a captive audience of 500 people: Ka-ching! That their actions could be intrusive or insensitive mattered little. They were after a body count.

Having been known to stretch numbers myself, I understood, but I did not like it. Our volunteers deserved the highest of praise for their efforts, with the focus on them. But it was not to be.

Usually we are accustomed to two or three alcohol-induced mishaps during such parties, but this year, following the illuminating slide show, which Glenn narrated to the piano strains of "Silent Night," we had 12 bouts of vomiting, none triggered by alcohol consumption.

Crisis #3 occurred when our muscle Santa, who looked so hot in his thong, found himself a half hour into the evening with a severe case of diarrhea. Unable to sit on our velvet throne and having soiled his thong, we sent him home. In a moment of P.C. blindness, I replaced him with a naked Sandra Bernhardt look-alike whose tits and crotch we covered in spray whipped cream. Although the few ladies present queued up quickly, the men smartly cleared out soon after and our annual holiday extravaganza was over by 9 p.m.

I took no pleasure in seeing Glenn proven the imbecile.

Despite his glorious debacle, he somehow managed to convince himself that the pained faces staring up at him were not repulsed, but rather greatly moved by the poignancy of his presentation. Not even Ed was fazed by the spectacle. This was because, as I later discovered, at the time of Glenn's slideshow, Ed was in the alleyway outside, giving one of my best volunteers head. Evidently, he wasn't very good. And, truly, if you are going to be the top executive of an AIDS organization, shouldn't you be proficient in such things?

Even if I'd wanted to gloat, I had no time for it, so packed was my calendar. Between holiday brunches, doctor's visits, bazaars, and bizarres, I barely had enough time to shop. Hailing a cab, figuring that taxi fare couldn't count as part of that 30 bucks, I perused the racks at Macy's, but was stumped as to what to get Jon. Clothes were too impersonal, cologne seemed tacky, and jewelry inappropriate. Nothing was quite right, and anything that did was priced substantially higher than our agreed-upon limit. I debated purchasing something outrageously expensive and thinking up a clever lie about finding it at some thrift shop, like Out of the Closet, but then quickly came to my senses. It was not until I had walked every inch of the Beverly Center, resting every few yards, that I gave up and returned home.

It was there, after a nap, that inspiration finally struck. I could make something. That would be incredibly personal, thoughtful, and—above all else—cheap. But what? What could I possibly make that would look good after a bottle of wine had worn off? Gazing about, my eyes went to the window and lingered on our meager garden. Although fairly picked over from summer and fall, we still had some rosemary, oregano, and basil. Lots, in fact. But what could I make with those?

Pouring through a book on herbs, I came up with several great ideas and, unable to settle on one, decided to make them all. I made soaps and oils for Jon's baths, created exotic infused olive oils for cooking, made dried arrangements for our kitchen décor, and even came across an intriguing recipe for a basil-scented sexual lubricant.

On Christmas Eve, I am happy to report, all were greatly received, save for the lube. While we sampled it that very evening, Jon was unenthusiastic, and ended our tryst by saying that he felt like he was fucking a salad.

Later, as the embers of our heaven-sent fire began to wane and we giddily awaited the arrival of Santa, Jon pulled me closer, cradling me in his arms.

"Thank you for the gifts," he cooed. "Especially the sex."

"You too," I blushed, grateful for the cover of darkness, unwilling to let him see just how much energy the simple act of intercourse had taken. But considering his relative patience in abstaining these past months, it was the least I could do. "I really love the tapes. How long did it take you to make them?"

"Well, the hard part was figuring out the order." He kissed my cheek. "You see, if you listen to them, back to back, the songs tell a story. Our story."

My breathing stopped, ever so slightly, as I let his thoughtfulness run through me, warming me more than the fire ever could. Instead of brushing my emotion aside, as usual, I tried to remember what my old therapist Roberta had taught. I lay for a moment, savoring, hoping to commit every detail, every emotion, to memory, letting it linger, to be replayed again when needed. Then I sat straight up. "Wait a minute. Wasn't one of the songs 'The Bitch is Back'?"

"Well, you have to admit, that is one aspect of your personality."

"And Merry Fucking Christmas to you, too." I sulked for a moment, wanting him to pull me back in. As if I didn't trust all that was happening and needed even further proof of his love.

"Gabey, you can't pick one song and expect it to define you. You have to look at the whole."

I relaxed, snuggling in closer, wishing I hadn't spoken. "I suppose."

"Know what inspired me?"

"What?"

"Andrew Lloyd Webber."

"Please," I cried. "Don't irritate me any more than you already have."

"Really!" he protested. "It's true. A couple of weeks ago, I was listening to *Song and Dance*. 'An Unexpected Song.' You know it?"

"Don't I look like a homosexual?"

"Okay, then you know how it says something about never feeling like this before? Being so lost for words because you've found happiness?"

I nodded.

"Well, that's us, Gabey. That kind of out-of-the-blue high is what I feel when I'm with you." Jon rolled over, taking my hands in his. "Do you think I ever imagined anything could be this good? Not in a million. And so I wanted to put it all down. My whole experience with you. And a tape of songs made the most sense, because, with you, I feel like singing."

I didn't respond. I felt stupid for putting Jon through so many games. Here he was, loving me, just as I'd always wanted, and I was doing the very things that could push him away. Pulling his hands to my lips, I made a silent vow, as I kissed his fingertips, to grow up then and there. From this point forward, no silly games, no manufactured doubts, nor feeble insecurities. I would treat him with the utmost respect, just as he had me, and demonstrate my appreciation daily, showering him with boundless love and endless gumdrop kisses.

Despite my optimism, a chill soon filled the air, not altogether caused by weather alone, and I knew that my time was limited. Jon had taken note of my quickly declining state, which now includes problems with speech. My words have begun to slur, coming forth slowly, strung together like gloppy strings of cheese fondue. I can no longer function at work, and am put on disability from LA-DE-DA, "Just until you get better!" Their irritatingly buoyant outlook makes me want to scream, especially as they are each AIDS experts and know far better than anyone where I am headed.

It seems a crime that at age 36 I should be robbed of my future. I have done so much in my life, yet have accomplished so little. Although I realize that accomplishment alone is not the true and final measure of a man, I am still terrified, for I know that what is in my soul is not entirely worthy, either.

I have followed, at times, my sense of morality and let it be my guide. But there have been other times when I threw right and wrong out the window, settling too quickly for here, now, and sticky. Although I have also been kind, loving, and caring, there is much in my history that proves the reverse true as well. And when that final tally comes and deeds totaled, I am afraid that good and bad will cancel out, leaving me with a draw.

If there is a God, what will he make of my case? Will he be forgiving? Spiteful? What happens to those neither entirely good nor evil? If you are not quite John Wayne, but not John Wayne Gacy, either? Is there a place, other than heaven or hell, for the rest of us?

I have never been one to embrace that which I cannot see, taste, smell, touch, or hear. My life has been built on the tangible, and now, I fear, I will pay the price. It was the coldness of a quenching beer that drew me back to Keith, after so long apart. It was the smell of his neck that moved me to pull him closer. And it is the taint of his deep, rich blood that infected me, tying the two of us, collectively, forever.

God would have to be infinitely understanding to be able to erase such incidents, to close eyes to all of which he disapproves. But, to be capable of such, God would have to be female. The sainted wife of an errant husband, ready and willing to take him back, forgive, and love, love, love. But if God is a man, I am screwed, for there is nothing men like more than to show their omnipotence over others, leaving in their path only scorched earth.

Please, God, when I arrive, let you be like Betty Buckley's warm and forgiving Abby on my old TV favorite *Eight is Enough*. That will be more than enough for me.

In the panoply of human maladies, HIV is hardly the worst. And yet, now that I have it, nothing else seems worse. There are many others for which, given the option, I would gladly exchange. Blindness could be a lot of fun. Cancer, a blessing. With either, the attempt could be made to alter or improve. A stroke would have been efficient and direct. Malaria would have at least required a tropical getaway. But to know that your body is infested with disease, with the only uncertainty being how or when...? I have spent countless hours speculating about both.

Will I be struck with pneumonia? Thrush? Kaposi's sarcoma? Will my weight drop? Will my vision go? Will I need a PICC line inserted into my vein? Or will I wheel an oxygen cart about the dance floor? So many opportunistic infections, so little time.

Given that my T cells had been stable for so long, a tiny part of me started envisioning a future. Nothing grand, mind you, but a future nonetheless. In my thoughts, I invariably picture a brownstone, somewhere cool and crisp. Yellow and rust-colored leaves blanket the sidewalk, crunching under foot. Through a window, Jon and I sit separately in front of a blazing fire. I am stretched out on the couch, a Springer Spaniel puppy at my feet. Maybe Maxie's offspring? In my hands, the latest Maeve Binchy; true to form, her heroines are heroic, her villains are men, and her endings empowering, if bittersweet. Closing the last page, I glance first to the Springer, who snuggles even closer, then past the fire to Jon.

Biting the cap of his pen, he carefully studies the crossword in front of him. Thinking of an answer at last, he meticulously and confidently fills in the blanks. As he lays the completed puzzle onto his lap, his lips part, revealing the trace of a satisfied grin. Removing his glasses, he rubs the small of his nose and smoothes his graying temples. Realizing that I am staring, he glances at me with a warm smile. Though he speaks, I cannot hear the words. But I see my response. Stretching out my hand to his, he grasps it, bending to offer my fingers a light kiss. I sigh, so happy and contented.

Outside the door, a burst of giggles and stomping feet: children. I look to the door, see the brass knob turn...

It is at this point that I can imagine no more.

I long to linger in that image, wrapping it around my shoulders like a warm woolen blanket. But, instead, I glance to the catheter tube sending urine into a pouch beneath my bed. The idea that my daydream might actually become a reality grows increasingly dim, and I am troubled by the lack of another image with which to replace it. If you have nothing left to dream, are you really still alive?

That the course of a human life can change direction so suddenly is unsettling, to say the least. Though ripe with possibilities, both positive and negative, once cast to the wind, it can be difficult to recover. Such change can happen at any time and come in any form. Unexpected love or the death of such, the entrance of a friend, a change of locale, or the onset of illness.

The doctors have finally agreed on a diagnosis: Progressive Multifocal Leukoencephalopothy. While that certainly is a mouthful, they've come up with the cute little acronym PML, which somehow makes the disease sound almost pleasurable. Basically, with PML, a virus creates lesions on the brain, eating through it vigorously and systematically like some deranged Pac-Man. Those with PML are usually dead within four months of diagnosis. And my symptoms began over three months ago. In short, I am fucked.

Given that it has begun its diet on the area governing motor skills, my issues of mobility and speech are easily explained. Though I also have pneumonia, as it is not pneumocystis, it is the least of my worries. PML, they tell me, has no cure.

However, there is an experimental treatment that sounds not only promising, but fun! A device is implanted into your head, just under your skin, which administers medication directly to the affected area. For the most fleeting of moments, I see myself parading around West Hollywood, showing off my newfound accessory, and launching a news-making fashion trend. After piercings and tattoos, under-the-skin implants are certain to become all the rage. Think of all the different designs. Imagine what fun you could have with your very own raised-skin Bart Simpson implant!

If I've been honest at all, by now you understand that, for me, vanity has always been job one. The idea of an implant being lodged into my skull is not remotely appealing. Especially since I will eventually die from AIDS, regardless of how this particular episode ends. But I see the look in Jon's eyes. He wants me to live. And for me, right now, that is reason enough.

I nod, almost imperceptibly, to the doctor, who nods back.

"You understand the risks, don't you?" The mop-topped doctor asks. "For some, we see a reversal. For others, they continue on the path they are on. And still others—"

"Yes?" Jon implores, putting voice to my question.

"It may halt the disease, but leave you in the state you're currently in."

I feel Jon look at me, but do not have it within me to glance back. I know how much he wants this. He needs to believe I will get better, that everything possible has been tried. He needs to believe that I will survive. Though I know the opposite to be true, I concede. Death is not a time to be proud.

The pain slices through me like a cleaver, ripping against the grain, through the bone, straight into the marrow of my soul. It is not, however, the ache doled out by disease or medication. Rather, it is wrought from the destruction I have left, deliberately, in my wake. Saying simply that I have made mistakes or done harm markedly diminishes the severity, the enormity of my actions. For I have behaved quite consciously, viciously, and with purpose and skill.

Whereas bullets may pierce the skin, the tools in my arsenal are words, and they are far more deadly. I have used these weapons to maim and kill, and have rarely missed my target. For far too long, my every thought and action centered on the total annihilation of those who had offended. The easy explanation would be that I've been hurt and therefore hurt others in turn. But such rage-fueled intention cannot be attributed to mere reflex. The link between mind and mouth was malice, most pure.

My acuity in assessing the weakness of my foes and aiming straight for their kneecaps cannot be underestimated. To see one's prey crumpled, lying shattered in a heap, was exhilarating. At the time, my actions seemed almost heroic. *Look how clever I am! How swiftly my words draw blood!* Truly, my serpent's tongue had no equal, and I remained immune to all slings and arrows, fortified by my malevolence.

But now, as I lay motionless, unable to respond, the faces of those I've harmed prowl toward me, parading surreally through my head like disjointed marionettes. They neither judge, nor absolve, nor rebuke. But stare.

And in those eyes, I see what they felt the moment my words hurled forth, hitting them smack in the face. Eyes, pained and shocked, moist with coming tears, unable to comprehend how innocuous chatter such as theirs had provoked the proceeding firestorm of brutality.

The eyes of one in particular return again and again, floating just above my hospital bed. They are the pale blues of one Debi Beckett. Cursed with poor genetics, a healthy appetite, and glasses, she was ripe for a strike. That she was too easy a target, too much of a cliché, is perhaps the reason she so haunts me.

The moment was junior high, a difficult time for all, let alone one who does not fit into a mold. The place was a roller rink. Why she had come with my girlfriend and I remained unclear, as Renee regarded Debi with even more disdain than I. It is the curse of the beautiful to have such gangly parasites attaching themselves, hoping to benefit by sheer proximity. But there she was, nonetheless, teetering behind as we skated faster and faster, trying to outrun the raging hippo nipping at our ankles. Her innate awkwardness, compounded by considerate girth, made it impossible for her to ever have hope of catching us. We skated circles around her, dizzying her with our speed, launching vicious zingers her way each time we passed.

I can no longer recall my final bon mot, but it almost certainly entailed Debi's weight. What I *do* remember is skating backwards from her, bomb dropped, and looking arrogantly into her eyes. So brave was she, or shell-shocked, that she never dropped her eyes from mine—even for a second—which allowed for the briefest, unrestricted glimpse into her soul. The staggering waves of despair, hidden just below the surface, so alarmed me that I tripped, sprawling backwards into nearby skaters. Looking up, I saw that Debi had vanished.

Meeting Renee at the snack bar, she laughed heartily at my retold narrative, offering a reward of Red Vines for a job well done. Debi, I noticed, had made her way to the lockers, silent tears streaming, refusing all offers of assistance. Those around likely assumed that her injury was purely physical, the result of a slippery floor or an unruly skater, never suspecting that she had been felled solely by an unkind word. But, as the one bearing the dagger, I knew better.

A few years later, starring in Tiger High's production of *Our Town*, I unexpectedly found myself being directed by Debi. Wracked by guilt, envisioning laborious rehearsals where my every dramatic flourish was criticized, I somehow found it within to step up and apologize. Interestingly, she said that she didn't even recall the incident. Though she stared blankly, I knew that I had seen more in those eyes than she showed, and wondered if I alone was responsible for the impenetrable wall that now greeted me.

That I could have caused such pain eats at me still. That I did so, saw the results, and chose to wound again is almost unfathomable.

But I did.

Again, and again, and again.

It's 6:00 a.m., and the tiny stripes of sky are the bluest yet. Though the louvered blinds stand open, allowing full view for anyone with the capability of movement, for me all that is visible is the tiniest of fork-like slivers. I can no longer even direct my eyes to view it. Instead, whatever impression I have is the culmination of reflected images, memory of color, and wishful thinking.

I am struck by how, right now, I would kill to make even the smallest of decisions for myself. I am bathed, fed, and turned according to the nurses' schedule. Though the TV is on, it is not by my choosing. Even my bowels empty without regard to intent. Jon's kisses, though sweetly given, come and go without heed.

You'd think that, at prior points in my life, little actions such as these would have registered their importance. But when they did, I turned a blind eye. I have lived my life focused on the big picture, going after LOVE! MONEY! SELF! SEX! with ferocious conviction. I have focused on the big brushstrokes, when I should have been studying pointillism.

Paintings by Seurat and such can be easy to dismiss. After all, each is just a collection of dots. And a dot by itself is fairly insignificant. Really, if one dot were to be changed from green to orange, would it substantially alter the artist's landscape? But consider if ten dots were to be changed, or twenty. Eventually, these collective changes impact the canvas, creating a far different mood and, indeed, an entirely different painting.

These choices are not unlike the wooden blocks I once played with as a child. One block is only a block, inconsequential, but twenty blocks can be a castle.

I'm thinking now of all the blocks I've played with, and the importance I once assigned to them. When had I decided that I was somehow above reproach, that rules and etiquette did not apply to me? How many times have I pushed a shopping cart into others, ignoring clearly marked return stands? When speeding well above the posted limit, why did I think that sign did not apply to me? How could I have viewed it as a suggestion and not a rule? And if I did view it as a rule, what made me feel that I was somehow superior to it?

My landscape is littered with such choices. And in almost every case, including the one which brought me here, I have chosen incorrectly. But despite this, and all of my misgivings and insecurities, the presence of Jon tells me that somewhere, as Julie Andrews famously sang, *I must have done something good.*

A nurse comes in, I am not sure who, and turns the TV to Katie, my sassy morning pal. *My* Katie; she of stylish bob and toothy grin. For a moment, listening to her authoritatively recap the latest on the trashy O.J. murder trial, I can't help but think that all is truly well with the world. Her tone flows effortlessly, with a hint of mischief just beneath the surface. She gets the joke, the irony. She is one straight-up, sassy, smart, don't-fuck-with-me bitch. Ms. Couric is no fool—no sir!—no matter what her high school cheerleader appearance might convey.

They cut to someone else. The tone changes. It is huskier now, even more inviting. Less toothy, but somehow more... mysterious. If I could actually get a hard-on, I am certain that I would. I wish that I could force my eyes up to the screen, hovering several miles above my bed, to more fully focus on

Matt Lauer's gently glistening lips. But such choices are beyond me now.

God, I wish I could sleep. Although sleep is about the only activity I can now fully engage in, my body resists, as if knowing that slumber is just one step removed from death. Jon sits nearby, reading a magazine. I sense him look up, trying to catch my eye. I can tell he is offering a smile.

He is truly, at heart, a good man. Nevertheless, I hate him. Why does he insist on staying here? This hospital offers no amenities over which to linger. Under the harsh fluorescents, the cool designer-toned walls look as appetizing as the food. In all, there is no reason for Jon to remain, and yet he does.

More than anyone, he has stepped naturally into his caregiver role, becoming the perfect picture of dutiful, patient wife. Although it is pure evil on my part, I cannot help but wonder if he actually gets some pleasure from all of this. It is not that he is inappropriately giddy or overly maternal. Rather, he slipped so easily into his role, greeting visitors, arranging the proffered flowers, distributing the strange homemade confections to the nurses and others who can actually move their mouths to chew.

By now, though, I am familiar with his canned patter, expressing his thanks at the visitor's gift and appearance, oblique update on my health, then slightly-forced frivolity as he escorts the visitor to my side.

Warmly grasping my hand, though I cannot squeeze back, he'll say, "Gabey, look—", as if I were capable of turning my head, "Tina is here, and she brought macaroons!"

I wish I *could* turn my head, to see if there is a smile in his eyes. He genuinely seems grateful for the trickle of visitors, while I simply wish they would go away. Had I been able to plan this hospital stay, I would have chosen to be admitted in Puerto Rico, where I don't know a soul, and spend my last days far from hushed voices and well-meaning gestures.

Why is it that I hate people so? Although I sometimes react out of general discomfort, other times find my cauldron boiling over with the soup of unbridled animosity, which I can only partially disguise. Though there are some who are truly deserving of my vitriol, such as the clique of co-workers from LA-DE-DA who have just left, rushing off to tweak themselves to death at a circuit party, there are countless other innocents who receive my poisonous, if veiled, sting.

An hour ago, an older woman, immaculately dressed, yet unadorned, wandered into my room to talk to me about Jesus. Jon was out, likely cruising the cafeteria in search of his next project, and unable to rescue me.

Though she was warm and loving, sitting beside me, holding my hand, seemingly unafraid of the dark-cloaked specter floating just above my bed, and though there was nothing said that was, in itself, offensive, I couldn't help but wish to see this sweet elderly woman pushed out the window to her death. Even now I am unsure whether my rage toward her was fueled by disagreement with her message; irritation that she had managed to penetrate my fortress (Jon); jealousy, that she could be at peace with this concept of life and death, whereas I seethed and fought for every breath; catty pettiness that this old bat so much closer to death should walk freely, while I rolled more quickly toward the precipice; uncontested revulsion that though I disagreed with her so vehemently, I was unable to voice my protest; pity that she would take advantage of those unable to resist; or, finally, resentment that, aside from age, gender, and belief in the Holy Trinity, this serene, loving person is who I had always yearned to be.

The door opens and Jon enters with Clare. I can hear her step toward me, hesitantly, before Jon ushers her into my field of vision. I wish I could somehow make peace with her; to once again apologize for my callousness. Jon stands behind her, looking at me with such love, and I am almost blinded by their combined goodness.

Clare pulls over a chair, close to the bed, and sits. Reaching into her purse, she pulls out a stack of letters and notes, bound with a rubber band. Taking my hand, she opens my palm, and places them into it, wrapping my fingers around them as best she can.

Exhaling a long, low sigh, she looks directly into my eyes.

"I'm sorry I couldn't respond to you before... but I'm here now. Is that okay?"

I try to reply, but as I can no longer even blink at will, Clare is left to decipher my reaction on her own.

She smiles slightly, taking my blank stare as a "yes", then looks up to my hair. Again digging into her purse, she pulls out a brush, then looks me in the eye. "Gloria would be furious with you, you know." She glances to Jon, "You, too."

Standing, Clare authoritatively begins to work on my hair. "Remember—above all else—presentation counts."

It is quiet; late. Jon sleeps in an empty bed down the hall. Every so often, a nurse enters, checking my vitals, which are not remotely vital. The lights are never fully extinguished, and my sleep is never restful.

As the faces of those I've hurt yet again fleet through my mind, I search for closure. Some means of making amends. But what, at this juncture, are my options? Is it enough to merely say "I'm sorry" in my head?

For I am.

Jon has told me countless times that my very employment, my work in the community, is my penance, but it doesn't feel nearly substantial enough. It hasn't eased my regret in the slightest. Though I may have done my darndest to smile each day like my beloved Katie, inside, I fully feel the depth of the pain I've inflicted. That never goes away.

In my twenties, every thought, every utterance, was delivered with a smile, but came loaded with bile. Could it all be traced to that single evening with Joey and Kid, and the subsequent failings of Gloria and Lenny? Was it a result of trying desperately to succeed at L.A. life, where sex and status were all that mattered? Or was this viciousness simply an underlying and unalterable element of my persona?

Undoubtedly, through the years I'd made great strides, but while subtle and steady progress had been made, it seemed increasingly clear that there *was* no ultimate finish line. And the thought that I should die without redemption is disquieting, to say the least.

The door opens, and a squat woman enters. I see her shape, out of the corner of my eye, and wonder why she stands so silently. Surely she is a relief nurse, checking on my status. But as she quietly inches closer, I smell the faint, familiar scent of sugary grape, and realize it is Pastor Sally.

She sits, snuggling her hips onto the edge of the bed, then takes my hand in hers. She says nothing, but gently strokes her fingertips over my now-prominent veins, tracing each deviation. I wait for her to speak, to offer a greeting. Instead, she stretches out, lying beside me. Her arm encircles my shoulders, and I recognize that I am being hugged.

Sally says not a word, but holds me until morning.

"Give him another bump," I hear someone say, ever so softly. Probably Jon.

Had I winced? Moaned? What prompted the increase? I no longer know which actions are mine and which are imagined. Reality, for me, is now streaked with pinks and grays as the cool ice is pumped into my veins.

Someone pats my head, I think. Maybe a wash cloth, caressing my forehead. Who it is, I am not certain. For some reason, I envision Pastor Sally, and it is she who I imagine proffering relief.

Why is it that I don't visualize Jon or my mother in that role? Perhaps I am being prepared for the hereafter, whether I want to be or not. Or perhaps it is that I do not want Gloria or Jon to get that close, to see the decimation in my face. They will have more than enough time later for sorrow.

How I wish I could scream. Every muscle in my body is tense with the message that this is not what I want. There is so much left undone. So much I haven't said.

"Please," I cry, "not yet! Reverse the clock, if only two weeks, when my words at least came forth, though not easily. I want to tell you how much I love you, Jon. How I can't imagine what would have become of me if I had not known your kindness. To have died without knowing that; to have entered this state without having felt your gentleness; to have not had you by my side, even now." These phrases reverberate through my head with the timber of cymbal crashes, yet no one in the room seems to detect even the slightest of changes.

Someone inserts a tape.

As much time as I'd spent picking out music for my funeral, I hadn't yet thought of this scenario: music to die to. I hear the boom box door snap close and know that this particular cassette has been chosen for my benefit. But between the gentle hiss of the oxygen and the quiet murmur of the room, the song becomes lost in the vast expanse of white.

Voices call to me. Soft whispers, beckoning, offering tales of the sea. Suddenly I am in the sails of a pirate ship, adjusting my cap, a gull perched at my side. The wind cools my sunburned face.

Below, the men, my brothers, count towering stacks of gold coins while eating gigantic turkey legs. It is odd, though, that the turkey heads and bodies are still attached.

Even odder still is one pirate in a wheelchair, dressed as a mermaid. He looks to me, knowingly. Though I cannot place his face or the long ringlets of hair, I am certain we once shared a meal or conversation.

The bell clangs as I glance to the stern, my father at the wheel. He winks at me, playfully, before turning the boat toward open sea. As he does, a purr, sad and resigned, plays through my head.

Shiver me timbers, it whispers, and before I can fully grasp what is happening, I find myself sailing away...

PART II
GABE: 1986

"Samedi et Vendredi" by Bette Midler & Moogy Klingman
Track 1B, Side B of Bette Midler's album,
Songs for the New Depression

GABE: 1986

"OOOOH, THAT'S IT. Eat it. Eat that ass like you haven't had breakfast."

Pulling back slightly, I stared at the pulsating asterisk in front of me. Had this sphincter just spoken?

The folds of skin tensed, then relaxed, silently pleading for my tongue's return. Numbingly, I obliged. Lapping about like a dehydrated terrier, I speculated as to whom this rectum belonged.

The surrounding hair could have been brown, or blonde, or black, so wet were they. Had the lighting been better, it might have been easier to discern, but given the mango-scented candles that perfumed the air, this guy obviously took his cues from *Homo Digest*. The sheets were a high-thread count Ralph Lauren, so at least he had money or a decent line of credit.

"Yeah, baby, that's it," the stranger sighed. "Gonna give you somethin'... something good to eat."

Given that I am presently munching on your ass, asshole, please tell me that your idea of a wholesome breakfast does not include a piping hot loaf. Think of the sheets...

I shoved my tongue deeper, to which the body responded by dropping down from its perch onto all fours.

"Shove it in, baby. Get me ready for your big dick. Your big, beautiful dick!" I shoved my tongue so far in that I almost expected it to dart out from his open mouth. "Yeah, that's it—

Oh, you are so fucking hot!"

While I wasn't about to contradict him, I wondered if he were as clueless as I about our respective identities. I inserted a finger into his trough.

"God, that's it—right there..."

That we had met only tonight was a given, but where...? I hadn't had a steady for months, having stopped going to the baths after that last bout of gonorrhea. After all, I don't even like to *eat* cottage cheese.

Perhaps we met at the Mother Lode? No, the only person there worth having had been the bartender, whose lover with the comb-over kept giving me the evil eye. The bar had been dead, for a Wednesday. Or was it Tuesday? Definitely not Friday or Saturday. No matter, really. But where had I gone next?

"Um—are you gonna, uh—?" The hole again spoke.

I stared down at my inert finger, hanging limply out of his ass. Had I even moved it since penetration? That had been several minutes ago. Usually I wouldn't even question it, so proficient was I in the art of love. Where was my head?

"Can you just—do something?" the guy pleaded. To silence him, I pulled my single finger out with a plop, quickly replacing it with three. "Jeez! Watch it—"

I pummeled his ass furiously, trying to keep him quiet long enough for me to remember who he was.

Let's see: Rage had been playing Human League, which meant it wasn't retro night, so today was likely Thursday. And after Jasper and I had finished dancing, we stopped for pizza to check out the other losers who hadn't hooked up either. The pizza had been warm, but hard, having congealed behind glass all night. Jazz and I had selected a prominent table facing the sidewalk, the better to greet our adoring public.

Tow-headed Charlie stopped by, undoubtedly high, with a passably cute friend named _____. God, was this him? He'd had olive skin (check), darker hair (check), and a devilish grin (can't see it). We had flirted, him docking his head to the side, with studied affect. He was only here for the week, on break from—where?—Vegas, I think, and he was staying with Charlie.

Which meant either we were at Charlie's (unlikely, as no smell of cat), a hotel (again unlikely, as neither of us had cash), or at my place. Quickly glancing about, I searched for clues: standard issue futon sofa with tasseled throw pillows; copy of *Frontiers* magazine on the nightstand, next to the bottle of lube; a grab bag mix of condoms, procured from bars throughout the greater L.A. area and artfully displayed in a wicker basket; and, most damaging, *my* mango-scented candles, polluting the air with the smell of piña colada vomitation.

Jeez, when had I become such a fag? I mean, yes, I am gay, but does bad taste have to automatically accompany one's desire for cock? I made a mental note: call credit card company for higher credit limit; need new décor.

"Yeah, that's it." God, was he still here? "Come on, Greg, give it to me good!"

Incensed, I pulled my fingers out, shoving him onto his back. (Yes, this indeed was—*Alex.* Alex.)

"Are you gonna fuck me, Greg? Please? I need your big tool in me..."

"My name is Gabe, asshole. Gabe. Don't you even know who you're fucking?"

"Sorry. I mean, hey, we just met—"

"All the more reason for you to remember. When you get back to Nevada—"

"Utah—"

"You're going to remember this fuck. Gabe Travers is one orgiastic, memorable fuck!" Reaching over, I ripped open a rubber, shoving it down my prick with the skilled touch of a professional.

Lifting his feet onto my shoulders, I paused, allowing the head of my cock to push firmly into him.

"Hey, wait, Gabe! I need more lube!"

Ignoring his plea, I thrust forward, smothering the ensuing scream with my mouth, ensuring that his lips would forever remember my name.

Alex finally gone, having limped rather quickly to Charlie's borrowed car, I closed the door and turned to survey my apartment.

Euphemistically called a studio, there was little here to conjure up the image of a creative soul, at one with his palette. Instead, the Navajo white walls, cream sheets, and light-colored bookcase seemed antiseptic. What about this room is unique, I wondered?

Looking about desperately, my eyes finally rested on the three framed photos, grouped artfully on the bookcase.

In one, I smiled, popping out of a cardboard chimney, wearing a Santa outfit. And, no, this was not taken last Christmas. I was three years old, and in that photo I look so jubilant that I can scarcely believe that child and I are one and the same.

Another photo shows my mom and dad, neither exactly smiling, their arms draped around each other limply, much as a hug you would give your butcher. Behind them is a mountain, exactly which I cannot say. A telescope jutting into frame suggests that they are at a roadside turnout, in between destinations, which somehow seems fitting.

The third photograph, newer and yet not, shows me with Keith. It was taken at our Tiger High graduation, and the smiles on our faces are pure, secure in the mistaken belief that better, happier days lie ahead.

In the photo, his dirty blonde bangs fall across one eye. I knew that his father had pestered him for weeks to get his hair cut, if only for the big event, but Keith had refused. Stubborn to the core, he never allowed anyone to tell him what to do. Initially, that had been part of the attraction.

My first recollection of him was as juniors in gym class. Although trimly built and a natural athlete, Keith despised the formulaic routine of Phys Ed, fighting it at every turn. Whereas I played sick, especially on days when we'd be asked to do something solo, such as shooting free throws, Keith would participate only when deemed necessary to achieve his personal objective.

To Keith, more important than anything was the idea of "getting out." Whether he meant getting out of high school, out of town, or something larger was never quite clear, but the refrain "I'm getting out" could easily have been the quote beneath his yearbook picture. And if getting out meant that he had to pass P.E., he would do it, but with only the barest of efforts.

Sitting on the bleachers one day, watching sexy Joey Tatolla jump toward the basket, lean legs outstretched below, my attention was disrupted by the noisy arrival of Keith, plopping himself down a few feet away. He wore the regulation red and blue gym clothes of the Tigers, but protruding from his shorts were striped boxers—in clear violation of Tiger High rules.

Catching my eye, he slid over slightly. "What're you out for?"

"Um, sprained ankle," I lied, eyes darting away.

He leaned closer, conspiratorially. "Didn't you have one of those last month?"

"It never really, uh, healed—you know?" I fumbled, uncertain of his sudden interest. "It still acts up, sometimes. Now and then."

"On a full moon, right? Or on days when Coach Beeson might call on you—like today? I get it," he nodded, grinning. "Gym, my friend, is fucked. I mean, how is shooting hoops gonna prepare us for life, right?"

"Yeah," I nodded sagely, not knowing what he meant, but feeling close to him nonetheless.

"Think about what we do here... Every day, for 35 minutes, we either run around in loops, or kick a ball down a field, or— oh yeah—tether ball. What the fuck is that? Then we all romp back to the locker room and have a big old homo moment."

I looked away quickly, praying that the burning sensation flooding my face wasn't visible.

He looked at me for confirmation. On my unknowing shrug, he continued. "What's the goal, you know? I mean, if they want us physically fit, there are better ways to do it. Put us on treadmills. Show us proper stretching. Give us classes in nutrition. Whatever. Or if the real goal is teamwork, then don't just throw us all together and expect us to act as one. The guys who are good always end up in front, with the rest of us just staring at their asses."

Again, he looked at me for confirmation. What on earth for? Had he seen me checking out the other guys in the showers?

Did he know that, late at night in my darkened room, I'd stroke myself, fantasizing about being held tenderly by the very guys who had harassed me throughout the day? Regardless, I had no response. Sitting silently, we watched as the other kids practiced pivot turns.

"Your name is Gabriel, right?" he prodded.

"Yeah," I almost smiled, flattered that he'd even noticed me, let alone remembered by name. "Gabriel, or Gabe—whichever. How'd you know?"

"I was in your English class last year. Mrs. Gunther."

"Oh yeah!" I confirmed, clearly not remembering.

"I sat in the back," he ducked his head, shyly. How sad to have spent an entire school year within 15 feet of someone and not to have made some impact. "You did that presentation on Tennessee Williams, right? Where you did the speech from that play?"

Indeed I had. One of my many crowning achievements. When asked to give both an oral and written presentation on an author, composer, or artist whose personal life impacted their craft, I had chosen Williams. Although I skirted his sexuality altogether, unwilling to supply my classmates with the ammunition necessary to link his desires with my own, I had calculatingly selected him so that I could discover as much about homosexuality as possible, under the guise of research.

My presentation met with great success, topped only by Hal Chauncey's presentation on Michelangelo. Had he not brought in a scale replica of *David*, my report would have remained the class favorite. But the impact of male genitalia in a high-school classroom, no matter how miniscule, cannot be underestimated.

"You know Tennessee Williams is a homosexualist, don't you?" Keith squinted.

"Uh, yeah. I found that out."

"Is that why you chose him?"

Caught in his gaze, I stammered. "No, I—he's a great writer, whose plays forever—"

"Forever changed the tenor of American drama. Yadda yadda ya." His legs swung, absentmindedly kicking the bleachers.

Now, I stared. Had he read my report? I had worked for hours on that line, trying to end my paper on just the right powerful note. Keith looked back at the basketball court. "It was a good presentation."

"Thanks." We both watched the players, relieved not to be among them.

As covertly as I could, I allowed my eyes to take in his tennis shoes, slowly working my way up his pale legs. The hair was almost golden, purer than that on his head. It was clear that, once summer had arrived, the mantle of Bronzed God would be his. Though his knees were a bit wobbly, his thighs—oh! My eyes rested on the bit of boxers, teasingly hanging beneath his shorts. The act seemed highly erotic and calculatingly subversive. Keith clearly made his own rules, challenging all who would oppose him.

I stared at the thin blue stripes, willing the fabric to shift higher and expose more of his smooth skin. How I longed to lick the inside of his thigh. I couldn't imagine if it would taste sweet, or salty—like tears, or something else—perhaps smoky and sexy, as yet indescribable.

Feeling his stare, my eyes jumped to his and he steadily held my gaze. As the warning bell rang, sending all Tigers, including Keith, into the locker room, I sat, still and silent, lecturing my erection to return to dormancy so I could move on to class.

I last saw Keith at the Burbank airport, August of our graduation summer. Keith's grandmother had died, so his dad rounded up the boys for the funeral in Kentucky, and off they went. Keith wouldn't let me go to the airport with them, despite my pleas, even to say goodbye. But I went anyway.

Seated at the gate opposite, the chair's worn rubber arm disintegrating against my fingers, I watched as the family checked in, willing Keith to turn and notice me. He didn't right away, but later, as they announced boarding, Keith finally looked up from his magazine, directly into my eyes. And what I saw in those familiar, nurturing, alluring eyes, seeping through, was sadness. At his grandmother's death; at not being able to say goodbye; and, sadness too, for upon his return, I would be gone, off to college.

But beneath it all though—and I could be wrong, given how far away I sat—I could swear that I detected a glimmer of something else. Whether of hope or excitement, I wasn't quite sure. But Keith had long dreamt of going someplace—anyplace—and this trip would be his first. Perhaps, even in the aftermath of death, Keith would find a place he belonged.

In my prized photo, he and I stand side-by-side, graduation caps askew, arms pumped high into the air, as if we'd been unexpectedly released from a 20-year prison term. Our shared joy at having escaped reads clearly on our faces, and just looking into his eyes in that fading photograph, I am reminded of how very much I loved him.

If his grandmother had not died, if I had not gone out of state, if we had made other choices, would we have remained together? It seemed an impossible question to answer, especially given our quixotic personalities and naïve immaturity, yet in my heart, I knew that it was a possibility.

That I have unexplored depths and caverns didn't scare him; in fact, he became my own personal spelunker, and I—in every way possible—his hole. He climbed so deep within that it seemed he had left a part of himself inside.

There were moments, often late at night, when I heard him calling out for me. It was an insistent cry, one of desperation, as if only by finding and reuniting would our souls ever be healed and harmony restored. Nothing except our coupling made any sense. We were meant to be together, one. Through that fog of impenetrable sadness, his cries would become more ravaged, scraping at my flesh, bringing tears to my eyes as I found myself calling out for him in return. "Keith! I'm here! Where *are* you?" But eventually a car would honk, or a dog bark, or the neighbor upstairs would yell at his TV or at me, and the cavernous echoes faded until I was again in my studio, uncomfortably alone.

How was it, then, that with all that I felt inside, that deep well of emotion, my apartment remained so bleakly unaffected? From the books on the shelf to the carefully coordinated furnishings of muted hue, nothing gave hint of any substance, or emotion, or character. Rather, it seemed more like the home of a eunuch with fashion sense; not quite one thing, nor the other, but nevertheless very smartly dressed.

With a melodramatic sigh, I reached into the closet for my well-worn apron, then turned to address my tie. My hair was flawless, my complexion unmarred, and my eyes disturbingly blank. If, as they said, the eyes were the window to the soul, why were mine perpetually shuttered?

Heading for the door, I dug within, summoning energy and boundless positivity, and prepared myself for yet another life-changing shift at The Happy Tomato.

The following Saturday, by the time Jasper and Charlie arrived, my apartment had been completely redone.

"Um, wow—", Jasper mumbled, taking in the brilliance of my golden velvet chair and frosted glass fruit bowl. "What do you call this look?"

"Venetian," I smiled, pleased with my handiwork. "Don't you think it's me?"

"You know," smirked Charlie, "this *does* look like a whorehouse."

I balked, tossing a gold-painted apple at him. "It's Italian, thank you very much. I wanted something to express myself."

"But you're not Italian," quibbled Jasper, his blondness showing.

"I'm expressing my individuality," I stressed, "not my ethnicity."

"And by putting up red flocked-wallpaper, you think people will attribute to you certain qualities?" Charlie laughed.

"Designer not being one of them," Jasper muttered.

"Gabey," purred Charlie, "to express your individuality, you first have to be an individual. And, honey, you're not. Now, you are a lovely and charming person, I'll give you that. But, at heart, you're no different than us. We're all just WEHO star-fuckers, looking for the next big dick to suck. But if you now desire only the gondoliers, at least that leaves the rest of the populace for us."

During Charlie's obviously drunken rant, Jasper had walked over to my new hand-painted armoire with Venetian crests on it.

Opening it—

"Hey, where'd you put your porn collection?"

"It's gone."

"Gone? Gone where?" Jasper looked faint.

"I sold it."

They gasped.

"Not all of them!" Jasper was clearly going into shock. "Even the Rex Chandler?"

"Every single one."

"But, Jeff Stryker, too—?"

"Yard sale. By 8:30 this morning, everything had been snapped up."

"That's what happens when you live up the street from Revolver," Charlie mumbled.

Jasper's eyes fluttered, uncomprehending. "Gabey, just because those guys weren't Venetian—"

"You're missing the point, Jasper. As always. It's not about Venice, or my apartment, or porn. This is a new me. I'm now a kinder, gentler Gabe. I want people to see past my veneer. I am more than the clothes I put on. I am more than just sex. I am a person with a multitude of thoughts and emotions. I am an individual!"

"Hear you roar," Charlie muttered.

"Fuck you, Charlie," I snarled. "At least I'm trying to change."

"But your porn?!?" Jasper choked, still looking weak.

I sank into my new chair, reveling in the velvety texture. "I just—I finally realized that I have been far too consumed with sex. I have let my desire for intimacy create a falsehood. I have become a shell, with only one goal: orgasm. And I am done. Finished. From here on out," I proclaimed, "it's just me, flaws and all."

For a moment, all was quiet. Jasper stared intently at the armoire's empty shelves, hoping that this bad dream would end, and the videos he had once savored would be returned to their rightful home.

Charlie surveyed the room, then turned to me, lips pursed, unflatteringly. "Tell me, hon, how is this any different from six months ago, when you got bored with the Santa Fe look? Or before that, art deco? Changing a room doesn't change who you are."

He had a point. There was no proof, no assurance I could give, that all this would lead to actual change. Looking over my carefully selected furniture, my eyes returned to Charlie.

"You're right, guys. Maybe just redoing this room won't change anything. Who I am... But it's a start."

The next months saw a flurry of activity, as my vows to better myself first became plans, then actions. And one important step in that was finding more rewarding, fulfilling work. To that end, I happily hung up my apron, said "Good-bye" to the Happy Tomato, and "Hello" to the e.e. come-on-in gallery.

Parking my car somewhat illegally across the street, I glanced over at my new place of employ. Through the window, even at that distance, I could spot the glare in Clare's eyes. The look softened somewhat by the time I dodged the Melrose traffic and reached the door, but it had not entirely dissipated.

"You're late," she complained flatly. "And what are those?" she cringed, pointing to my socks.

"It's the latest thing," I noted proudly, showing off my recent purchase. "Kind of like leg-warmer socks. But butch-er."

"If you say so... But Gabey, I told you—here at the gallery, we have a very specific look. Clean, all black, simple lines."

I nodded, to give her the impression that I actually cared.

"The goal," she stated, "is to look subservient. Refined, elegant—but not so wealthy as for our patrons to think that we could actually afford these paintings. We want to look smart, but not smarter than our clientele."

Turning, she pulled something from a drawer. "Here. I want you to wear these..."

Unfolding the black framed eyeglasses, I was uncertain as to why they were for me. "My vision is perfect."

"You need to look smarter. With all the highlights in your hair, and that outfit, you look more Denny Terrio than is healthy."

"But I have a reputation!" I protested.

"Honey—let's not talk about that. No need to scare the customers." She turned to face me. "The point is, you need a job."

Knowing this to be true, I placed the glasses onto my head and blinked.

Suddenly, I did feel smarter. More certain of myself.

Perhaps this gallery would prove to be the perfect fit after all! An art career would provide entrée to the life of which I'd dreamed: champagne-filled openings with glittering glitterati, traveling the globe in search of the next hot thing, heady conversations with earnest young artists about cubism, famine, and Guatemalan politics. Life would surely be good.

Later, as I once again dodged Melrose traffic to reach my now-ticketed car, I glanced back, only to see Clare sadly fold my glasses and return them to their drawer. While it wasn't her fault, after all, that I'd been fired, I wanted to strangle her. She should've known better than to hire me. As she fully knew, better than anyone, whenever I am asked for an opinion, I give it, bones and all. Was it my fault that David Hockney failed to first introduce himself? There were others, after all, who would also put him in the same category as Nagel, but you didn't see them losing their jobs over it. Prissy little queen. And what was with that hair?

Sitting in my car, keys in the ignition, I couldn't even start the car. Here it was, a beautiful Friday afternoon, and the sun was shining so brightly that my eyes began to tear. I had nowhere to go.

The classifieds were useless. Almost any job I'd ever gotten had been through friends, but as I had very few of those left, I was reluctant to chance it. If it came down to food or friends, I would, of course, eat. But at the moment, my pantry was well-stocked with both Top Ramen and Kraft Macaroni and Cheese, so all was semi-well in my noodle world.

Four art history books lie on the floor, an ill-considered investment in my short-lived gallery career. At least they related to my Italianate décor and, even if unread, would not go wasted.

Perhaps next to the golden fruit?

A pet would be nice. Nothing big, mind you, like a dog—too much commitment. And a cat, too little. And that hair, rubbing against the flocked wallpaper...

An aquarium could be festive. With miniature Roman ruins on the bottom, continuing the Italian motif? But, then again, tanks have to be cleaned, and I don't do well with pond scum.

Back to the newspaper. Sale at Bullock's. But no money. Job. Must have job. Look for job later. First, update resumé to include recent gallery experience. Put Clare as reference. Stretch length of stay to account for prior unemployed period... There. Six months, six hours—it's all relative.

Relative. Shit—got to call Gloria.

"What did you expect? You majored in Literature."

"Don't do this, Gloria."

"Didn't I tell you? I warned you."

"Yeah, I remember how supportive you were."

"Don't get smart with me, Mr. Career-Man. I have a job."

"What you have isn't a job," I shot back. "It's a prison cell."

"Working in a cubicle may not be glamorous, but at least it's honest," she prattled. "The problem, son, is that you are afraid of work. You are afraid of tedious, mundane, push-through-the-week work. Somehow you got the short-sighted idea that a job is supposed to be fun and fashionable. That it says something about you."

"Doesn't it?" I argued. "You think the girl working the beauty counter at Saks has the same life as the woman at Woolworth's lunch counter?"

The sigh on the other end of the phone told me that while Gloria saw my point, she wasn't ready to concede, so I continued, putting the exclamation point on the end of my sentence. "The choices we make do define us. And ordinary isn't me!"

"So it's high life or no life?" she queried. "Caviar or crap? There is a middle ground, Gabe, of people who work and enjoy their lives. You need a reality check. Maybe being unemployed will be it."

Later, over my fifth serving of noodles in a cup, I thought of a million comebacks as to why I was somehow more worthy and deserving of success than others. Then I flipped on NBC and settled into one of my favorite episodes of *Fame.*

Throughout my life, I had made various attempts to change, but it never seemed to stick. Shouldn't desire for transformation be enough? What more was needed to open the door? Despite my repeated efforts to move ahead, it seemed increasingly likely that I was destined to remain as I am. Much like my stereo needle, I am stuck in a groove in the middle of a song.

In some respects, though, my recent efforts had paid off: I was at the gym every day for 2 hours, no matter what. I had begun Learning Annex classes in Conversational French (though who knows when or if I will ever have the chance to use it.) I filled my days with trips to the museum, zoo, botanical gardens, art house flicks, and started a morning love affair with the *L.A. Times.* I successfully avoided all gay bars, bathhouses, and cruising areas. And, most remarkably, I pulled away from Jasper and Charlie, my formerly forever friends.

I had cast off my WEHO shackles and emerged from the Coliseum unscathed, having defeated the lions. I was pumped, primped, primed, and proud. For once in my life, I felt relatively capable and confident, stable and secure. I knew who I was and what I wanted.

So how was it, then, that with all of this, I was so alone?

I tried calling Jasper, but his machine picked up again, as did Charlie's. In the past, I had angrily pushed them away, only to find them happily scampering back when summoned. But it seemed this time I had gone too far. Calling Charlie an 'evil cock queen whose only hope for regaining the hair on his head was to save up those found in his teeth' probably didn't help. But still, aren't true friends supposed to be there for you, no matter what?

Staring at my wall, the velvety fleur-de-lis, swept up with swirls that repeated endlessly across the wall, drew my focus. The look was clearly royal and I had always loved the emblem's symmetry. "Fleur", as I had recently learned in class, means flower in French, so—SHIT! Did I just buy French wallpaper for my fucking Venetian walls? How stupid can you get? I should've chosen something with a more authentic and recognizably "Italian" motif, like elbow macaroni or a big nose.

Still, it did look good, which in the end was really all that mattered. And I did like the phallic quality of the strong pointed iris, jutting out from the flowering balls.

Going without sex for two weeks had been harder than I thought. The videos I did not miss at all. Well, that wasn't entirely true, but the absence of another's touch, of someone's skin against mine, telling me that I was not alone...

Staring again at the wallpaper, I decided to create transformation on my own terms. I would change. I would be a better person. And I'd still have everything else I'd ever wanted: friends, family, home, wealth, and happiness. And so, focusing on the latter, I grabbed my genuine Italian leather jacket and headed out to "1", in search of sexual pleasure in the form of a rock hard fleur-de-lis.

Despite having spent the better part of my life in the gay world, I have never felt truly at home within it. Try as I might, each time I walk through the doorway of a gay bar, it feels eerily similar to first. My stomach churns, I clench my jaw, suck in my gut, and become hyperaware of my immediate surroundings, while simultaneously ignoring those who occupy it. Though part of that nervousness is rooted in sex and my ache for embrace, the bulk of that nervousness revolves around approval: I want to know if others think I'm okay.

The collective hours I have spent prepping for such outings could have been better spent on any number of endeavors. In the time I've spent simply spraying my hair, I could've cured cancer.

Tonight was no different. Pulling my Camaro Z28 with moon roof and Space Mountain-y seats into a prime spot just south of the bar, I checked my rearview mirror for signs of imperfection. Miraculously, I found little had changed from my apartment mirror 10 minutes ago.

Walking the short block to Melrose, I took in the surrounding homes, whose windows shone like lanterns, illuminating the happy families within. Though, at this late hour, many shades were drawn, I caught brief glimpses: a couple bathed in the blue glow of the TV; the abandoned remains of a dinner party; a young child running down the stairs... I longed to be with them, to feel connected to a place and people. I longed to glow as they did.

Instead, it was the familiar red neon glow of the numeral "1" sign which greeted me, its comforting buzz beckoning entrance into *my* world.

Surveying the crowd, there was little here that would normally catch my eye, but tonight was not normal. Having gone two weeks without sex, I was desperately in need of meat, no matter how fleeting.

After snagging a drink, however, I lingered on the edge. My initial attempt at assertiveness disappeared. Perhaps I made no move because I knew in my heart that disappointment would ultimately follow. Or maybe I did not because I needed someone else to take the lead, to show me that I was desired.

A man stepped into my path. A hot, sexy man—not unlike myself.

"Hey there, handsome—whatcha drinkin'?" He nodded, glancing at the cocktail in my hand.

"The name's Gabe, Ugly."

"Ha! Very funny."

"And it's a screwdriver."

He nodded to the bartender. "Gimme one of those as well. And another for my friend Gabe here." Turning back to me, he extended his hand, which I shook, reluctantly. "My name's Tom, by the way—not Ugly. And if you really found me repulsive, Gabe, you'd have just kept on walkin', right?"

"What? And pass up a free drink?" Despite myself, I smiled. This guy did repulse me—his attitude, at least. But his eyes... And his jaw...

"You've got spunk, huh? I like that." He grinned, flirtatiously. I'm sure his smile had worked on a million other guys, but at that moment, I didn't care. It was working its magic on me, too.

Still, I hated him for it. For having that kind of power. And I hated myself even more, because I was such a hopeless sucker for faces such as his, especially those wearing cowboy boots.

Where was my dignity? Where was the inner good guy that I longed to be?

"Look, Tom, I appreciate the drink—really. Maybe I'm giving off the wrong signals. I'm just here, looking for my friends."

He glanced around, doubtful. "Did they, uh, stand you up?"

"They didn't—I—look. I just came to relax, okay?"

"You *are* tense—I'll give you that. Want a massage?"

"That is the worst line," I laughed, shaking my head, as he leaned in closer.

"I'm serious," he insisted. "I've got all kinds of oils at my place. I'm training."

"For what?" I smiled, despite myself. "The Lube Olympics?"

He grinned. "I go to massage school."

"You have to go to school for that?"

"If you want to be legit."

"And you are?"

"Usually," he smiled. "But with a gorgeous guy like you..."

He sent the thought drifting across the cocktails. God, this guy was so fucking hot, by anyone's standards, and yet—.

"My friends should've been here by now," I looked around, pushing myself away from the bar. "Maybe I should call them."

Tom pulled me back to him. Leaning in, he whispered, "There are no friends, Gabe." I stammered, but he shushed me. "You came here for one thing, like all the rest of us." Sliding his hand down my back, his fingers played with the top of my jeans before inching down my ass. "Let's just cut the crap and save us both a lot of time... What are you into?"

I pulled away. "If I haven't made it clear enough already, it isn't you! Jesus," I turned, ready to leave.

"Touchy, huh? Obviously a bottom."

I whirled about. "What the fuck is your problem? 'What am I into?' 'Top or bottom?' Is that really what sex is to you? A laundry list?" I could feel people staring, but I didn't care.

"What I'm *into*, Tom, really isn't any of your business, unless I happen to have my dick up your ass. We shouldn't have to compare notes before we even kiss! Sex is supposed to be organic. Fluid."

He laughed, "It's *orgasmic*, first, *then* fluid."

Steam poured from my ears. "You're a pig, you know that? But, okay, for the sake of argument, let's say that most of us are here just for the sex. And maybe we do prefer certain roles or activities... In the end, though, isn't it really about more than that? Isn't it really love and affection that we crave? An arm around us in the middle of the night? Isn't the sex just an excuse for the other?"

My Julia Sugarbaker tirade over, those around us turned back to their friends, breathlessly repeating our interaction.

Tom, however, looked me straight in the eye. "Okay, handsome, okay. I got you. I might disagree, but I got you. I'll leave you now—Let you look for your 'friends.' But you know what?"

Defiantly, I faced him.

He leaned in closer, his voice a low rumble. "You can protest all you want, but you're really just one hungry bottom, waiting to be gorged by my big man-dick." Tom reached around, grabbing my butt. "And I know just how to make you happy." He shoved his fingers roughly against my ass.

Jostling him aside, I pushed past, through the crowd.

"Hope you find your friends!" he shouted with a self-satisfied grin.

I burst from the bar, fuming. Ignoring my parked car, I headed down Melrose, walking quickly, with purpose, but with no defined destination. My skin was hot, flushed, as if on fire, with the night air a freezing burst, intended to douse the flames.

I inhaled deeply, willing the air to enter me and tame my body down. I was infuriated, both with Tom and myself. Why had I allowed myself to be treated like that? To be humiliated? Degraded? And why did that smug bastard seem so certain that I would eventually bend his way? Confident that his fucking beautiful teeth and knowing smile would somehow entrance me, despite his shallow persona and irritating arrogance?

That he would have felt empowered enough to actually finger my ass, without first handing over a dollar? And what was this aggravating top/bottom shit? Wasn't it enough that I had defined myself as gay? Was a further refinement really necessary?

Back in school, I had to grapple with the considerable concept that I preferred sex with my fellow gym buddies to the more accepted female option. Now, it seemed that I must return to biology, dissect my inner frog, determine exactly which activities I prefer, categorize and rate them, so that I would then be prepared to offer my top 10 list to any potential herpetologist who inquired. Although there are certain acts which I enjoyed and participated in more often than others, the idea that I could be restricted in my selection disturbed me.

It was not only the idea of restriction that bothered me, but the social perceptions that accompanied such labels. When you hear, "Oh, he's a top," you immediately picture a Tom-of-Finland hunk, complete with leather armband and armpits smelling of cheap cologne and raw sewage. You do not envision a lanky thing with wispy hair, wearing a kimono and slippers. That would clearly be a "bottom."

Although far from butch, I really like to fuck. And, though not incredibly femme, I also enjoy a hard dick shoved up my ass. That these acts should somehow become confused with personal characteristics was both unfair and misleading. In my not-so-distant past, I have been fucked silly by a rather overweight bald man, who favored lavender and pearls and, the very next day, served my saucisson to a ravenous French marine. Both proved thoroughly enjoyable, but what label did these experiences warrant? (Please don't say "whore.")

To say that I am simply "versatile" is also misleading, as it implies that I am capable of performing stupendous circus tricks at will ("And, folks, you should see what he can do with a cantaloupe!") Basically, "versatile" means you have no morals and will open your ass for anyone. Although I am not always incredibly picky about my choice of partners, I do like to think that I have guidelines, however mutable.

Stopping, I realized that the heat of my body was now

tempered, as was my anger. Looking about, it hit me that my endless wandering had actually led me back to where I started, in front of "1".

It was disquieting, but I knew why I had engineered a return to this place, despite my earlier humiliation.

Entering, resigned, I looked about. Tom was still there, leaning against the pinball machine. He eyed me with a self-righteous smile, knowing that he'd won.

I knew he wouldn't come over to me. I had to show him that I had caved, submitted to his will. That I was what he knew me to be from the beginning. Walking toward him, the crowd parted, sensing that I would give myself, submit, in any way that he wanted. I both hated and wanted him completely.

Upon reaching him, he slowly and deliberately finished his drink, and then set it quietly onto the counter. Without even a "hello", he grabbed my belt loops, pulling me to him. Holding my stare, I felt him unbutton the front of my Levis, and his hand once again slid down my back, pushing firmly into my jeans. With a tug, he yanked my briefs to one side, forcing a finger into my ass. I grimaced as he shoved harder, but didn't look away. I stared right back, letting him know that he could use me, but that I was giving myself willingly, on my own terms. He finally leaned into me, his stubble grazing my lips as he shoved in yet another finger, stretching me roughly. I took it, like the whore I am. Finally, his tongue probed my mouth, jabbing inside with all of the passion of a man insatiable for sex and empty of affection. I returned that passion, sending the message that I could just as easily top him as he me. My energy only served to make him angry, though, and he roughly pushed me into the corner, his hands all over me, grasping, pinching, pulling.

At that moment, my political convictions went out the window, and all I wanted was for this man to fuck me. I didn't care who witnessed my degradation. I was a willing participant in my own abuse. Flashing on my tormentors in high school, I wondered why the line of sexual tension was so close to that of humiliation. When had love been replaced by cruelty?

But it really didn't matter, because like it or not, right now I was getting exactly what I wanted. Tom bent down, biting my nipple through my shirt. He kissed me again, roughly, then brought his hand up from my ass. He held his pungent fingers beneath my nostrils, nodding for me to inhale. And I did.

At that moment, my eyes locked with those of the one person I did not want witnessing this stupefying act of desperation. After so many years, I almost wasn't certain it was him, but the look of sadness that greeted me confirmed that indeed it was Keith. His face was strained, if still beautiful, but his eyes—. His eyes didn't so much look at me as penetrate. They peeled back layers of skin and tissue, his X-ray vision piercing through to my clearly-troubled soul. I held his laser force glare, watching as he registered an encyclopedia of emotions: confusion, disbelief, anger, fury, and an oddly curious touch of gentle and unyielding kindness. And it killed me to see that spark of goodness.

Tom noticed that my attention had been drawn elsewhere, and twisted my nipples violently to regain his advantage. This time, however, his actions provoked a torrent of pain, rushing through me, and my body convulsed as if punched in the gut.

Breaking from Tom, I blindly pushed through the crowd toward Keith. Stumbling urgently toward him, I cried out, pleading for his rescue. Hearing my call, through the sea of faces, Keith offered a quick, forced smile before darting out of the bar.

Racing out onto the street, I strained for a glimpse of him. His face. A car. His shirt. His scent. Some sign, anything, that he had actually been here. That I hadn't imagined him.

But he was gone.

Later, beyond exhausted, I entered my apartment. Bathed in the red glow of light reflected off my flocked wallpaper, I realized that it was I who was actually flocked. This was not the life I wanted or planned, so why was I living it?

The bathroom light was on, ignored in my primped rush out the door. Stepping inside, I peered into the mirror and saw a haggard face staring back. This is who I am now, I thought. And the sad thing is, I created this monster. No one else is to blame, despite the many I have. And yet, somewhere within, there must be some remaining humanity, right?

Hoisting myself onto the bathroom counter, I pulled the mirrored medicine cabinet open, triggering reflection upon reflection. In the seemingly hundreds of Gabeys staring back, I searched the eyes of each, hoping for some hint of my childhood optimism. A flicker of innocence; a trace of light, joy, hope.

Instead, what jumped out were the crow's feet, splintering from my eyes like the quick crack of ice breaking on a frozen pond. They were not so much wrinkles, gentle reminders of time, as bloody gouges; scratches from the sharpened claw of a spurned lover or a rabidly pissed kitty. These grave trenches poured forth from my eyes, so red, so veined, apparently crying bloody tears over my currently ailing state.

I knew I had to find Keith. He, more than Gloria or Clare or anyone else, knew the goodness that existed within me. Only he knew the course I have charted in attempting to outrun my past. And only he could rekindle that goodness, transforming me into the person I so desired and had once been destined to be.

The next day I scoured my apartment, overturning everything until I finally found my old Day Runner. Pouring over each page, I was assaulted by the names and faces of past lovers and friends. These were my friends; *mes amis*. Fellow journeymen. And yet as important as each had been, I'd lost touch with all. When had I decided that friendships were as disposable as soiled tissue?

Finding Keith's listing, I tried the numbers. None worked, but I knew he probably wouldn't talk to me anyway. Not after the look he gave me. I called high-school classmates I hadn't spoken to in years, but none knew his whereabouts. Information had no listing either.

Getting in my car, I made the familiar trek into the Valley and drove to his father's home. Aside from a recent coat of paint, little had changed. Walking up the steps, I wondered if his dad would recognize me, this boy who had poisoned his son. Having been banished from this house once before, I knew the likelihood of a warm embrace, let alone information, was doubtful. Still, I had to try. Pushing the Gambles' doorbell, I listened to the footsteps within, drawing closer.

But the eyes that greeted me were not those of Keith, nor his father, nor anyone else remotely familiar. A small Asian woman peeked out, unwilling to unleash the chain.

"Hi, uh, is Keith here? Keith Gamble?"

The woman shook her head, "No. No Gamble. Move six years ago."

The door started to shut.

"Wait!" I shouted, wanting to throw myself against the closing barrier. "Do you have an address? A phone number?"

But the door locked decisively, prompting the rants of the crazy man outside to escalate as the echo of shuffling footsteps faded, quietly recessing into the distance.

In times of crisis, there are only two people I call. One, my mother, usually makes me feel worse about myself, and was called only as a last resort. Clare, the other option, made me feel better, yet was exhausting.

Just anticipating picking up the phone, I felt tired.

To some degree, I think I withheld calling simply so that I could wallow in self-pity a bit, as for in that moment, enveloped in sadness, I felt somewhat human. I let myself sink into the quicksand of depression, allowing my chest to open, ever so slightly; but when the feelings increase and begin overflowing, that panic of true desperation, of drowning, forces a call to "Clare 911," before rescue is actually out of reach.

Why did these emotions scare me? Most times I felt impervious to pain. Others could shoot endless rounds of bullets, they'd just bounce right off my Teflon-coated breastplate. But put me in a quiet space, and I was left utterly defenseless to all invaders.

"Is the low-cal Italian as low as you have?" Clare peered intently at the waiter, a pimply kid of 16.

"Ma'am, it's low-cal Italian."

She nodded, knowingly. "Right. But, I mean, is there a nonfat? Do you have a nonfat dressing?"

His eyes rolled up into his head, leaving us with a zombie

food servant.   Mechanically, he recounted, "We have Ranch, Blue Cheese, French, Italian, and low-cal Italian. That's it."

Again, she nodded hopefully. "And those others—?"

I jumped in, hoping to spare the waiter's life. "—Are all fat. They're high fat. The highest-of-the-high fat. The 'Call-the-Sally-Jesse-Raphael-show-I'm-ready-for-my-close-up' fat. Clare, get the low-cal Italian."

"But do you think that the low-cal Italian will be—"

"Clare, we could have eaten by now!" I threw down my napkin. "If you're not happy with the Italian, get some fucking lemon wedges!"

"Ew—no! Gross. I'd rather have the low-cal! I'm not some purist." She smiled to the waiter, who didn't smile back. "Oh, and a glass of Chardonnay."

"And you, sir?"

"Gimme the potato skins with Ranch, a side of onion rings with BBQ, and a vanilla shake," I smiled. "All with extra fat."

I ordered this purely to watch Clare squirm with envy, happily knowing that she will eventually devour the remains.

"Do you realize," she said, sipping her water, "that all of our interactions now involve a meal?"

"What do you mean?"

"Well, we used to hang out. Go clubbing. Chat all the time. Now, we just—eat."

"No, we don't."

"The only time I hear from you is when you're in trouble. And soothing the pain means comfort food." Reaching for her water, she sipped contentedly.

"That's not entirely true," I objected.

"Oh yeah? Then why are we here?"

As I fumbled for an answer, the waiter arrived with my onion rings and her Chardonnay.

"How're Charlie and Jasper?" Clare asked innocently, taking a sip.

"I wouldn't know," I admitted. "They're—"

"Not returning your calls. Got it." She reached across the table, snagging three rings. With a crunch, "So, what this time?"

As the chain of events unfolded, Clare nodded at all the right places, proffering her familiar platitudes. When I finished, Clare stared at me for a moment.

"Do you like having no friends, Gabey?"

"Well, you're my friend, right?"

"You know what I'm talking about."

I looked away. "You don't know what it's like."

"Try me."

"Look—You have a terrific job at the gallery, which you love. You've got your mom, who isn't half as crazy as mine—"

"Oh yeah?"

"Your sister, and you've always had a good circle of friends..."

"And why do you think that is?"

"Beats the hell out of me."

Taking another onion ring, Clare eyed me quizzically. "Did you see what you just did?"

"What?"

"Here we are, having a serious conversation. I ask you a question, an important question, and you spew out a one-liner."

"I thought you liked my humor."

Clare slid from the table and stood.

"What did I say—?" I was certain I'd once again fucked up the moment.

Ushering me to scoot, she slid into my side of the booth, then turned, taking my hands in hers.

"Clare," I managed, suddenly uncomfortable. "I know people here."

"Shush. This is important."

"Okay..." I droned.

"I said, 'shush!'" she demanded. "Are you listening?"

On my petulant nod, she smiled, squeezing my hands. "Good. I love you, Mr. Gabriel Charles Travers."

"Oh, fuck! I knew it."

"Right," she laughed. "Believe me, I know where your thing has been, and that ain't for me!"

I grinned, but somehow wished that I somehow *had* inspired some degree of lust in her. Not that I wanted Clare sexually, but that kind of passion I fully understood. It was the more muted sentiments that caused me pause.

"What I'm trying to say," she managed, "and not very well, given that glass of Chard, is that I know you. I know the you *within*. The one that others don't even know exists. I just—I look at you, hon, and see such amazing things. I'm not gonna list 'em all, because you know what they are—"

"I do?"

"Think back to when we first met."

I nodded. "I remember."

"We had such fun, right? Planning our futures, joking about all the funny people around us, laughing our heads off—"

"But you just said that my humor is all wrong."

"That's not what I said," she countered, still holding my hands. I was beginning to wish we'd gone somewhere more private, as her intimate gesture felt entirely awkward in the midst of my cruising grounds. "It used to be, your humor was light, funny. Jokes about situations, or people's hair, you know? But somewhere along the way, this bitter, snarky edge crept in."

"You think I don't know that?"

Clare was quiet. "We both know what I'm talking about, as well as where it came from."

I looked away.

"You remember," she said softly, "back then? We talked about me being some big-time artist—"

"—And me writing for the *New Yorker*," I finished with a sigh, shaking my head at the idea.

"It's not too late, sweetie. For either of us. Dreams don't end, just because we have responsibilities and rent."

"You think that I don't have dreams?"

"I think you did have dreams," she said, speaking more gently than her norm.

Staring into my drink, I knew that she was right. I flashed over the long list of both things and people I had loved and lost.

She took another sip of her wine, then grabbed her napkin, dotting her lips. "I read a great quote today."

"Of course you did."

"Some philosopher—Jewish."

"Which makes it even better."

"What was it?" Clare wavered. "Oh yeah. 'The course of life is unpredictable. No one can write his autobiography in advance.'"

"That is good," I nodded, all too aware that I'd already written my own destiny, pushed people away, just as easily as flipping a light switch.

As Clare offered a kiss, heading back to the gallery, I ruminated on my current state. My desire for change was what drove me to act, as evidenced by my Venetian Palazzo. I had gone to great lengths to change my façade, when the problems were purely internal; it was my plumbing and electricity that were in need of repair. Somewhere, at my core, the sheathed wiring was entangled, short-circuiting my efforts, and I had yet to find an affordable electrician. Is that what I'd been searching for in bar after bar? A humpy electrician with reasonable rates?

While I realized that it was time to put away the spackle, the path to such a sharp inward turn remained unclear. I'd read piles of self-help books and attended motivational lectures, but aside from the recurring and feverish insistence that I needed a positive attitude, I'd found no guidance. Desire for change, in and of itself, was but one step. Without the accompanying tools, it was like being handed a scalpel and assuming you could perform surgery.

I fully acknowledged that I had no equipment or training for such a trek; I needed guidance.

My sherpa came, surprisingly, in the most innocent note card imaginable. A petrified cat, clinging perilously to a bar, accompanied by a jaunty font: "Hang In There!"

Where Clare managed to find such anachronistic greetings was a mystery, but my hunch was that this box had sat in the bottom of her desk drawer for several years, waiting for just the right occasion. Her painstaking cursive resembled the bouncy script on the card's cover, and I winced at the carefully crafted message:

Gabey,

So great to see you! We need to do that more often! After our "chat", I thought about you, me, us... and how hard "moving on" has been. Maybe it would help to talk over stuff with someone. You never know - in no time you just might be able to turn that frown upside down!!! ☺

With Much Love (but not in "that" way),

Clare

As much as I appreciated her note, and that she cared enough about me to send it, it was what she enclosed that would launch me onto a new path: a business card.

"I think it's a good idea," Gloria chattered. "Remember how I used to beg, after——?"

"I remember. Thanks for bringing all that up."

"You were so stubborn, as was your father... Getting Lenny to go, I practically had to twist his arm."

"He didn't want to face what he'd done."

"Who does, honey?" she chortled. I was sure she was enjoying a martini. "We all make mistakes."

"You're talking as if he just spilt some milk or broke a plate."

"I'm not making excuses for him," she muttered. "I hope this helps, honey. Really, I do. And if it doesn't, maybe try a good cry or a heating pad."

"You think I haven't cried? I've cried, yelled, screamed—I've overhauled my entire life trying to be a better person."

Gloria's long sigh filled the empty space. "Hon, I'm gonna tell you exactly the same thing your shrink is gonna tell you five long, expensive years from now: There is no 'better person.' You are you—like it or not. And the trick about life is getting to accept yourself as flawed. That's it. No pixie dust or Jack's magic beans. You are flawed—just like everyone else."

"You think I don't know how screwed up I am?"

"I raised you, remember?"

"Yeah—and thanks for that, by the way. Stellar job."

"And that's the other thing."

"What?"

"At some point, you'll want to blame me. Or your father. To blame anyone but yourself for the shitty state you're in."

"Mom—"

"And you know what? It's okay. Blame away. I can live with that. Because there is a lot we should have done differently. Better. But Lenny and I—we were just as flawed as you. So there."

Later, as I replayed what she'd said, much of what she'd said was true: damaged kid, check; damaged parents, check; totally damaged adult, double check. But just knowing that I came from a flawed gene pool was not enough.

Driving to my appointment, it occurred to me that perhaps Clare was not the most ideal person to rely on for a referral. Not that she was any more screwed up than anyone else, but whether Clare had said she'd stubbed her toe, was suicidal, or envisioning herself in a bell tower with an AK 47, I imagined her therapist gently entreating, "Come on Clare, let's turn that rain into a rainbow!"

While positive reinforcement might work for Clare, I did not want coddling or hand-holding or pleasantries; I wanted a dominatrix. Due to my precarious financial situation, my therapy had to be aggressive, succinct, and kick-ass productive.

Riding up in the elevator, I wished that I'd asked for more information about this woman. I really knew very little, other than, being a woman, she had a vagina, which could be problematic. How, after all, could I possibly discuss my odd aversion to female genitalia, when labia would be sitting not three feet away? Regardless, it was too late now.

Entering the waiting area, I saw a row of buttons on the wall, and found her business card below one of them. "Dr. Roberta Heinlich." Seeing her name, I couldn't help but giggle "Hiney-lick!" But hey, maybe with a name like that, she'd be my kind of gal after all.

I crossed my fingers, then pushed the button.

The door opened and a warm, welcoming red head extended her hand. "You must be Gabe. I'm Roberta. How are you?"

Was that a trick question? Why would a therapist even ask that? I wondered if she wanted the truth. Instead of responding directly, I smiled pleasantly, trying to return her warmth, and shook her hand, "Nice to meet you."

And, thus, ushering me into her office, we began.

It occurred, as I left her building, that I hadn't yet mentioned Keith, or Joey and Kid. I'd talked about myself: my goals, my doubts, my lack of money, my sex life, my family... all of which is fundamental. And yet, the truly momentous events, I'd left to a later date.

Perhaps that was normal, needing to feel more secure with Roberta, more certain of her abilities. But part of me questioned the need to rehash all. Keith was my first, and only, love; sacred. While potentially beneficial, dissecting that relationship would likely dull its gentle patina. I had so few good memories to hang on to, and I wasn't about to let one go.

In the weeks since locking eyes, I'd utilized every possible source to locate Keith. Wherever I'd been, throughout the city, I'd kept my eyes peeled. I returned to the scene of the crime, "1", several times, hoping he would return as well, but only ended up bumping into Tom, whose look of scorn could be felt clear across the room.

I searched other bars as well. Out-of-the-way places that would've appealed to Keith. The S.S. Friendship in Santa Monica, Venice's RoosterFish, and countless Valley dives. While I couldn't imagine Keith in West Hollywood, given his aversion to all things mainstream, that didn't stop me from looking. While Keith was the reason I gave myself as I headed out each night, I fully realized that I was using him as an excuse. But so what if I returned home with some other toy instead? Wasn't I entitled to a bit of happiness? A hobby is a hobby, after all. Some people crochet; I fuck.

In pursuit of Keith, I always set out alone. Clearly, the wreckage I'd wrought with Charlie and Jasper was irreversible.

And Clare had grown tired of the bar scene, having been my right arm for so many years. So I told myself that such evenings were not only in pursuit of Keith, but also of new friends.

Perhaps I'd connect with someone with whom I could actually talk. Converse. Exchange something more than pleasantries or bodily fluids. While I was sure that some of the guys whose dicks I'd sucked were dandy gents, in the heat of the moment, communication meant speaking in grunts and groans. From the taste of their cocks, I couldn't be certain whether one had worked in a quarry or were poet laureate.

Occasionally, however, I would meet people with whom friendship seemed a real possibility, such as Ric and Tim. We met at Marix one Sunday afternoon, giggling together over a drunken Brazilian god wearing Dolphin shorts, then sealed the deal over a shared meal of fajitas. They taught me that the true way to eat fajitas was to order a side of mashed potatoes and gravy, and to spread it onto the tortilla before adding the rest.

That this pair had a never-ending stream of fabulous friends to join them on trips, dinners, and evenings out was understandable, for they were truly good people and deserved to share their lives with the same.

But to have been granted such endless bounty—kindness, effortless good taste, good humor, looks, friends, money— seemed excessive to a fault. "God divides," some would say. But doesn't that statement imply that those of us not blessed in such a manner would have received other, equally-worthy compensatory attributes?

Quite honestly, the only endowment I received was my ample endowment. And though thousands have benefited, it is hardly the attribute that induces desirable dinner invitations. ("Hey, what a great story from Danny! And now, Gabe, why don't you tell us more about your big crank?")

It wasn't that I was not friendly or funny. I *was*, wickedly so. But every action felt forced, never germane. While I may have engendered a hearty laugh or a kind word, the sheen from those such as Tim and Ric contrasted too starkly with my own lackluster-finish, magnifying my inadequacy.

Although there were elements to my persona that were

appealing, I, as a whole, was not.   Too many similar dark characteristics had obscured my gentle side, forming a mask with perpetual sneer.   That I felt tenderness, sadness, or even kindness remained unnoticed, so overpowering were my defenses.

It is difficult, once you've found parts of yourself that serve to amuse or entice, to break free of such nooses, and let the more nuanced sides emerge. I wondered if my disparate parts would ever become cohesive, coming together to form the man I wished to be.

It seems, at times, that God does indeed divide. But only into the "have's" and "have not's."

Looking at the clock, I realized that it was getting closer to Keith hour. My energy picked up, and I began my familiar prep of hair (mousse, light blow dry, spray), skin (equal parts Clinique moisturizer and bronzer, mixed together before application), and uniform (tight aqua T, white Bike jock, and my favorite crotch-worn Levi 501's). The key was to look both put together and effortless at the same time.

My West Hollywood circuit started, as always, at Revolver, which was not yet happening. Not seeing anything delectable, I meandered down to Rage. Happily, Tony was working the door, and I floated past the waiting queue, drawing both criticism and appreciation in my wake. Then a cursory cruise through Studio One and Mother Lode, before ending back, full circle, at Revolver.

While no one in my journey struck my fancy, the streets were alive with the fervor that precedes Halloween. People were happy, celebratory, and for a moment, West Hollywood actually seemed like a community, rather than a loose grouping of condominiums and gay bars.

At Revolver, a line had since formed, but Eddie nodded me in. I smiled, grateful to be acknowledged as one of the chosen. Steve slid me a drink and a wink: his signal that if I didn't find Prince Charming by midnight, he would charmingly shove his pumpkin dick up my ass slipper.

Turning, however, a young man caught my eye. His hair was

brown, and long enough to brush his shoulders. His eyes were penetratingly dark and focused right on me. I blushed, and looked away, uncharacteristically. Why? What about him had removed my usual projection of confidence?

He approached. "Hi there. I'm Jahn."

"Gabe," I smiled, shaking his hand. "So, Jahn—Is that Swedish?"

"Most people think that. I guess it's pretty common there. But I'm from New York, originally. Upstate. A little town called Fishkill."

"Really?" I couldn't help but laugh. "Never heard of Fishkill before. Or met a Jahn, either."

"Well, I guess tonight is your lucky night."

I was beginning to think so myself. "Was Jahn a family name?"

"Kind of," he nodded, leaning forward. "My dad's name is John. And he's the fourth. Jonathan Carter Butler, the fourth, to be precise."

"Sounds impressive."

"He's a librarian," he laughed. "Anyhoo—he was insistent that I carry on the family lineage, but my mom wasn't having any of that. To her 'John' was just too pedestrian. So, as a compromise, they settled on Jahn Carter Butler, the only."

"So 'Jahn'—"

"Jahn, Johan, Gianni—all just variations of John."

"Well, Jahn definitely sounds more exotic."

He agreed. "Plus, it also means, 'God is gracious.'"

Despite my years fighting against his very existence, perhaps God indeed was gracious, to have created someone like Jahn.

Our introductions complete, our discussion progressed, moving quickly from the typical bar talk. We dissected the upcoming election. Who did we favor? What would be the implications if George Bush were elected? Why had the Dukakis campaign been so lousy?

Jahn laughed when I told him how Clare had been so excited at Paul Simon's candidacy, only to be heartbroken upon discovering that he wasn't the singer.

Talking with Jahn, I was charged with the kind of electricity you picture surging through power plants. Not only was Jahn to-die-for, but he knew the value of responsibility and social service. Of our inherent duty to leave this world better off than when we first came into it.

His remarks were not off-the-cuff, nor simply calculated to impress, but substantive responses to questions long pondered.

As we talked, I tried to follow Roberta's advice and remain in the moment. Whenever I veered into my head to begin planning our lives together, I immediately refocused myself on what he was saying. And, surprisingly, it was working.

At some point we moved our conversation outside and strolled the boulevard. Engaging with Jahn, I realized that life could indeed be lived on all cylinders, and that part of the surging vitality I felt was a direct reaction to feeling valued and appreciated. What a change! To be prized by someone, not just for my wit or dick, but for my insight and views.

Looking about, I took in all that surrounded us: the sights, the smells, the assorted drag queens and Halloween revelers sauntering past. Breathing it in, I vowed to always be so keyed into life, not just in passing moments, but in each moment of every single day.

I felt, for the first time with anyone since Keith, entirely comfortable and at ease. We wandered through A Different Light, perusing the latest bestsellers and sharing with each other our favorite novels. We stopped for coffee, settling in to our chairs, and it just felt so right. I felt close and connected, and was certain that he felt the same.

It was getting late, the bars were closing, and I knew we'd eventually end up at my place. But I wasn't ready yet. I wanted this feeling, this connection of souls, to continue. Suggesting a bite to eat, we walked the many blocks up to Ben Frank's, which was packed, despite the hour.

Jahn told me about his relationships; what had worked, and what hadn't. I shared my experience with Keith, and my discouraging track record since. I told him of Gloria, and Lenny, and even a bit of what had happened that night. I was trying to be honest, unguarded, and authentic, just as Roberta had instructed.

But later, pancakes finished, as we walked back to my place, I sensed that something had changed. Whether with Jahn, or me, or both, I didn't know. Though we continued to talk, the spark had somehow been extinguished. I knew, even as he swallowed my shaft, that we would not see each other again. Whatever flame had been lit had been doused by an unseen bucket, ending the date as so many before, with a fake phone number scrawled on a realtor's notepad.

Driving blindly, it barely registered where I was. All I could think about was Jahn. What had I done? Where had I messed up? He was everything I'd ever wanted and, at least for a few hours, it seemed that I fulfilled his needs as well. How, then, could something so right go so unbelievably wrong?

I'd tried calling Roberta, but as it was a Saturday, she wasn't working, and wouldn't be in the office until Monday. While I thought about calling Clare, I couldn't bring myself to the energy level necessary for her relentless good cheer. I knew that I had screwed up, and needed to know exactly how. Replaying the evening, though, everything seemed perfect, until I had invited him back to my place.

Was it the sexual immediacy that had turned him off? He had agreed to it, after all. Or had I rushed in too quickly? Had I shared too much, or too little? Roberta had said to be honest, to be my authentic self, and I was, for the most part. So was this, then, a rejection of the authentic me?

The Palm Springs turn-off came into view, with the wind farm stretching out for miles. The mills turned, unceasing, and there was something so repetitive about their round and round that felt very much like my life. Old patterns are hard to break, as I was finding, but I truly had tried to do as Roberta had suggested.

Did that mean that her advice was incorrect? Or that I had somehow not followed it to the letter? Where, exactly, had I so entirely fucked things up?

All I knew, now, was that I wanted to be fucked. I turned off Ramon and onto Warm Sands, feeling the constriction around my chest like a too-tight belt. I pulled into the gravel drive, then entered the dingy office. Every single piece of wood that I saw was disintegrating, and I couldn't help but wonder if staying here would do the same to my soul. Still, I was undeterred.

The fat old fart at the desk gave a knowing smile, as if he could read my thoughts, then waddled down a path, much as a walrus, beckoning me to follow. I spotted people lounging by the pool, but was more focused on the room I was faced with. The single light bulb bathed the wood paneled walls in harsh and unforgiving tones. I set my suitcase down, staring glumly at the hideous blue floral bedspread, covering what was surely a multi-stained mattress. The bedspread was so off-putting that any thought I'd had of laying outstretched on it, being pummeled by faceless strangers, was instantly gone.

"I did the needle point myself, you know," noted the man proudly, nodding toward the gnome wall-covering. I attempted a smile. "There's a continental breakfast from 8:00 until 10:30 on the patio. Just help yourself."

"Great." Again, I faked a smile, knowing full well that I would not eat food prepared on the premises. After he left, a knowing wink his parting gift, I slipped into my Speedo. Assessing myself in the mirror, I realized that one benefit from being unemployed was that, due to countless hours spent at the gym, I now had infinitely lickable abs.

At the pool, I got a lot of stares, which caused my dick to plump a bit. Lying down on my stomach, the itchy hotel towel beneath me, I assessed my fellow leisure-goers, determining which lucky fellow would be my evening's fuck.

A few twinks frolicked in the pool with a beach ball. What the hell did they think this was? A scene from *Beach Blanket Bingo*? They seemed so unearthly, all stick arms and legs, mops of stringy hair and pale skin. As if they'd somehow fallen directly out from a vat of formaldehyde. Definitely not my type, and I wondered how they could possibly be anyone else's either. Their giggles crescendoed into a group squeal, rendering them entirely sexless to me.

There were a few older, solitary guys, both in the pool and lounging, but they all seemed to be covertly ogling the prancing pre-pubescents to take much notice of me. Directly across, I noted a couple about my age, discreetly eyeing me from behind their home décor magazines.   Both were cute, and they exchanged arched eyebrows and whispers, as they apparently discussed me. But, unfortunately for them, a couple's scene and all the drama that entailed was not what I needed. My mission was clear: I wanted someone to take me and make me their own. No need for fuss, or muss, or tender glances. Just fuck me, please—hard—and all would be well.

When I opened my eyes again, the only other poolside inhabitant was the innkeeper, dozing beneath his large straw sunbonnet, needlepoint clutched firmly in hand. As if anyone would steal it. Rising, I ran my hands over my mottled skin, the affects from the overly-starched hotel towel made plain for all to witness, if only someone had been around to see it.

In a way, it was a relief that no one remained to observe my less than stellar appearance, but the lack of prospective nighttime partners meant that I would have to travel further still on my quest.

The Barracks was packed, as I knew it would be. Surveying the crowd, I was certain that almost any of them would be adequate for my purpose. Big builds, cropped hair, leather, Levi's—exactly the crowd for me. If only I could somehow prevent them from speaking, destroying the illusion, I would prevail.

My first few attempts were absolute disasters, prompting countless bottles of beer. While visually intriguing, in a beat-me-up sort of way, Prospect Number 1 ruined it the minute he mentioned that he'd seen me in L.A. at El Coyote. "Aren't their margies totally yummy?" he purred with a smile. I excused myself and went to piss.

The trough was full and, as I waited, I could feel the sexual tension in the air as the three men before me eyed each other's cocks. While one actually attempted to pee, another began stroking himself to full erection. As I did in fact have to urinate, I tried to clear my throat as politely as possible, but it didn't work.

I waited as long as I could, hoping one of them would cum

already, but this threesome was all about foreplay.

"Hello—I need to *pee*!" I stated, the grimace plain on my face.

"Jeez, Mary!" one cried. "Lighten up—"

"I am trying to lighten up, asshole, by lightening the load in my bladder. Can't you take this someplace else?"

One guy turned to me, erection in hand. "If you want," he grinned, "you can spray on me."

"Get the fuck out of my way," I growled, pushing my way to the urinal. Erection Man backed away, but the others remained, with all eyes upon my cock.

Now, as big as it normally grew to be, having three sets of strange eyes on it was having the opposite effect, and I could feel it pulling inside myself. I couldn't pee to save my life. The strain was almost unbearable, and I tried everything I could to go.

"Do you want me to turn on a faucet, honey?" one said gently.

"Jesus Christ!" I erupted. "I don't need an audience."

"Performance anxiety," one muttered.

"Let's sing," said another. "That'll distract him!"

"You are not going to fucking sing," I demanded. "Just leave me alone."

The room quieted when, behind me, Erection Man turned on the faucet, sending the sink gushing. Just then, I did as well, and in my anger, I spun toward Erection Man, spraying all over his pants. I was shocked and embarrassed, but the smile Erection Man gave me told me all was forgiven.

"Happy?" I queried, zipping up.

"Oh honey," Erection Man winked, "you have no idea."

As I headed back into the bar, the three regrouped at the trough to continue their urinary bacchanalia.

Stumbling out onto the darkened patio, its army netting obscuring any hint of moonlight, I wondered if I was the only sane person on the planet.

What if there had been some alien invasion, and I alone remained, uncontaminated? Perhaps I was doomed to forever be on the lam, and visions of *Logan's Run* filled my head.

Suddenly I desired a sheer dress exactly like Jenny Agutter's. Maybe there was a diaphanous dress shop on El Paseo, full of mannequins wearing see-through dresses and Farrah Fawcett wigs.

My attention was refocused, immediately, by a man rubbing my crotch. In the murky shadows, and given how many beers I'd had, I hadn't realized anyone was near, but, as evidenced by the tongue shoving its way into my mouth, there was. I returned his kiss, grabbing his ass and pulling him closer. He did the same, grinding his crotch into mine. I pushed him downward, and he rubbed his face into my jeans, tonguing the outline of my growing member. See, Urine Boys, it does get bigger! Actually, I could *feel* people watching us, perhaps the Urine Boys among them. All I could make out, though, was the glowing embers from cigarettes, and the breathless anticipation of the gathering throng. We were obviously providing a show, and, trooper that I was, I was determined not to disappoint.

I could feel Shadow Man unzipping my pants, and the sigh that slipped from his lips told me that he was quite content indeed. He licked it all over, lathering it with love, then pulled my balls out. As he lapped and sucked, he brought me closer and closer, until I was on edge.

"Open up," I ordered, and he obeyed. I shoved in and out of his mouth, gently at first, allowing him to get used to the size, and then faster. He was an eager apprentice, taking me, every inch; deep throating me with the skill of a seasoned professional. Not that it mattered, of course. I wanted to use him, just as I had been used. He was a repository, nothing more, and I had a huge load ready.

I shoved in and out, even faster, holding his head in my hands. I was close, on the verge.

"I'm coming," I yelled, to him and to all.

The crowd circled closer, members out, stroking themselves as I came. "Yeah!"

The little fucker swallowed my spunk, slut that he was, either uninformed or uncaring that my load might be toxic.

Around us, I could tell others were getting off as well, and I was happy to have been able to provide fodder for their fantasies.

Beneath, *ma petite prostituée* licked me clean, determined to get every drop. Finally, he rose, giving me a salty kiss. Leaning into me, he whispered, "If you want a repeat, I'm just out highway 111 at the Motel 6. Room 143." I smiled to myself, knowing that I'd made him happy, while also acknowledging that I'd never go.

As he pulled away, he turned back for the briefest of moments. "By the way," he said, "my name is Keith."

The sea of men on the patio parted and then engulfed him as Keith made his way inside. I stood, stock still, trying to put the pieces together of who this was and what we'd just done. Keith? My Keith?

I ran for him, as I had before, calling his name. Through the crowd, I could see him stop and turn, eyes scanning.

I called out again, "Keith!", and he finally saw me. His eyes registered with—what?—terror? Regret? Then he bolted, pushing his way to the door.

Shoving people aside, garnering cries and protests as I forged ahead, I didn't care. There was no way I would let him get away again.

Regardless of what had just happened, how we'd reconnected, I had to see him. To talk with him. Keith, whatever he may be, regardless of the path he'd chosen, held the key to my future and I *would not* let him slip away.

Up the street, a red Mustang started up, pulling a quick U-turn. As I ran to my car, I could see Keith's eyes, scanning the parking lot. Trapped at the light, the gas station's glow showed him drumming the steering wheel impatiently, urging the light to change. It did, just as I reached my car, and I cursed as his car peeled north on 111.

Gunning it, I was soon after him. Though I could no longer see him, I had a destination. And, based on the look he gave me, he—better than anyone—knew that nothing could get in the way of a Motel 6 and a deranged Gabriel Travers.

Driving up, I was startled to see just how desolate the motel was, and how worn it looked, compared to my prior visits as a boy. Despite being high season, the lot was oddly empty, making Keith's red Mustang easy to spot. I parked next to him and scanned the row of rooms for number 143. Running up, I pounded on the door.

"Keith, let me in! Keith!" No light shined from within, but I was certain he was there. Again, I knocked, so hard my knuckles ached. But no one responded. He had said 143, right? Or was it 134?

I ran down the corridor, footsteps echoing, and stopped at 134. No lights were on there either, but that didn't prevent me from pounding anyway.

"Hey—you!" An older man tottered out from the office. "What do you think you're doing?"

Truly, old man, I have no idea. Ignoring him, I ran back to Keith's car, then turned to face the strip of rooms that held him.

"Keith! Come out here! I need you!" Getting no response, I uttered one more long, painful, "Stella" cry: "Keith!"

Though lights switched on in various rooms and doors opened to view the psychotic man in the parking lot, none were the person I sought. Knowing that the manager of the flea trap likely had the cops on speed dial, I decided to cut my losses. Grabbing a napkin and pen from my car, I scribbled down a note, tucking it under Keith's wiper blade.

The next morning, I sat at the Denny's I'd designated, certain that, in the light of day, Keith would relent. Scents of pancakes and eggs drifted past as a busy waitress carried a full tray to a large family, both in number and weight. My cup of coffee was repeatedly filled. I kept one eye on the door, but all I saw was tourist after tourist. Who else ate at Denny's anyway, right? Can you imagine anyone with a remote knowledge of a city suggesting Denny's? Surely not. Well, no gay folks at any rate.

I'd been up all night, running over the chain of events and trying desperately to hang on to that vision of Keith, so close, and yet so far. What did he taste like? Smell like? How is it possible that I didn't realize it was him? Certainly some imprint from our past remained within me. Shouldn't the grazing of his teeth on my cockhead have summoned up some memory of our glory days of yore? Some flicker of recognition? And why did he keep running away?

After three hours, it was apparent that Keith was not coming, so I methodically downed a Grand Slam, willing its carbohydrate-laden fatness to nourish my shattered soul, as I would surely need sustenance to resume my search.

Though a few people hung at the pool, the Motel 6 seemed largely quiet. The echoed laughter of playing children hung in the air as I crossed to the office. A kindly grandmother-type greeted me, inquiring if I was checking in. "Here?" I wanted to reply, "Hardly. I have better taste than that!" Then, realizing the hotel I'd chosen for myself, I stopped.

"I'm looking for a Keith? Keith Gamble?" She stared at me blankly. "He's in Room 143—?"

Eyeing me, she crossed to the mail slots and returned with an envelope.

"You Gabe?"

I nodded.

"Here," she said, handing me the envelope, "Mr. Gamble checked out. But he wanted you to have this."

I stared at the envelope in my hand. Would this be it, after all of my wandering? Could one slight envelope contain all of the answers to the long list of questions I'd compiled?

Exiting, I walked back to the car, noticing both how hot and how light the packet felt in my hand. Regardless of the contents, I refused to open it within the confines of this soul-sapping motel. I started to head toward my hotel, then recognized that it wouldn't be an improvement. Pulling off Palm Canyon Drive into an empty lot, I parked, rolling down my windows.

The note was short and unadorned:

Gabey,

I am not sure what you want from me, but I know that I don't have it to give. If this means that I have failed you,

I'm sorry, but I failed myself first, long ago.

Much love,

Keith

I turned the note over, hoping for an address or phone number. A clue. Some way to contact him. Surely this couldn't be it, could it? I wanted answers! Some fucking closure. He ditches me, but signs the note "much love"? I'd been looking for Keith to help solve my problems, but instead found myself with even more questions.

Who is Keith now? How could he have changed so dramatically in only—what?—10 years? What had led him onto the path he'd chosen? And when did he become such a whore? I used to be the bad one. Now, it seemed, we were both on the dark side. And yet, despite some distaste for who he'd evidently become, I couldn't help but think that evil never looked so good.

Winding through the desert, I found myself turning off the highway, onto Monterey, and ascending into the hills. I'd come to the desert for comfort, in the hopes that I'd find someone who'd help banish Jahn from my thoughts, only to find myself rejected again, by the very person I thought could save me.

While road signs ahead warned of the presence of Bighorn sheep, in all of my years of coming here, I had yet to see one. But they must exist, right? Just as Keith existed, though only a scrawled note proved it. Surely he knew how much he had hurt me. How hard I'd tried to find him. Had he known it was me as he dropped to his knees? I thought not, but still—. He was my last hope in making sense of the jumbled mess I'd created. How could he have no interest in even talking to me? Wasn't he remotely curious about the Gabey he once knew? What had I ever done to Keith, except love him?

And now, without him, I was so alone, not even tears would share my sorrow. No friends, no lover, no one to laugh and play and cry with. What kind of future was that? When there is no joy, what is the fucking point?

Swinging the car back and forth, banking into the curves, I envisioned myself locking arms against the wheel, unwilling to turn. With a silent scream, I plow through the silver rusted railing, hurtling down into the dried brush and invisible bighorn sheep below.

But that, of course, was the road not taken. No matter how desperate I felt, dying in Palm Desert would be redundant.

Instead, I journeyed on, searching for solace. The widening turns through the chaparral gave way to Garner Valley, with its pine trees and sprawling horse ranches. Part of me longed to linger, but it seemed better to just keep moving. Soon after passing Lake Hemet, I hung right, climbing into the familiar mountain village of Idyllwild.

Parking the Z, I found that the drive had done nothing to relieve my anxiety. If anything, I was even more tense. Hoping to walk it off, I poked through metaphysical shops, art galleries, antiques and collectibles, and the tackiest Christmas shop I had ever laid eyes on. All the ornaments in it appeared to be made of cheap shiny plastic; the same kind used for toys in Happy Meals.

Finally, I sat, treating myself to an ice cream, but even that ooey comfort didn't help. The knot in my chest still surged, and seemed to be growing. It felt like a grapefruit, and I couldn't fathom why others did not see it. Surely it must be protruding, turning me into some sort of reversed hunchback. Once known far and wide for being a great hump, I'd now be known for having one. Throwing my napkin away, I licked the remaining stickiness from my fingers and continued through town.

I couldn't believe, at almost 27 years old, I was alone, friendless, unemployed, and so utterly clueless as to how to change my current state. No one seemed to want me—that much was clear. I'd been rejected at every turn, and part of me just wanted to run away and hide.

At Bearly Heaven, a shop in which I normally would not step foot, I found myself lingering amongst the teddy bear paraphernalia. What lured me, I cannot say, but once inside, I stayed, surrounded by all things furry. I found myself looking not at the various bear t-shirts, soap dispensers, nor embroidered bear tapestries, but rather, at the shopkeeper, a big old bear himself. Passably attractive, but somewhat thick around the middle, it was his shy smile and warm laugh that caught my eye. As he was chatting away with another local, also somewhat bearish, I hadn't yet drawn his attention, but I could not pull mine away.

He seemed solid. Grounded. Just observing him, his easy way of talking and the focus he showered on his friend, made me want to jump the counter, bury him in kisses, and hold him as my own.

Please do not turn me away, I cried silently. *Want me. Love me, in any way possible, but want me.*

I imagined his bemused (or is it frightened?) response. Unable to draw his arms around this clearly insane stranger, he instead stands stiffly, too polite to push me away.

I know you don't love me, or even know me, but I want you, I plead. *Let's run away together! We'll find our own little cabin in the woods, where we can bolt the door, and snuggle warmly, keeping the outside world at bay. You can even decorate the entire thing in teddies! Do whatever you like— anything. It doesn't matter. Just love me.*

As the local headed out the door, my beloved finally noticed me, standing near the brown bear hand puppets, and sauntered toward me.

"Hi," he smiled, ripe with possibility. "What can I do for you today?"

I hesitated, wondering if this man had a clue as to the implications of his harmless query. Over his shoulder, a wall clock ticked impatiently, a smiling bear swinging on the pendulum beneath. "Oh, uh—" I muttered, "just browsing."

"You realize what you're doing, don't you?"

"What?"

Dr. Heinlich peered over her glasses, expectantly. "With these rejections, in each case, you automatically assume that it is somehow your fault."

"I think it's obvious."

She shook her head, insistently. "I don't see it that way. You view yourself, Gabe, as damaged, and somehow deserving of rejection. And you paint everyone who rejects you as perfect, blameless."

"I know everyone else isn't perfect."

"Is that so?" She peered at me. "Then why is it that Jahn 'rejected you'? Did he say that?"

"No."

"So maybe he's the one with the issue. Maybe he can't commit, or was just looking for some fun, or—I don't know. Or take Keith. Maybe he ran because he was frightened, or didn't want you to get too close—who knows? The point is that other people are battling insecurities, Gabe. And while you don't have to take on their struggles, you do have to realize that it's not all about you." She sat back in her overstuffed chair, on her overstuffed ass, and removed her oversized glasses. "How long have you been coming here?"

"You should know—just count the stacks of money you've made."

"Exactly," she nodded. "You've been coming here weekly, for several months. And what have you gotten out of it?"

I stared at her, uncertain as to where this is headed. "Are you dumping me?"

She laughed, "This isn't a date!"

Peering at her, I wondered exactly what she was thinking. I wished that I could dive headfirst over the table and rip the transcripts of our sessions from her oversized fingers. It would likely read something to the effect of: *This guy is really fucked. This guy is really fucked. This guy is really fucked.*

Perhaps realizing that her oversized jowls missed her oversized glasses, she slipped them back on with a sigh. "Have you learned anything, anything at all, during our time together?"

"Aside from the fact that I'm a loser?" I joked flatly. "Well, I mean, I feel better about myself. Is that what you're asking? I feel more comfortable in my own..." I tapered off.

"Right," she nodded, biting the top of her pen. I wondered if she sucked her husband's cock, and imagined her biting down hard, making him squirm just as she was doing to me.

"You don't believe me?" I frowned.

Shaking her head, she leaned closer. "When you first came

here, you said that you wanted to have deeper connections. Better relationships. 'Break through' was how you put it. You wanted more emotional ties, with both yourself and with others."

"Yeah?" I replied cautiously.

"Do you feel that you've found that?" she prompted.

"A deeper connection?" I stammered. "Well, kind of."

"Because my sense... is that you haven't. Perhaps because you come here regularly, and share things with me about your feelings and experiences, you feel that you have in fact reached the end of the journey. But sharing intellectually is only the first step. Right now, you're giving book reports."

"I'm telling you about myself," I protested, louder than warranted.

"Telling," she nodded, somehow satisfied with herself. "Exactly. But not on a deeper, core level."

"That is why I'm paying *you*! To get me to that place." Sputtering, I rose, trying to grab hold of my thoughts. "God, woman—if I knew how to do it myself, do you think I'd waste my time here? You think driving to Pasadena every Friday is fun for me? Starting the weekend on such a high note? I used to love my Fridays and Saturdays. Now, I start off with a healthy dose of self-examination, which leads to self-recrimination, which leads to a Chardonnay bottle full of self-loathing. Great. Yep. You just send me off on a weekend full of fun-fun-fun."

Silently, Dr. Heinlich again bit the top of her pen.

"Do you have an oral fixation, Doctor?"

Stopping, she put the pen down. "Does that bother you?"

I shrugged. "Guess I just figured that, for you to work in this field, you would've first worked through your own issues before attempting to lead others."

Again, she was silent.

From the side table came the ticking of the clock, facing toward her alone. Each tick noted another second of uncomfortable stillness. In my stomach, a gopher was busy, digging away, wedging himself deeper and deeper into my gastrointestinal tract.

"So, we're just going to sit here?" I prodded.

"Is that what you want?" The clock ticked, filling the dead space of my non-reply. "We still have 20 minutes," she added, so smug in the knowledge that she had me trapped.

I nodded, contemplating my options. If I suddenly bolted, I just might make it to the door, but I knew that would likely prompt her to launch out of her seat, taking me down with the full, furious power of a psychiatrist scorned.

Why was I so uncomfortable? She was, after all, only a woman. An inferior being. And an ugly one, at that. An ugly, inferior being who *I* had sought out for help.

At what point had I turned her into the enemy? She was to be my savior, but I had sabotaged this, as so many before. Friendships, jobs, lovers; each had been eviscerated, cut from end to end and the guts splayed out, just as you'd disembowel a fish, by this tired fisherman's own hand. As I aged, growing older and even more bitter, my bounty would surely lessen, until there were no fish left stupid enough to be enticed into my net. Unless I made a change, I would end up in isolation; a solitary figure, silhouetted on a bluff above the craggy sea, in an unappealing yellow slicker that smelled of vagina.

I did not want my net to remain empty. I wanted to cast it into the sea and pull out armfuls of slick, squiggly creatures, gasping for breath and slathering me with slimy affection.

The clock ticked, reminding me that whatever decision I made would ultimately impact the rest of my life.

"How do I start?" I queried, so quietly I wondered if I had indeed verbalized the thought.

"You just have," she smiled. And not with the smugness I thought I'd detected earlier, but with tenderness. Someone was looking at me the way that I wanted to look at others: with compassion.

"Getting angry with me, showing me that, that's a big step." She offered me that thought gently, tentatively, as if she knew I would likely strike at it; an attempt to eradicate the infinitesimal gain I'd made. I knew that possibility was there, and so chose to remain silent.

"Because, for that moment, Gabe," she continued, "probably for the very first time since I've seen you—you were not in your head, but in your heart. That emotional connection is the one we need to explore."

"So you want me to yell at you every week?"

"If that is what it takes, yes! Yell or scream or cry or just—be in touch with what's inside. As we've talked about, the trick here is to not shut down. Try to hang onto that feeling, whatever it is, and just let it be. Don't push it aside." She held her hand to her heart, patting it. "Let it resonate."

"You make it sound like that's easy," I stated, my skepticism barely veiled.

"I'm not saying that," she says, shaking her head. "We need to explore what led you to this place, where you've shut so many out—including your own emotions. There are times where I feel like you're not telling me everything."

Despite my best effort, I looked away. I still wasn't sure that resurrecting the horrors of the past was the best of ideas.

She prodded, "Did your father play a role? Keith? Gloria? All of them?"

"Blaming them isn't going to suddenly make things right, is it?" I stammered.

Dr. Heinlich shook her head. "We're not talking about casting blame. We're trying to find out why you feel you are unworthy of love. We're searching for the key—the key to unlock yourself."

In the months that followed, I alternated between visits with Dr. Heinlich and hunting for Keith. After scouring the city, fruitlessly pursuing him through darkened alleys, bars, and overly-lit laundromats, his face reflected in each glass of beer or whirling collage of damp clothing, I finally gave up. Clearly, I dreamt him; saw his face in the face of a stranger; conjured up a rescuer at my last desperate hour. Even the note he'd left on my windshield I'd somehow mislaid, so even that worn piece of paper seemed more and more like an apparition.

And whether it was in letting go that I found release, or due to something else entirely, I felt as if my cloud had begun to lift, the tension in my chest to ease, and my need for metaphor substantially decreased.

This was likely due to not only Roberta, but my new job as well.   Through a fluke, I'd ended up temping at Amblin Entertainment, home of the ever-cuddly E.T. and the less-cuddly, more-awarded and overrated Steven Spielberg.

I'd yet to see the mother ship himself, full frontal, though I had caught glimpses.   Delivering scripts to his office, I peered past the imperious guardian assistants with mountainous breasts, through the blazing glare of bright endless light, until I could just make out Mr. Spielberg's bony finger, shakily extended toward me through the ever-present fog.

As tiring as being a production assistant was, just to be in that environment, surrounded by masses of creativity (or, better stated, creativity for the masses) was exhilarating.   Finally it felt that I'd found a workplace where I belonged.   I copied and delivered scripts, helped out in the story department, and even managed to read Steve's—er, Mr. Spielberg's—top-secret draft for a sequel to one of his biggest hits, which I had to sign a non-disclosure agreement just to read.   Could anything have been more glamorous?

Though Northridge and Universal City were both in the Valley, a mere 10 miles apart, the miles seemed to have somehow elongated, creating an untraversable chasm between this city of twinkling starlight and the dowdy suburbs of my youth.   Not only was I working on amazing projects, but here I'd seen the Toms (Hanks and Cruise), Richard Dreyfuss, Holly Hunter, Denzel Washington, and had just missed Dustin Hoffman.   Still, knowing that he'd walked the same halls as I, minutes prior, was enough for me.   I bumped into Valerie Perrine one day, and gaped, wondering who on earth she could possibly be here to see—surely not Steve?   Seeing me staring, she gave a giggly "Hello" and winked before heading toward her car.   And that single gesture, of noticing my existence, was enough for me to defend her at dinner parties forever after.

I finally made a new friend, too, Timmy.   A slight but perpetually sunny 35-year old, he'd somehow garnered the nickname "Thunder".   While Thunder didn't really suit him, it was at least preferable to calling a grown man Timmy. Knowledgeable and eager to please, Thunder taught me virtually everything I'd need to succeed in the Amblin universe, leaving out only key items, to ensure that I didn't get promoted before him. I understood, however, and would have done the same.

This new job also boosted my social status, short-listing me onto the gay "Hollywood" circuit, where to be beautiful is nothing if not backed up with legitimate credits. I suddenly found myself being invited to parties in the hills, in spectacular historic homes, surrounded by boys in Speedos, who drank shimmering cocktails while ignoring the buffet. And while the gay power moguls could be a bit more difficult to spot, they were at every party: older balding men, standing on the sidelines, their plates overflowing with free food and a gleam of hunger in their eyes. The moguls remained invisible to the younger guys, until their identities were strategically revealed, causing them to then become swarmed by the cannibalistic crowd of actor-cater-waiters, who took sudden interest in the size of the power brokers' cocks and bank accounts.

Now, albeit tangentially, I *was* one of those power brokers, and though I didn't have any pull to speak of, to the hoards of climbers, I was a stepping stone, and I didn't mind getting stepped on as long as the hunk was hot.

Soon I was balancing long days at Amblin with romantic dates with actors, each more stunning than the last. I attended screenings, wrap parties, networking events, read scripts and the trades, and make sure that everyone at Amblin knew my name. And once they did, I found myself quickly promoted up to Assistant Story Editor, which meant that I was no longer a bottom-feeder.

Thunder, however, seemed to find my quick rise suspect, and initiated a coordinated response to knock me from my pedestal. But his sabotage efforts were no match for my well-honed skills. I chose to treat him with sweet condescension, much as you would an indigent child. "Timmy, would you mind picking up my lunch? Steven has me working on something very important. I'd tell you, but it's very hush-hush." Or, "Oh Timmy, Cindy asked if you'd stop at her office. She needs her trash emptied." And my favorite, "Timmy, Mark brought in some Girl Scout cookies to share with everyone. Can you please put them on a tray and walk them through the building? Oh, you are so nice!" In each case, Thunder submitted, knowing that my smooth smile and killer instincts were no match for his gap-toothed grin. Behind his back, I whispered to others about his curious lack of height, and speculated as to how he got his job, given his obvious autism.

Thunder soon turned to Rain, then was downgraded to a Trickle, and then finally, disappeared altogether. I missed him a bit, I guess, as he had been my only friend, but that quickly passed. He had been intent on only one thing: getting ahead. And I just didn't have time for self-centered people like that.

As I walked up the steps of Acapulco's Mexican Restaurant on La Cienega, the loud blare of a mariachi's trumpet pierced my ear more painfully than the needle from an actual piercing. I'd been skeptical after receiving the invitation to the first-ever meeting of the Rainbow Connection, a gay entertainment networking group. After all, wasn't every entertainment networking event gay? And naming the group after Kermit the Frog's theme song seemed tacky, at best.

Heading into the generic fiesta palace, my cynicism increased as I took in the peeling paint on the fake toucans perched overhead. There was nothing remotely authentic or swank about the locale, and certainly nothing that read "Hollywood" either. It occurred to me that there was no way this gathering could have been planned by a gay man. And the 300-lb. lesbian who greeted me, crushing every bone in her dykey death grip, confirmed my suspicion.

Janice worked at Warner Bros. in scheduling, and this event had been her brainchild. While working in scheduling *technically* meant that she worked in entertainment, shouldn't this event have been restricted to those professionals who actually mattered? Agents, producers, actors, directors, development folks such as myself, fine. Craft service, grips, electricians, and honey wagon "professionals," not so much. I was tempted to run, but couldn't pull free, as her boa constrictor fingers were wrapped around my arm, guiding me into the banquet room.

In any event, meeting fellow professionals hadn't been my

goal in attending, as I knew most every mover who shaked. But meeting hunky guys who shared my top primary interests of movies and cock, well—there were worse ways to spend an evening.

And Devon Ackerby, a doe-eyed newbie fresh off the Iowa corn train, was exactly what I was looking for. We ended up standing next to each other at the bar, both reaching for the same tortilla chip, at exactly the same moment. In Hollywood, this is called "meet cute", but I just called it hunger.

Somewhat slight, with dark blonde bangs cut almost straight across, everything about Devon, from his hairstyle to his clothes to his shoes, were completely old-fashioned, which only added to his charm. In a way, he reminded me of Keith. But I quickly pushed that thought aside, determined to remain in the moment, as Roberta had suggested. Over my margarita on the rocks with salt, and his frozen strawberry daiquiri, I learned that he was a screenwriter, trying to make it in the big city.

While he kept trying to pitch me his latest script—"It would be perfect for Bette Midler!"—I kept trying to pitch him a trip back to my place.

Just when I was getting close to signing him to a deal, adding him to my list of conquered "artistes", Janice rather roughly intervened.

"Time to mingle, fellow craftsmen," she bellowed, shepherding Devon into another part of the bar.

Later, having suffered through several rounds of weak margaritas and endless small talk, I left. Walking to my car, which I'd parked down the street, I massaged my arm, certain that Janice's fingerprints would forever remain imprinted. A figure stepped from the shadows, script in hand, and I could tell from the bowl haircut it was Devon.

"I, uh, thought you might like to read this," he offered. "Everyone in my screenwriting class loved it, even Mr. Beeker, and it would make the perfect—"

"—movie for Bette Midler," I nodded. "Got it."

We stood closely, the streetlight casting our faces in odd geometric patterns.

"So, you'll read it?" Devon pressed.

I took the script from him, flipping it open and holding it up toward the light.

"*Big Business*?" I frowned. "I can't see Bette doing a workplace comedy, especially after her uptown role in *Down and Out*."

"It's not really a workplace—"

I stopped him, moving in closer. "Listen, Devon. I like you," I grinned. "I don't know why—maybe it's your sweet nature..."

Even in the bad lighting I could tell he was blushing.

"Maybe it's your persistence. Or maybe it's just the amazing tightness of your ass." Even as he looked away with a nervous smile, I could tell that he was excited. "But I'll tell you what. I'll read your script."

"You will?" He lit up like a Christmas tree.

"I know some folks over at Bette's company, *All Girl Productions*, and if the script is any good, I'll pass it on to them."

"That is terrific—" he gushed. "Wow—I can't tell you how much I—this is just great!"

I held up a finger to silence him. "On one condition."

"What's that?" he squinted, warily.

I grinned, confident of my position. "That we complete that little dance we started earlier."

"Dance?" he looked confused. "There wasn't any dancing."

I moved in closer, wrapping my arms around his waist. "What? You didn't hear the music?" I nuzzled his ear with my nose.

"I, uh—"

"Come on, Devon—when was the last time you got laid?"

"Back home, in Iowa."

"Well, let me show you how we do things here in Hollywood." Devon sighed as I gave his neck a soft kiss, whispering in his ear, "I'm gonna lick every inch of your amazing body until you are so close you're about to burst. I don't think I've ever wanted anyone so much..."

He pulled back, as if no one had ever said anything nice to him before. He needed to believe that my words were not just a line, but fully supported. "I—do you really think I'm hot?"

"Oh baby..." I zeroed back in and started gently kissing his neck.

"And..." he confirmed, showing his true colors, "you'll read my screenplay?"

I gave him my best Tom Cruise smile, copied from his new *Top Gun* film. "First thing in the morning."

As we entered mi palazzo, I spotted the blinking red light, alerting me to messages on my machine, but chose to ignore it. It had taken so long to charm Devon that I didn't want any interference. And if it was Gloria, well—that was a buzz-kill I just didn't need.

Moving to Devon, who seemed in awe of my design aesthetic, I tossed his script onto a rather large pile of others.

Later, after I'd feasted on Devon's corn-cob cock and pork-roast rump, we lay, entirely spent. As I started nodding off, he began telling me a story, his story, of two sets of twins, mistakenly switched at birth, and the supposed hilarity that ensues.

"Too bad," I thought, as I drifted toward peaceful slumber. "He's a really sweet guy, cute and all, but his screenplay will never sell..."

The next morning, after a hurried shower and bowl of *Cracklin' Oats*, I finally remembered the answering machine. As I crossed to it, it seemed the red light blinked even more insistently. As Gloria's voice filled the room, I moved to turn it off, until—

"Son? Darling?" She never called me that. I froze in my tracks. "I—uh—Keith is here. Keith Gamble. I know you two used to be—close. And I—. Well, I was going to put you on the line with him, but since you're out—"

After sitting on the 134 for what seemed like hours, I finally arrived and waited for Gloria to open the door. I needed to hear from her, directly, what had happened last night. What had Keith said? How did he look? Did he give her a phone number? But the door remained closed.

"Hurry up, woman," I sighed, giving the door another knock.

I knew that my boss hadn't bought my "cold" excuse, but given that I'd covered for her bathroom abortion, just down the hall from Steve, no less, I knew she wouldn't rat me out.

Perhaps I should've called Gloria to let her know I was coming, but my only thought was to get here, without fail, as quickly as my monkey wings would carry me.

I pounded on the door. "Gloria, come on!"

I rang the doorbell again, finally hearing footsteps approach. "Jeez, I haven't got all—"

The door opened, and a frazzled-looking Keith stared at me.

"Hey Gabey," he said, "come on in..." Holding the door open, he ushered me into my childhood home as if it were his own.

"I—" I stammered, following him into the living room. "Where's Gloria?"

"Oh. Shopping. I think." He sighed, sinking onto the couch. "Yes, she's shopping. For supplies. She wants to fatten me up."

Not knowing what to do, for a moment, I didn't do anything.

"Would you like me to make you some coffee?" He asked. "Something to eat?"

"I—no. No, I just ate." I stood a moment longer, until I could no longer remain silent. "Keith, what are you doing here?"

"Your mom let me crash here—it was so late. So—"

"I get that..." I said. "What I mean is—I've looked for you everywhere. For the past several months, since that night at the '1', almost every single day, I've searched. I finally find you in Palm Springs, and you again run away? Do you know how hard—? How much I've wanted to see you?"

He stood and crossed to me. I could scarcely believe it as he reached out, taking my hands in his.

"I'm sick, Gabey," he said softly, eyes watering.

I laughed, "You're screwed up; I'll give you that!"

"No, Gabey," he shook his head, guiding me to the couch to sit. "I'm sick." He sat beside me, focusing his eyes on mine.

"You've heard of AIDS?"

I nodded, dimly. Who hadn't heard? The gay cancer; eating up men in metropolitan cities around the globe. But those were the guys into crazy, hardcore stuff—right? The dungeons, and fucking themselves silly every night in bathhouses and parks, partner after partner. Those guys weren't me. They weren't Keith. We were good people. Maybe messed up, but good, somehow, somewhere. I only wanted love, damn it! The sex, okay—it was great—but—FUCK! AIDS? AIDS? That death could come from longing was too tangled a concept for me to even contemplate.

Looking down, I saw that Keith still held my hand in his. I followed the course of his veins, just under the surface of the skin, from his wrist and down into his fingers. That these veins carried poison... That the man I loved—.

I looked back into his eyes, and what I saw was transforming. Keith looked at me with all the love and passion that I'd felt all these years for him. And yet under that gentle gaze, sadness remained.

"I couldn't tell you, Gabey," he sighed, so quietly it sounded like a sob. "That's why I ran. I saw you, and I thought, how can I ever tell—?" He stopped, his eyes filling with tears. "I guess I'm ashamed, you know?"

"You never need to hide anything," I squeezed his hand in mine, insistently. "Do you hear me? After all we've been through—All these years? Our entire friendship? As much as we've loved each other—?"

"That was long ago, Gabey. Another lifetime."

"Still."

"I'm not sure anyone could love me, now."

"Forget about the AIDS—"

"It's not that," he looked down at our joined hands. "It's who I am. The life I've led..."

"But I love you—"

Keith paused, taking me in, in the way only he had been able to do. "What I need right now, Gabe, more than anything, is a friend."

I pulled his hands up to my lips, and gave his fingertips a

tender kiss. "I still care, you know? I always have. And who you are—what you've done—. We're not that different." Reaching for him, I sensed a slight hesitation, but hugged him anyway. I held him, finally, after so much searching. I was holding my Keith, and I knew that I would never, ever let go of him again.

The next few days seemed as if a dream. That Keith was here, with me... To be able to look at that face, into those eyes, both ever-so-slightly changed. And yet to know that the wrong question, or unintended signal, might frighten him back into the ether...

I didn't dare ask where he'd been. How he'd been infected. And it really wasn't any of my business, was it?

While I *was* curious, it was more important that I hold him, comfort him, and show him in every way possible that he was loved.

We moved him into my apartment. And the minute he walked through the door, he burst out laughing. Looking around at my studio with him, I finally saw what so many others had before. I'd created a ridiculous set piece, which no one could feel comfortable in. My attempt at beauty had been a miserable failure, and one of Keith's first projects was to help me strip off that flocked wallpaper, reclaiming both the room and some sense of normalcy.

It seemed that, despite the health challenges Keith faced, each day was blessed by sunshine. After rising to a pot of coffee and Jane Pauley and Bryant Gumbel chirping from the TV, I'd leave for the Amblin magic factory with a firmly planted kiss on my cheek. And throughout the day, while Keith visited doctors, herbalists, motivational healers, pharmacists, and Reiki specialists, that blush where he had kissed me remained, warming me. I finally knew what it felt like to be loved. It was a feeling not only of passion, but of comfort. The security of knowing that, as I slowly made the crawl back over Laurel Canyon, there would be a light on when I got home, and another kiss, to warm me while I slept.

I was fully aware of how schmaltzy how I sounded. But it was difficult to describe how I felt without sounding like a recipe for Tollhouse cookies. Was that what love was? A simple mixture of ingredients?

We search so desperately for something "special" that we forget: love is not a secret tonic or magic elixir. It is there, available for all, with the recipe printed right on the label. You just needed to know the proper measurements, and be able to get out of your own damn way.

Maybe it was the security I felt that lulled me into asking. Or stupidity. Had I kept my mouth shut and stayed out of my own way, he could have taken his time, and told me when he was ready. But that would have been too mature.

And why did I care, anyway? It's not as if there was any information that I truly needed to know. It wouldn't affect me in any way. And still, I asked. "How did you get it?"

Keith looked at me, as if he'd known I would eventually inquire, but surprised nonetheless. "How do you think? Sex."

"I know that—I mean—"

"I know what you mean, Gabey." He smiled, to put me at ease, then laid down his journal. My eyes lingered on it. Had he always kept a journal? How could I not have known that? Had he written about me? And, if so, what?

He gestured for me to sit. Maxie, sensing a chance for attention, pranced over, dropping at my feet. I stroked her back, absentmindedly. She was a recent purchase; the embodiment of our newfound domestic bliss.

"Forget it—you don't have to answer," I stated, more to seem mature than really meaning it.

"It's okay, Gabey," he laughed. "I'd want to know, too."

I was quiet. He'd called my bluff. And the truth was, I did want to know. But not out of jealousy, or needing the salacious details.

I'd missed so much of Keith's life that any opportunity to fill in the blanks was welcome. After a moment, he continued. "I was living in New York..."

"Really?" I hadn't meant to cut him off, but New York

surprised me. "That doesn't seem like your kind of place."

"I know. I just—." His head hung low. "That last time I saw you, at the airport—seems like several lifetimes ago."

I nodded, for it definitely felt like it.

"I felt really lost." I stared at him, but he couldn't raise his eyes to meet mine. "I couldn't stay with my dad. He was an ass, day in and out. Watching my every move. Studying me for any sign of gayness. Asking where I was going, who I was seeing, when I'd be home—I couldn't live like that." He shrugged. "So, I left."

"But why New York?"

"First it was San Francisco," he laughed. "I mean, I was young, gay, and unwanted. Where else would've been so obvious?"

"You weren't unwanted, Keith. I wanted you."

His eyes met mine. "You left."

"To school," I clarified.

"So you wanted me to wait? To hang on for your periodic returns? I couldn't do that, Gabey. I couldn't live under his roof any longer."

Mr. Gamble had always been an ass. I'd initially chalked it up to his lot as widower, left to raise his sons alone. But I think he would've been an ass regardless. The widower label was just an easy way to assure continued sympathy.

I looked at Keith. "I never should have left you."

"You didn't have a choice, Gabey," he insisted. "Neither of us did. We had to follow our own paths—and grow up."

"And did we? Grow up, I mean?"

"I don't know," Keith frowned. "When you're a kid, thinking about life, you always see it as a storybook. Handsome prince, white knight, dragons slain, a magic kiss that awakens the dead... Even if you see the adults around you struggling, and maybe on some level understand that life might be a bit more difficult than you imagine, no one ever tells you the whole truth about adulthood. How it tears at you. How heavy the burden truly is. That's a bigger lie than Santa Claus."

With a sigh, I stood. "Do you want a glass of wine?"

Keith nodded. "Desperately."

Heading into the kitchen, I pulled out a chilled chardonnay. "So, San Francisco, huh? That must've been cool. What a scene in those days... Were you in the Castro?"

"At first," Keith said, loud enough for me to hear. "I mean, I arrived with a backpack and whatever cash I could gather. I relied, as they say, on the kindness of strangers."

I entered with the wine. "You hustled?"

"Well, I wouldn't say that," he demurred. "I crashed where I could, took any job offered. Just, tried to get by."

"Did you make any friends?"

"Some," he offered. "I didn't find the people all that... I mean, I had no money. No degree. No exciting job. I just... I was a bit out of my league."

"That must've been hard."

"It was. And then, just when I thought I couldn't take it anymore, I met Lark."

On that, I perked up. "You met Lark on a lark?"

"Never heard that one before!" he laughed, then clarified, in a haughty tone, "Larkin Lowenstein."

"Very fancy."

"He was. Handsome, well off, charming conversationalist, great in the sack... Everything I'd always wanted."

For some reason, no matter how many men I'd had in the years since, hearing Keith express his feelings about another cut me to the core. I looked away.

"We met at the Elephant Walk during happy hour. He was chatting with a friend when I walked in, but when he saw me, he just—honed in. I felt special. And for the next six years, we were never apart."

"Sounds perfect."

Pondering my assessment, Keith frowned, then took a sip of wine. "I guess."

"So the two of you went to New York?"

"Lark was in finance, and kept getting promoted, so we landed in a bunch of places. My favorite was Chicago, which I loved. And then New York, which—"

"You didn't?"

"It was just, in Chicago, I was in my element. Friendly

people, nice community.   No pretense.   I had an amazing partner, great home..."

"What did you do for work?"

"I didn't."

"You were kept?"

Keith lowered his head. "I was loved. Or so I thought."

I knew I shouldn't have opened this particular door, but it was too late now to close it, or to erase the words I'd just uttered. "Go on."

"When we moved to New York, it—everything changed. What was day became night. The city was overwhelming and he worked *all* the time. So I'd go out. Movies, shows, galleries, whatever. Anything to fill the time. But Lark—he got paranoid. He imagined I was cheating."

"Were you?"

"Not then.   But as time went on, and the questions persisted—where were you, what did you do, who were you with—it was just like living with my dad," he admitted. "Those eyes, which used to look at me with such kindness, greeted me with suspicion. I couldn't breathe. It was like, suddenly he saw me as the opposition, the enemy. And so I did go out, and I did meet others, because at least they saw me as something good. Lark—he just—gave up. And once he did, he showed me the door."

"He kicked you out?"

"He was far too refined for that. Larkin paid me off, very generously. He dismissed me, as you would a maid."

I wasn't sure of the wisdom of my next move, but I couldn't stay quiet. "So, Lark infected you?"

After a long moment's silence, Keith finally responded. "Who knows? It could have been him, or anyone, really. Back then, there was nothing safe about sex. It was reckless. It is *supposed* to be reckless... but Larkin thinks I infected him. Even though he was unfaithful, too. To this day, he sees me as this vampire, who snuck into his unsuspecting bed in the middle of the night, blindly ignoring all who came before me, or since."

I poured us both another glass.

He took a sip, then sighed. "I thought my life would be so

different, you know? That it would've meant something."

"It has to me."

He reached towards me, grabbing my arm. "I don't deserve you, Gabey."

"Why the hell not?" I responded, taking his hand in mine. "Just because we're flawed doesn't mean we can't be happy. No matter what you think, and all the years, I've never stopped loving you."

"I admire your passion," Keith smiled, somewhat indulgently. "You were always more confident than me."

"Not always," I said, pointedly. He looked into my eyes, nodding sadly, and I knew he understood. "You gave me confidence, Keith. You helped me see that night for what it was. I truly believed my life had ended, and you built me back up. Let me do that for you."

He closed his eyes, leaning back with a sigh. When he opened them again, I saw that he was crying. "You'll never know how long I've waited for someone to love me like that. Not as an object. But as a person."

I leaned over, giving him a kiss. First on the lips, then one on the cheek. I hoped that the warmth from my lips would provide the same strength as his had for me, giving him the necessary fuel to power himself through the day.

At first I wasn't sure that I'd done the right thing, ripping off the Band-Aid that Keith had firmly taped over his wound. Would such an impetus scare him? Make him resent me? Cause the wound to resume its flow, bringing forth more painful memories?

Exactly the opposite occurred, as facing his past seemed to bring us even closer. We began to open up, honestly, in other areas, freeing ourselves of both past and present cares. There was no pretense, no masques. Together, we allowed ourselves to just "be", regardless of whatever "being" meant at any particular moment. And as we did, our hearts opened, embracing each other's authenticity. Maybe there was something, after all, to what my good doctor had tried to teach.

My sessions with Roberta continued to progress as well, and I began to feel as if I could handle anything. We talked about my self-esteem, and where those feelings of inadequacy had come from. We talked about Lenny; his utter failings as a father. We talked about Gloria, and the strange brew of emotions she continually stirred within me. And we finally talked about what had happened.

In many ways, I'd begun to feel as if I had dreamt it. Aside from Keith, few knew the truth. That I was even talking about it felt both freeing and scary. The rawness came back and lived just beneath my surface, just as Keith's had when we'd discussed his relationship with Lark. But now I had some basic tools to help me deal emotionally, however inexperienced I was in using them, and I refused to ever shove those roiled emotions away, unexamined, again.

It felt as if I finally had a unit, a family. People who cared about me and accepted who I was and hoped to be. Both Keith and Clare had been there for me in my darkest moments, and would be there for the best. Even Roberta felt part of the family, albeit a paid member. And Gloria, well... she was family, my only remaining blood family, and yet I wondered if I would ever truly forgive her.

She could be brutally honest, which I fully appreciated, but had enormous blind spots to any unpleasantness she wished to ignore. Perhaps, though, she was simply doing exactly what I'd done all these years, burying the disagreeable in order to survive. For if she had fully examined Lenny and all of his failings, then she would have to face her choice of him as husband, and why, knowing all, she continued to choose him over her son.

In an attempt to get closer and improve our relationship, I invited Gloria to lunch. Ca Del Sole, given its proximity to Universal, seemed like a good choice, and I knew she'd get a kick out of rubbing elbows with the stars. Unfortunately, the only recognizable one that afternoon was Jasmine Guy, of the new *Cosby* spin-off, *A Different World*. Gloria, however, was thrilled. So much so that she bossily interrupted Jasmine's business lunch to ask for an autograph. While Jasmine happily acquiesced, I was mortified. Here I was, in my element, surrounded by the crème de la crème of Hollywood, or at least the crème de menthe of it, and my mother asked for an autograph.

As Gloria proudly sashayed back to the table, showing off her signed napkin to all in her path, I buried my head in my hands.

"Look," she said proudly, thrusting her treasure into my face. "She even did a lip print."

"That's great, mom," I smiled, for there was truly nothing else I could possibly do.

"Do you think she's mulatto?" she queried, loud enough for all to hear. "I mean, she can't be fully black, right? She's more like a frothy cappuccino."

I busied myself with the menu.

"And, in person, her voice isn't half so annoying as on that show."

Staring at the overpriced salmon, I wondered why I hadn't taken Gloria to the Bob's Big Boy on Riverside Drive instead. The only celebrity I'd ever seen there was Tyne Daly, and she appeared to be lunching in her bathrobe. Besides, I sincerely doubt Gloria could've caused much damage over Pappy Parker's fried chicken and hot fudge cake. But then again, that would be underestimating Gloria.

"So," said Gloria, as we finished our meal. "Do I get a tour?"

"Of what?" I asked, wiping my mouth.

"Come on, Mister Fancy Pants. Big new job, Amblin Entertainment. Universal Studio. You can't keep all that from your mother," she prodded.

"I'll put you on the tour list," I offered, afraid of where this was headed.

"Like hell you will!" Gloria puffed. "I'm not some tourist from the hinterlands."

"You're from Northridge, Gloria. Same thing."

"This is the first job you've had that I can actually brag about to my friends," she persisted. "You have no idea how hard it is explaining to your bridge club what exactly a bathhouse attendant does."

She did have a point. Still...

"But best of all, Gabe, you seem happy. I've always hoped

I'd see a day like this, where you are content. Great partner, a career you love. It's all I've ever wanted for you."

And so it was that, against all natural instincts, I tried to remain in the moment and acknowledge my conflicting emotions, just as Roberta had encouraged. Every bone in my body was saying to just put Gloria on the next passing tour bus, but there was a nagging part of me that said, *Isn't this what you always do? Compartmentalize your life? Your mother is reaching out. She's proud of you. Hold onto that—place it inside your heart, on a little shelf—and honor it.*

If I was ever going to fully integrate my assorted parts, a tour of Amblin for my sometimes-beloved mother was the least I could do. After all, it was just a simple tour. What could possibly go wrong?

It started out well enough. That is, at least our drive into the parking lot was uneventful. Gloria pulled in behind me and asked why I didn't yet have my own parking space.

"I've been here four months. What did you expect?"

"They'll see your worth soon; mark my words." She came up, hugged me, and I immediately pulled back. "You are meant for great things. I believe that. You are so much better than you know." She kissed my cheek, causing me to blush as I ducked my head, embarrassed. "Hold on," she motioned, reaching up to wipe her lipstick from my cheek.

"Thanks, Gloria."

I'm not sure why, but at that exact moment I knew that this visit would not go well. Perhaps it was the martinis she'd downed at lunch. Perhaps it was her unexpected intimacy. Her perplexing faith in me, although I'd begun to share in it myself. And maybe that's just it. Whenever I have a good groove going, something always causes it to derail. *I* cause it to derail.

But even I had no idea just how spectacular that derailment would be.

Despite her obvious pride in my having obtained such a prestigious and glamorous job, as we toured the Amblin compound, it seemed that at every introduction, Gloria managed to take me down a notch. The considerable time I'd spent at Amblin cultivating a witty, sophisticated, and utterly urbane persona was flushed away the minute Gloria opened her mouth. Without warning, I was suddenly reduced to just another desperate kid from Northridge, trying to make it in the land of milk and honey.

She talked about my past jobs. Brought up my first attempt at anal sex. And, of course, just how perfect I was for this particular job. After all, as she said, "You've got to have a gay in the story department, right? Otherwise, how good can it be?"

I hurried Gloria through the main building, attempting to minimize the damage, and would have forcibly ejected her, booting her ass right into her car seat, had we not then run into Steven Spielberg himself. I would've kept walking, but Gloria was much too quick for me. Getting between her and a celebrity would be like trying to intercept a runaway freight train.

"Steve, hi!" She rushed over, hand outstretched. He took it, uncertain who either Gloria or I were. "Gloria Travers. A pleasure to meet you, sir."

"Well, thank you, Mrs. Travers. Welcome to Amblin. Now if you'll excuse me—"

"Of course, Steve. You're a busy man. Meetings at every hour. I get it, Mr. Showbiz!"

He looked at her warily, uncertain if she were being comical or dismissive. She continued, "My Gabey here has told me so much about you." As she gestured to me, Steve faced me, taking notice of me for the first time.

"He has?"

I tried to smile politely, to let him know that I was not in any way connected with the crazy woman gripping my arm. "I, uh, work in Development, Mr. Spielberg. Assistant Story Editor."

"And he started as a temp! Can you believe it?" Gloria blathered.

"Well, nice meeting you both," Steve grinned, through his teeth. His eyes searched about for security, to no avail. "Now, if you'll excuse me, I really have to—"

"Go. Right," Gloria nodded. "One quick question, Steve. *The Color Purple*. Loved it! Cried my eyes out. That Whoopi!

And the fat girl? Wow. Kudos to you! But my question, Steve—and I know you're pressed for time. The lesbian kiss. That interested me. In the book, the relationship between the gals is so complex. Nuanced. Complete. Yet you reduce it to a footnote. Less than a footnote, even. A comma. Steve, what happened?"

"Well, I—." Steve stopped and looked at us, really taking us in for the first time. I knew he was wishing he had a pad and pencil to make note of the name of the traitor within his midst.

"I mean," Gloria prodded, "your people. You're down with the gays and the blacks, right? A shared history of persecution. Discrimination. Of being *less than*. And here you have this chance—this opportunity—to do right by both groups, and what do we get? Soggy oatmeal."

I felt as if all of my skin was being pulled, peeling itself inside out, in a futile attempt at escape.

Instead of answering Gloria, Steve smiled tightly, turning to me. "Gabe Travers, is it?"

If I could have responded in any other way, I would've. "Yes."

Steve nodded, and then shook my hand. "Thunder told me all about you."

"Thunder?" I stared blankly, not putting the pieces together.

"Timmy Hughes," he said, pointedly. "He's an old friend of the family. We go way back."

He turned, with a wave, then entered the Amblin offices.

"Boy, he was nice. It's not every day I get to meet a TV star *and* a big-time director! Wait 'til the bridge club hears about this!" I stood, staring blankly ahead and trying to make sense of what had just happened, as Gloria continued her prattle. "Not a big talker, though—is he?"

She kissed my cheek and headed for her car. I stood watching, but couldn't bring myself to wave. My life at Amblin was over. In one brief afternoon of sightseeing, my entire career had come crashing down, and the sole reason for it was putting the key into her car. As she did so, she turned, saw me watching, and waved.

"I love you, son. I am so proud."

Somehow, I made it through the rest of the day. I kept waiting for security to arrive to escort me out, but they never did. Still, though no one mentioned a word to me, I could sense that my days at Amblin were numbered and began to make other plans. I must have come up with a thousand ideas, but none felt quite right. Keith said to follow my heart, but my heart wasn't speaking very loudly.

A career in entertainment was out. After all, once you've pissed off Steven Spielberg, there really is no place left to go. So I began making lists: what I did well, what I enjoyed, where I envisioned myself. But all I ended up with was a bunch of lists.

I knew that the reason I liked Amblin, as well as the reason I felt so comfortable with Keith, was because in each, I felt valued and appreciated. Plus, I was using my creativity. I couldn't take another job solely based on money, or status, or fame. I needed to find something which nourished me, on some inner level. But the path to that job was far from clear.

It was Keith's idea. And, at first, I resisted. I thought he was crazy. Truly, certifiably, off-his-meds crazy. Cashing in a life insurance policy? Trading in that security blanket for a joyride?

I'd never even heard of viaticals, but apparently everyone in the world of HIV had. Being, technically, close to death, anyone with a life insurance policy was basically sitting on a gold mine. Imagine, by selling that policy, you could reap the instant gratification that comes from a loaded bank account. Buy yourself a new wardrobe. A new car. Buy yourself 18 cases of frozen Pepperidge Farms chocolate cakes. Anything you desire could be had, for a price.

For Keith, it was much more than a store-bought trinket. It was much more than a car, or a nice jacket, or a stereo. His idea was this: Sell his policy. Put half into savings for me, so that, upon his death, I would have a nest egg. And the other share, put toward a trip to Paris.

Keith had always dreamt of "getting out", and Paris seemed like just the place to go. As I'd never been, the idea seemed completely fanciful and romantic. Me. In Paris. With Keith. Still, selling a life insurance policy... While I had no issue with it in terms of process, I pondered what psychological manifestations could arise for Keith.

He assured me, repeatedly, that he was merely being pragmatic. And the kisses I gave him in return told him that I understood. But I never quite bought it. For I felt that, even if unacknowledged, Keith was preparing for the end.

Regardless, though, he wanted to take *me*. After all the years of waiting, wishing, hoping—Keith was here, by my side, wanting to show me the world. And how could I say no to that?

I let Keith make all of the arrangements. And so it was that we found ourselves in a charmingly shabby walk-up in Montmartre. I could barely squeeze both body and luggage into the Escher-esque stairwell, and was reeling by the time I stumbled into nombre 15. But as I sank onto the bed, suitcases forgotten, I glanced over to Keith, standing at the window in awe. Rising, I was just about to ask him what he saw, when suddenly I saw it as well. Jutting just above the rooftops of the buildings opposite was the brilliant white dome of Sacré Coeur.

Wrapping my arms around his thin frame, I rested my head on his shoulder, taking in the city below. Keith stared, unable to take his eyes away, drinking it all in. "It feels like home."

I looked at him, waiting for more. But nothing came.

How was it that this man, who had looked for love, for home, in the arms of countless strangers, whose motto was "Getting out"—how could he be standing here, with me, in a foreign city, and think of this as home?

I looked closely at his face, so gentle. And his hair, still a bit in need of a trim, as his dad would've said. Eyes, so clear and understanding, if a bit sad. And I knew, then and there, that he was right. We were both finally home.

In Paris, I fell in love with everything. From the scale of the streets, to the food art of Fauchon, to the fonts on the Metro signs. From the painted street entertainers, frozen stock still; to the surging hoards on the Metro, constantly in motion. The quiet squares, with trickling fountains and sculpted topiaries; strolling Rue St. Honoré; sidewalk cafés, with their iconic rattan chairs, perfectly rowed; anything sweet from La Maison du Chocolat; hot Parisian men at every turn; museums to get lost in... To have all of your needs, wants, and desires so spectacularly brought to life; I kept pinching myself to make sure I was awake.

It was almost impossible, but this one city seemed to embrace every aspect of my disjointed interior. Paris took my love of food, culture, art, wit, cynicism, and sex, and wrapped it all up neatly with the prettiest of ribbons. I realized that the fragmented pie chart I'd been trying to make sense of had been instantly transformed, by a simple change of scene, into a glorious Tarte Tatin. Musky spices and tangy tartness were wrapped up and tucked into a butter crust that was—at once— flaky, crisp, layered, and multi-textured. Which was me. Sweet and sour. Soft and crisp. I discovered that these varied elements, that for so long had seemed at odds, were actually complementary.

I dashed off a postcard to Clare, touting the sights, and found that I sounded just as relentlessly upbeat as her. My next, far more perfunctory, was to Gloria. While she clearly had meant no ill-will, I couldn't help but blame her for my now-defunct career. But as Keith repeatedly and rightly pointed out, in truth it was my own actions, my poor treatment of Thunder, which had brought me down.

Why had I been so quick to cut him off? He'd been my only friend at Amblin, after all. Was that short-lived job really worth the anguish I had caused? Had I not treated him with complete disregard, I'd likely still have a job, and been writing him a postcard as well.

Instead, with only two cards written, I realized that there was no one left to whom I could write. Charlie and Jasper had long forgotten me; I was but a charming blip on their radar of fun. But would I have wanted them as friends, as I am now? Could they have provided the dimension of thought, the nourishment of soul, I now crave?

I vowed, upon our return, to cultivate a group of friends who would allow me to grow and be organically. My list would not

be long; there was no need to be greedy. But it must be solid.
No fly-by-night, good-time-Charlie-and-Jasper friends. Rather,
friends who would "get" and embrace me, fully. Whether
broken into infinitesimal crumbs or as a full-on Tarte; folks who
would lap me up, regardless. *Entièrement.*

With two weeks to spend, Keith and I felt no urgency, no
rush to cram it all in. Instead, we assumed the roles of Parisians,
with a leisurely, unhurried pace. Mornings brought petit
déjeuner, with its croissants, cheeses, and meat. Simple
sustenance, perfectly designed to provide ample nourishment for
the adventures ahead.

How was it that we Americans had taken this concept and
perverted it into a glass of Carnation Instant Breakfast drink or
an Egg McMuffin? So busy in our pursuit of promptness, we
mutilated the entire meal, merely to ensure that we arrived at our
cubicles a few minutes faster.

I spent a couple of hours yesterday at the D'Orsay, lingering
with Monet. While I normally wouldn't have gone on a
Saturday, given the crowds, Keith was napping, and it wasn't
long before I found myself communing with Claude. While all
of his work was entrancing, I was drawn to his paintings of the
Cathedral at Rouen, blending muted grays and blues through a
cloud-like prism. Had it simply been a foggy day? Early
morning? Or did the choice of palette speak to something in
Monet's soul? Was he depressed? Reverential? Angry with
God?

When I was young, we went to church habitually. I'm
uncertain as to why. My parents would sit dutifully in the same
pew each week and nod along with the sermon, but there was
never any follow up. No stories from the Bible. No prayers at
meals or bedtime. No dialogue about faith, or belief, or
morality. Once the service was over, and I had been collected
from Sunday school, we'd simply return home in the car, quietly,
save for Gloria's chatter and the radio, permanently set to news.

I wondered if Lenny and Gloria believed that our weekly
pilgrimage alone was sufficient in ensuring our entrance into the
holy kingdom. Or had the outings, instead, been engineered by

Gloria, designed solely to keep us "pure" in the eyes of the community?   Perhaps God had not even factored into the equation.

In my mind, God had never been settled. I kept changing my mind as to "who," "if," "any." The traditional image on which I had been raised never felt right, as I refused to believe that God would want us to fear him. I saw him as embracing, as love. God is that spark, the connectivity between us.   Like Bette Midler, whose concert patter is the glue between her songs, God threads through each of us, providing context and relevance. God lifts us up a level, so that we are more than mere animals, clawing about for our next meal.   God desires us to talk, to laugh, to cry, argue, think, fuck, decide, and take action. It is his will; all of it. We need God. Especially when we think we don't.

But simply visiting a church, or even joining one, doesn't make a person religious. Occupying a pew doesn't automatically imbue us with spirituality, regardless of what my parents may have thought. In fact, I believe that God requires nothing of us. There is no entrance fee or requirement for participation. He is there already, inside each of us, if only we'd stop and listen.

True listening, though, requires stillness. And in our rushed and hurried world, few pay heed to the more quiet moments. In fact, most people try to *quell* the clutter in their heads, not *listen* to it.   Even, if after a long night's rest, eyes not yet open and head on pillow, one had heard a voice, calling through the haze, we'd simply shush them to silence, preferring, instead, a few minutes more sleep.

Keith slumbered next to me, peacefully. I'd nabbed an extra pillow, so that I could easily take in the white dome opposite, jutting over the rooftops. Sacré Coeur translates into Sacred Heart, which sounded so base in English. It seemed the French did everything better

But was it even possible to have a sacred heart? Who, after all, has no impure or unkind thoughts? Or did having a sacred heart mean, rather, striving to be selfless, kind, more loving? To give oneself entirely to another, asking nothing in return.

If so, Keith had done that for me.

I wanted to be like that. True of heart. Pure. Selfless. And yet that ephemeral goodness still seemed precariously far from reach. Roberta had taught me to express myself, to not be afraid to go for what I want. So what, exactly, was it that I wanted?

Next to me, Keith's bare shoulder protruded from the sheet. He was so decent. Virtuous, even. I longed to be like him, to have just one ounce of his decency. I reached out, caressing his shoulder, when it registered: what I wanted was Keith. He had completed me. And yet, soon he would be gone, and everything good would disappear as well.

A thought occurred.

I immediately pushed it aside, rejecting it as ridiculous. But then I tried to refocus, to listen to that voice, to God. What was he telling me? What was my path forward? As I watched Keith breathe, I looked ahead, to a life without him, and the answer became clear.

Before waking him, I walked into the bathroom and found my toiletry kit. Looking in the mirror, I assessed myself, acknowledging what I was doing. I was becoming a better person. My life now had meaning. Keith had returned that sense of optimism, that spark of joy, which had been missing from my life for far too long. He was the source of all that was good.

There was no turning back.

As I lay back down, Keith opened his eyes and stared directly into me. Seeing the part of me that no one else sees. Pulling him close, I kissed him; slowly at first, then with mounting passion.

I grasped him, and yet his frame was so thin; close to transparent. He reached toward the night stand, but I pushed his hand away. He started to speak, but I quenched his voice with a kiss. In his eyes, there was a dart of fear. Of warning. But I persisted, nibbling his ear, his neck, his chest; wanting to devour all that he was.

He again reached toward the nightstand, but I grabbed his arm, holding it firmly. Maneuvering above him, I lowered myself gently, easing on. Nothing hurried or forced. I rode slowly at first, then faster. Tightening my muscles, I milked him,

squeezing him inside of me.   He gasped, eyes flashing another
dire warning, but I clenched my teeth, and rode even harder,
willing us to become one.

Our eyes locked.

Penetrate me, Keith.   Seep within.   Fill me until I am
overflowing.

Let your humanity take root, entangling our blood.

Fortify my core with your pure and sacred heart.

I need you, Keith. I need you within.

Sacré-Coeur.

PART III
GABE: 1976

"Let Me Just Follow Behind" by Moogy Klingman
Track 5, Side B of Bette Midler's album,
Songs for the New Depression

GABE: 1976

IN MY DREAM, I float effortlessly in the Seine. Sharks circle, serenely, as though the river their natural habitat. And although peaceful, I can feel their teeny tiny bites, as if they are nibbling on a bit of crusty bread and pâté de foie gras. While not painful, the prodding is dull and persistent, and the thought occurs that perhaps, if I just keep still, play dead long enough, the sharks might lose interest altogether.

The dream had played every night since, but despite its disturbing nature, I found it oddly comforting. That I was not dead, and in fact surviving, led me to believe that perhaps playing dead might be the solution to my problems.

Is that what high school was doomed to be? Inverting myself to avoid conflict? Closing everyone out? Each day spent walking the halls, eyes focused intently straight ahead, walking with purpose, as if I have somewhere important to be? Suffering through lunch, killing time until the bell rings and I can again return to the safety of class, where the jabs are only verbal and come with a swift from the teacher?

One odd thing happened in my dream, though. As I float, immobile, despite the sharks nibbling, I am able to shut my mind down, willing myself to another place. And as I do, a white dove swoops down from the heavens, landing on my shoulder. Whether it is a dove of peace, or justice, or just a stupid bird, I am never quite sure. But the face on it is strangely reminiscent of my father.

Yet another reason to hate him: he appears as my savior but doesn't bring a fucking life jacket. Loser.

The knocking jarred me from my slumber. I dug deeper into the bed, willing my mattress to swallow me whole. As my mother's voice droned on, like the steady whine of the clothes dryer, my mind whirled likewise, trying to come up with an excuse, but none came.

It had been a full week now. Seven long days. I could no longer avoid the inevitable return to school, and yet the thought of such gripped me so fiercely that a shudder wracked my body, like a sob, but made no sound.

Glancing to the clock, I realized that I'd already delayed long enough. If I waited any longer, I'd be late and would have to walk into class with a tardy slip. I knew that every eye would be on me, and soon, the word would spread: He's back! The little faggot finally returned. Did he think he could hide forever?

With a look into the mirror, I swept the trail of tears from my face and checked over my appearance. My now-red eyes would soon return to their normal brown. Maybe that soft green shirt would help highlight what little hazel my eyes possessed. Though just a mirror, as any other, I searched my face in it, hoping to spot that giveaway look, that pink triangle tattoo or lavender aura, that confirmed their whispered suspicions. Aside from my eyebrows, which were perpetually arched, making me appear awake and alert regardless of how I truly felt, I could see no remarkable features. My nose was there, where it was supposed to be, drawing a line to the inevitable mouth. A fairly strong jaw line, which I felt made me look somewhat masculine, was in truth the only remotely masculine thing about me.

Stepping back to get a fuller view, I removed my t-shirt and pajama bottoms. The overall effect of my nakedness was probably not unlike other 16-year-old boys. I was soft. Not fleshy, muscular, or bony; just soft. What tan I had possessed from summer had long since faded. My penis was, blessedly, enormous. And it worked wonderfully well, giving me endless pleasure when I treated it to an excursion in the fresh air. So I should have had some measure of self-esteem, right? I mean, average looks and gigantic dick—what's not to like?

I was sure someone, somewhere, would want to fuck me. The question was who? When? How would I find them? And would I first be able to survive high school?

The sharp rattle of the door sprang me from my reverie, reminding me of the coming horrors of the day ahead: school and breakfast.

"You'd better hurry. You're making us both late," my mother snapped as she grabbed a sip of O.J. before checking her lipstick in the oven door.

"I'm not the one who asked for pancakes, bacon, eggs, *and* sausage. What's wrong with the usual flakes?" I asked.

She moved quickly to her faux leather briefcase, checking to make sure her datebook was in it. "I just thought, with you going back and all—." Leaving the balance unsaid, she fluffed the frilled collar at her neck.

Shoveling in the food as quickly as I could, so as not to have to endure reheated eggs, I began to feel nauseous. Maybe that could be the excuse I needed! But mom moved more quickly than I—

"I'll heat up the car. Don't dawdle!"

Driving in silence, which was curious for her, my mom finally handed me my note. "I said 'flu' if anyone asks. Vomiting, fever, diarrhea—I put it all in. Sounds better that way."

Sinking down into my seat, I wondered what was worse: letting people know the truth, or having the details of my supposed upheaval and incontinence spread through the school like wildfire. When you're in high school, it's a toss-up.

As we approached the squat cluster of buildings that formed Tiger High, I flipped down the visor for a final check. True to form, my eyes were no longer red. The green shirt had been a good idea. The blush to my cheeks would disappear soon too, but I wished that it wouldn't. Somehow it gave the effect that I was alive, vibrant, and full of energy, providing a courageous look I could hold within, for I would surely need all the help I could get.

Help came in the unlikely form of Ms. Rice, my least favorite teacher—until today. Whether by premonition or shrewdness, Ms. Rice had rearranged all desks in my first-period French class so that they faced away from the door, allowing me to slip in unnoticed. As the desks were returned to normal in the days following, I'd like to believe that I shared some common bond with Ms. Rice. Some tic, some electrical spark, emanating from my brain to hers: "He's coming back today. Make it easy on him."

Perhaps she really was psychic, as some kids said. Or maybe it was just that listless right eye.

Years later I would learn that Ms. Rice had once been a man, but, quite frankly, as I pulled open the classroom door, even if she'd been standing in front of the class that morning butt-naked, sporting the biggest woody in the world, I would not likely have noticed, so preoccupied was I with my own terror.

Without a word or even a perceptible gesture, I felt her acknowledge me and will me into my seat. No one even seemed to realize that I was present until the bell sounded and we began filing out. Even then, with the rush to second period, I let the flow of the crowd carry me along into my next class, not acknowledging the few questioning eyes that caught mine.

By lunchtime, word of my return had spread, but I realized that the day would not be nearly as bad as I'd thought. Not only had Joey Tatolla and Kid Dollard been suspended for two weeks and not a threat at present, but an assembly had been held under the auspicious title, "The Golden Rule is in High School, too!" In some strange way, just by being a victim, I had been made a hero, as kids love any excuse that gets them out of class.

Despite this stature, throughout the day, it was as if I was a living form of kryptonite. I walked everywhere with an invisible bubble around me, so leery was anyone of getting too close. Even my teachers treated me timidly, with the exception of old Mrs. Karnes, who would have berated Anne Frank for missing class. "Hiding from the Nazis is no excuse, Anne! Now give me a three-page essay on 'Fulfilling Our Obligations.'"

During sixth-period study hall, the topic of my return was

finally broached, in the form of a note, slid to me across the library table by Clare Peer.

Though we knew each other and had shared some classes, we'd never spoken, imbuing her gesture with a small measure of bravery.

"So," the note read. "Is it true?"

I slid back my reply. "What did you hear?"

Clare looked at me hesitantly, and then wrote quickly: "That you were gang-raped by the football team."

Without thinking, I laughed. For the first time in a week, I actually laughed: a loud, deep-in-the-belly guffaw. Oh, if only that had been my fate! Getting plowed by the entire football team! I'd been dreaming about that since my first game of tackle.

Confused by my reaction, Clare looked around, checking to make sure no one was watching, then slid to the seat opposite.

"Why are you laughing? If something like that happened to me..."

"You don't know what happened?" I questioned.

"Well," Clare hedged, "I've heard stories."

"Like what?" I asked, genuinely curious. I'd always wanted to be popular, and to think that I was being discussed, even in this context, was kind of exhilarating.

"Okay—besides the gang-rape scenario, people are saying that you went crazy."

"Me? Crazy?"

"Something about how Joey and Kid beat you up, or taunted you, and how you went ballistic on them. Or—I don't know. But that doesn't really make a lot of sense, does it?"

"No."

She leaned in closer, conspiratorially. "So are you gonna tell me?"

"I just—you know," I tried to smile, but couldn't. Looking down at my homework, I was surprised to see a drop of water fall, obscuring the carefully written lines of cursive, the black ink liquefying, rendering the word "insignificant" illegible. Kind of like me.

Another drop fell, and I realized that the water was coming

from my eyes, trickling down in a silent stream. Looking up, I saw that Clare was tearing up as well. Behind her, I could see Mrs. Biddle pushing away from her desk, her eyes focused on our table.

Motioning, I gestured for Clare to wipe her eyes, as I did as well. Smiles were firmly affixed when Mrs. Biddle tottered up to check our work, and, in a way, I was relieved for the reprieve. While it was nice being able to bond with another, without pretense, I wasn't yet ready to share my story with Clare, or anyone else.

Luckily, by the time Mrs. Biddle departed, the scent of talcum powder wafting in her wake, the bell rang, leaving Clare's question happily unanswered. Still, I wanted to maintain our connection, so I tagged along to her locker, changing the subject-ever-so subtly.

"So, how'd you do?" I asked.

"Huh?" She stared blankly.

"The test," I persisted. "Weather? Science? Mr. Randall, second period...?"

"Oh," she laughed, "*that!* Duh. Well, at first, I was kind of struggling a bit, then I just kind of pulled myself together and thought—what's that great quote? You know—"

"What are you talking about?"

"I know! 'Success is not measured by what you accomplish—' blah-blah-blah."

"In high school it is."

"But high school isn't *it*, you know? There is life after high school."

"I sure hope so..."

"Anyway, just thinking about that quote made me, you know, sit up and think, and then the rest of the test came easy."

"Wow. Wish it were that way with me."

"So," she queried, "how'd you do on it?"

"Oh. I mixed up anemometer and hygrometer. Which is entirely stupid. Hy—hydro—water. Duh." I rolled my eyes, then picked up her backpack. "Wanna walk?"

"Sure."

"Plus my first boyfriend was named Hy, and he liked water

sports... So you'd have thought that'd be a no-brainer." I stopped in my tracks. "Um. Huh. No wonder I blacked that out—ew."

"What's wrong with water sports? I love to ski."

"Hello?!? *Water sports?* As in, *peeing on someone?*"

"Well they don't teach you that at Tiger High!" She laughed. "So... did Hy do that to you?"

"Once. Just once." I shuddered.

Curiosity got the best of her. "What was it like?"

"Hmm. Kind of like a nice warm tub, with asparagus bath salts." I grinned.

"Um, yuck. Okay, I'm not trying to be anti-gay, but that is just gross," she grimaced.

"I know."

"But listen, Gabey..." That was the first time she called me that. "If we're gonna be friends," she continued, "you gotta promise me something."

"Anything", I nodded, happy to keep this newfound friendship on track.

"Never, ever talk about water sports again. Unless you are referencing the beach."

While I knew that wouldn't be a problem, given the vegetable residue Hy had left in my mouth, it was also clear to me that Clare had her limits. As happy as I was to have made a new friend, I realized that, as much as I may want, I could never tell her *everything*.

After dropping Clare at home, I reflected on her family, whom I'd just met. Her mother, Betty, who plied us with cookies. Sister Sharla, walking quietly over to Clare and grasping her hand, almost desperately. And father Henry, eagerly explaining the differences between rare birds he had spotted. You could see the light in his eyes when he spoke of them, and the way he kept glancing to his daughters told me that he hoped they too would share his passion for winged creatures. But Clare and Sharla could not be bothered and did not disguise their outright embarrassment of him, which bordered on revulsion.

But passion *was* passion, right? And while I myself could not connect with his ornithological zeal, I admired him for so freely embracing it. My goodbye pat to his shoulder seemed to make an impression on him, as if he'd been heard and acknowledged by a kindred spirit. His smiling, grateful eyes bore into me, and I could feel his unsaid "thank you" clear across the room.

In the following weeks, school seemed almost normal, whatever that is. I'd see Joey and Kid in the halls, laughing, but they would never engage me. While admittedly for the best, part of me wanted them to recognize me. To pay homage to the experience we'd shared. Not that I wanted to be singled out for humiliation, or to be beaten or terrorized. But a simple look. A meeting of the eyes. Some acknowledgement. "Yes, it happened. We were there. Move on."

The only look that came, though, was from my father. Whether in passing as I glided through the family room, or sitting across from him at dinner, I could feel his eyes piercing through me. "This is my son," they say, "with whom I am displeased."

I did my best to ignore him, and mom helped tremendously, prattling on about all manner of unimportant topics. I wondered, watching her, if she ever thought for herself. Her patter seemed regurgitated, canned; coming forth exactly as she'd heard as expressed on TV, at work, or at the grocery store. After a long monologue on pretty ingénue Jessica Lange and her disastrous debut in *King Kong*, "She's cute and all, but I doubt we'll ever hear from her again," I half-expected my mom to robotically end with, "Paper or plastic?"

But at least she was talking. Her words filled the empty space around me, making me feel slightly less alone. When I later retreated to my bed, however, her words no longer clung, and I was left defenseless to the encroaching images. Aside from Clare, I had no other friends on whom to lean, and Clare couldn't be with me 24/7, which left a lot of time for solitude.

Yet when I was with Clare, she never again broached the topic of what had happened. Whether she was embarrassed, nervous, or simply waiting for me to bring it up, I was grateful not to discuss it. While it never really left my mind, it was as if it were a movie, playing in the room next door. Constantly looping, I could hear moments and see quick flashes, images, but never the entire thing.

Gloria offered that a therapist might be helpful, but one roll of my dad's eyes told me that therapy would not be an option. Therapy is for losers. Man up, boy—face your fears. Vomiting it all up ain't gonna do nothin' but throw good money after bad.

In a way, I saw his point. I'd asked for, and received, exactly what I'd gotten. I was not blameless, and they were just doing what boys do.

So who, exactly, was to blame?

Clare opened her closet, revealing two gowns.

"So," she smiled nervously, "which do you think?" Before I could even open my mouth to respond, she continued. "I mean, I love the pink, right? So cute and girly, but babyish, right? But the teal—"

"Would accentuate your eyes," I offered.

"Exactly!" she exclaimed. "And if people are focusing on my eyes, they'll forget how fat I am."

"Sweetie, for the last time, you are not fat!" I protested, to no avail.

"I have a mirror, Gabey."

"Then fucking use it!" I cry, exasperated with her undetectable obesity.

"Language, pet," she prompted.

"You are a twig! If you were any thinner, they'd roll you in salt and plop you into a bag of pretzel sticks."

"Aw—you are so sweet," Clare smiled. "Always trying to lift my spirits."

I quieted my voice, hoping to actually reach her. "It's true, Clare. You're beautiful. Smart, kick-ass skinny... And you're the only person I know who is eternally optimistic. Which is sort of sick and great, at the same time. I feel lucky to be taking you to Winter Formal."

"Oh!" she exclaimed, crossing to me and taking my hand in hers. "Can you believe we're juniors? Just one more year, then seniors!"

"You've always done well in math, hon."

"Well—you know what they say. 'He who asks a question is a fool for a minute; he who does not remains a fool for a lifetime.'"

"Who says that, huh? No one talks like that."

"Well, it was on my Daily Quotes calendar, so someone must have said it." Sighing, she sat back onto her bed and returned to the Winter Formal. "I am really, really happy you asked me. I mean, I know you'd rather go with some hot guy like Garrett Bradbury—"

"He is hot—"

"But I am grateful." She looked up at me. "I wouldn't be going, if not for you."

"You could've gone stag," I insisted.

"Right," she laughed, "and endured a night of watching Tiger High's finest slow dance? Trying to force a smile during my solo photo? No thanks. At least, for the dance, I'll be one of those people, on the arm of a really foxy guy."

"You know what they say, Clare. 'Beauty is in the eye of the beholder. It is only skin deep. And it fades, but strength of spirit remains.'"

She laughed, "Okay, I get it! Enough with the sayings, I promise. But seriously, Gabey—thanks. Thanks for letting me be a part of that world, even for one night."

My eyes clouded, remembering countless humiliations at the hands of Tiger High's "finest." "You know it's really not that great, right? Those kids are brats. They're gonna wake up some day, not too long from now, and wonder why their best years are behind them."

"You think?"

"We'll have a better life than all of them put together—just wait. You'll be hanging out with the art world crowd, showing off your latest painting, and I'll be writing brilliantly witty short stories. I bet we'll even share some cool studio in New York, where we'll throw amazing parties, with Warhol and Divine. We'll be the toast of the town. Nobody'll be able to beat us!"

Clare smiled, not sure whether to believe me. "Anything's gotta be better than high school, right?"

In the days following, we picked out my tux (black tails, teal cummerbund and tie), booked our dinner at The Fireside Room, and arranged our "limo," which meant washing the car and cajoling Lenny into wearing a suit and cap. He was none too thrilled, perhaps because he knew of the sham life I was leading, or perhaps because he was just a heartless prick. Either way, the peppermint schnapps we'd snuck into our mini-Scope bottles, with a dash of food coloring, helped make the evening fly, in spite of Lenny's attitude.

Dinner was great, though not as upscale as I'd imagined. We laughed over the looks we got from the older patrons, but the steak was good and it was nice, for once, to sit through an entire meal without hearing Clare complain about the imminent effect the food would have on her figure.

On the way to the dance, in the backseat, we covertly freshened our breath, though I knew Lenny's eyes were on us. I could sense a question in them, but wasn't certain what he was asking. *Do you really like this girl? Aren't you a homo? Are you really drinking Scope?*

Soon, we arrived at the Shriners Hall, and our last-minute primping began in earnest. I saw another question mark flash in my dad's eyes as I helped Clare redo her makeup, and yet another when she did my mascara. But I really didn't care. We were juniors, going to our first formal, and nothing else really much mattered.

Inside, I was pleased to see that my theme of Winter Wonderland had been beautifully executed. While I'd been happy, inspecting it with my design team earlier in the day, it was amazing to see how it came to life in the theatrical lighting.

The giant snowflakes twinkled—the glitter had been just the right touch—and the white lights everywhere transformed this dreary den of macho bull-wonky and stale cigar smoke into a brilliantly sparkling enchanted kingdom. Even Joey Tatolla seemed impressed. I was shocked, and Kid Dollard even more so, when Joey came toward me, hand outstretched and eyes never wavering. "Travers," he nodded, "nice job." And with that, we buried the hatchet.

Clare had been dubious when I first suggested we join the Winter Formal Committee. While she wondered if we would even be accepted, I had realized after what happened that the key to succeeding in high school was to fully show myself. No more lurking in the shadows. My enigma had been what singled me out as an object to ridicule, and I was determined not to let that happen again. I would no longer be a cipher, floating along the sidelines. I would join every group, every committee, and take on visible leadership roles. Not only would this lead to accomplishments, both for me and Tiger High, but it would ensure that every single person on campus would, if not like me, at least remember my name.

Clare and I became inseparable. We were co-chairs of countless groups, and to this day I am not entirely certain how or why we led the chess club, as neither of us play. Maybe no one else wanted the job, or, more likely, we steamrolled all applicants in our desire for school domination.

While not entirely "out," aside from Clare, I did begin to confide in a few others. I told them all about Hy, and how we'd met through a personal ad in the back of the *L.A. Free Press.* Clare thought the whole thing seedy and entirely too creepy—a 30-year-old man dating a 16-year-old kid. But I'd known I was gay since kindergarten, even if I hadn't known what to call it, and that feeling, tender desire toward other men, could not be ignored. It was who I was; normal. And no amount of fear-mongering or calling me deviant could dissuade me. I was not a scary man wearing a trench coat who would abscond with young children. I was simply a guy who liked other guys. Who wanted to be held, embraced. Yes, and even loved.

Still, I didn't feel the need to shout it from rooftops. My experiences with Joey and Kid had made clear that not everyone would be cool with a cocksucker in their midst, and so I became very picky about who would be worthy of my secret.

It was amazing, though, how many could detect I was gay just by looking at me. I was neither macho nor nelly, but something about me clearly communicated itself to others, even if I wasn't aware. Even when younger, I would find myself taunted, called sissy, queer, fag, long before I had chosen the same label myself. How had they known?

Just after turning 15, my mother took me with her to the optometrist. While she was seen, I was directed to the bookstore across the street, to bide my time and keep me out of trouble. Which didn't work out exactly as planned.

Wandering about the shop, through the dusty racks, I was suddenly confronted with a row marked "Gay Studies." While many text were clinical or self-help, interspersed were also *Giovanni's Room, The Front Runner,* and *City of Night.* I lingered as long as I dared, never even fingering a book, yet memorizing every spine. I was too afraid that someone would turn into the aisle and spot me holding one of the forbidden tomes. I pictured sirens, flashing lights, and being led out to a waiting police car, my hysterically-crying mother being comforted by a masculine lady cop.

That one visit might have been the end of it. But on my way out of the store, behind the counter, I spotted the man of my dreams. He was staring at me from the cover of *Mandate* magazine. And I could tell, from the way his denim shirt splayed open, revealing a thick mat of glorious hair, that I would return to this bookstore again and again, hoping to find him.

At home, I counted my allowance. Aside from recent covert purchases of a black jockstrap and a really nice makeup base, perfect for obscuring pimples, I'd barely dipped into it. Calling the bookshop, a tired man rotely announced the store name, followed by "How can I help you?"

I hung up. A few minutes later, I summoned my courage and called again. After receiving the same worn greeting, I spoke, deepening my voice. "Hi, uh—how old do you have to be to buy the gay porn magazines?"

After an unbearable delay came the drained reply, "Old enough to read."

I was out of the house in record time, hopping on my Schwinn for the ride. But even I was unprepared for the many-mile journey, and had to stop for breath on Ventura Boulevard several times. Luckily, Driver's Ed would be starting soon, so future trips would be easier, and I could hide my stash in the trunk.

As it was, I had to balance the black plastic bag on my bookrack, praying to God that it wouldn't slip out, littering the greater Northridge area with penises. Why on earth couldn't they use ordinary bags; something less overt? Everyone knows that only sex shops use black plastic, and this was a perfectly respectable shop. Gloria had even shopped there! There were no plastic vaginas or weird little glow-in-the-dark anal beads. It was a nice, normal little bookshop, from which I had just purchased works of reputable fiction, not to mention issues of *Mandate, Drummer,* and *Blueboy.*

Once home, I sought a suitable hiding place, but quickly came to the conclusion that the more fully I tried to hide it, the more likely prying eyes would find it. So I shoved them into my desk drawer, beneath a schoolbook. And over the next few months, as my collection grew, Lenny happily noted how muscular my legs were becoming, due to the increased cycling.

Still, while he showered me with praise for this newfound sign of masculinity, I could feel him waiting for the other shoe to drop. My protestation. An accusation, calling him out for his abandonment; his contempt. But I offered nothing except a smile, as no confrontation would compel him to see the harm his actions had caused. Lenny was clueless and utterly incurious as to the effect he had on others. Yet, for knowing so little about himself, he seemed immensely self-satisfied.

I often wondered why he'd married my mother. Why they'd started a family. And why they'd stopped with me.

I asked her once, "Was I a surprise?"

"Oh heavens no, son! You were fully planned and something I'd always wanted."

"Dad, too?" I persisted.

"Well, you know your father! Sometimes he has to be prodded along with a crowbar. But when you were born, he was so thrilled. Just your typical, proud papa. 'Look everybody—I got a boy!'"

At that moment, it dawned on me that it wasn't that Lenny never wanted kids, he just didn't want me.   He wanted a stereotypical boy who would hang in the garage with his old man, rebuilding car engines and wood-crafting. Not a boy who loved Easy Bake Ovens. Who loved coloring, and singing, and could devour *Little Women* in one sitting.

Both he and I were sad clichés. I, however, was determined to grow and break free from my mold, while he was determined to be unhappy. I think he chose the easier path.

My path became considerably easier, at least at school, over the next few days. Being integral to the functionality of Tiger High provided me with a certain cachet. Just walking around campus, people would call me out. But instead of "Hey faggot!", it would be "Hey Gabe—come sit with us!" or "Kate needs to talk with you about Spirit Week."

I loved being recognized and having my contributions noted. I doubted Tiger High would ever again see the likes of my Winter Wonderland splendor, or quite as successful a blood drive, or as many participants as my "Opposite Day Costume Contest" garnered.   And while this newfound recognition spread, it hadn't yet morphed from "well-known" to "popular", though surely that was just a matter of time.   Even Lenny seemed to acknowledge the advances I was making, and his glaring eyes glared not so much.

But the best part was meeting Keith. He was a total fox, into cool stuff, and really sweet, but didn't seem to know just what a catch he was. After meeting during gym class, we connected again at lunch, when he shyly waved me over to his open table. I couldn't believe this hot stud would sit alone. Flattered, I joined him, proud to have been asked. Our talk focused mainly on school, as we determined common ground before evolving to include other topics. He was into really weird groups like Cheap Trick, Patti Smith, and Kiss, all of which seemed incredibly illicit. I couldn't imagine mom allowing them to be played in our house, and thus began what was to become a familiar trek to the Gambles.

Lying on the orange-and-gold shag in his room, adorned with

posters of everyone from Jimmy Hendrix to Jimmy Connors to Jimmy Dean, I would gaze at Keith, listening as he played his favorite music. He'd tell me the back story on each band. Where they were from, how they met, who was fucking who... The music was all really—unusual. Sexual. Provocative. Poorly sung. And given that I was still mourning the cancellation of *The Partridge Family*, Keith's choice of tunes felt far removed from all things Northridge. Which was likely why they appealed to him, signaling a world beyond the monotony of our lives. Perhaps it spoke to a longing within.

If so, I was determined to find out exactly what he longed for, and to wrap it up and give it to him, a present for the much-needed friendship he had given me.

While Clare did not necessarily share my enthusiasm for "all things Keith," she also was smart enough not to bash him.

"He's really sweet, Gabey, but—"

"But what?" I persisted, "You're jealous?"

"Of course not! Friends are like Bacon Bits in the salad bowl of life. You can never have too many."

"So what's the problem?" I countered.

"I just don't want you to get hurt and all. I mean, we don't even know if the guy is—you know."

"I don't care about that, Clare. Just to have friends... Do you know how hard it's been? Before you came along, I had none! Zero. But to actually have a guy—another guy—think I'm okay? Who doesn't think I'm an idiot or prissy little queen—who wants to hang out with me? That in itself is a first."

"I love hanging with you, Gabey."

"But you also have Sharla, Christie, Betsy, Wetsy—"

"Stop, silly!"

"You have a whole bunch of folks who think you are terrific. But I've never had that—ever. When I was a kid, I didn't have any brothers or sisters or cousins to hang with. No built-in group. And it seemed like whenever I'd start to connect with a boy, to form a friendship, something would happen. I don't know if I'd say the wrong thing, or do the wrong thing, or if their parents suddenly noticed their kid hanging with the fairy, but it never, ever worked out."

"So, what are you saying?" Clare asked. "You're hanging all of your hopes on Keith?"

I didn't answer.

"That's a lot to ask, Gabey. Of anyone."

"I know."

"What do you even want from him? Friendship only? You'd really be okay with that? Because something tells me you'd want more."

"I don't know what I want."

"What if he rejects you? Or if he can't reciprocate your love?"

"What makes you think I love him?"

"Oh, honey—I've known since that day, when you came into Davenport's with that smile of yours. And you'd just come from gym class, which you never smile about. Clear giveaway."

We sat for a moment.

"You're right, you know," I said.

"About...?"

"Him. My expectations," I replied, sighing.

She took my hand in hers.

"I hope it works for you, Gabey. I really do. All I want is for you to be happy. Just—"

"What?"

"Enjoy it. For however long it lasts. Try not to over-think it or ask anything unreasonable. It's your first love, honey. Savor it."

The trip had been planned for months.

"He needs a change, Lenny," Gloria had prodded. "We all do."

"What?" I asked, entering the kitchen.

"We need a break. A little vacation. You know we haven't had one since Big Bear, and that was two years ago!"

"Now is not a good time," Lenny stated, as firmly as ever.

"When would be convenient, Lenny?" she persisted. "Our son needs a change of scene. To take his mind *off things*," she enunciated, as if neither of us could decipher her intended meaning.

"I'm fine, mom. Really." The idea of going somewhere, anywhere, with these two was really unappealing.

"Oh, I know you're fine, hon!" she smiled. "Still a week in the desert would be like a tonic, right? Soothing. All that sun!"

Lenny started to argue, then thought better of it, realizing this battle was not his to win. Still, at her next suggestion, his eyebrows raised.

"And Gabriel, why don't you invite your nice friend, Keith?"

"Keith?" I choked. The idea of both of us sleeping in the same room, changing, showering...

"Why not?" Gloria chortled, martini in hand, as Lenny rolled his eyes and turned away. "The more, the merrier!"

As I ran to call him, I could hear the low tones of my father, questioning Gloria's wisdom, and her resolute firmness in insisting that friends were just what I needed. I knew that my mother would be victorious, and Lenny would relent. And as I reached for the phone, I kept my fingers crossed that Mr. Gamble would readily consent as well.

Topic broached, Keith, while happy, didn't seem nearly as enthusiastic as I. Was he apprehensive? Had I crossed a line into inappropriate behavior? Was it too soon to vacation together? Had I misread his friendship, and not seen it for the charity case it was?

He'd been distant for weeks. I didn't know if it was simply that the original sheen cast from our initial meeting had now comfortably dulled, or if he was having concerns about me, or something else, but it never seemed the right time to ask. I got the sense that not all was right at home, but as he hadn't yet confided, I couldn't know for certain.

It seemed like forever before he came back on the line, but at least when he came back, I could hear excitement in his voice.

"I can't wait to get away," Keith groaned, his relief palpable over the phone.

"Me, either," I smiled, for altogether different reasons.

Driving east, I took in the 10 freeway, in all of its ugliness.

Countless billboards littered the passage with loud, faded, and peeling messages, which is the perfect entrée to Palm Springs, home of all things garish, wrinkled, and near death.   Palm Canyon Drive was simply storefront after storefront, offering tacky tourism in buildings shaped like squat shoeboxes.   There was nothing swank or classy or noble about the strip, no remnant of the movie-star days of years past.

As we drove, my eyes darted about, trying to spot the gay hotel I'd seen advertised in the *Advocate*, where clothing was entirely optional.   I'd fantasized about a beautifully-lush Polynesian resort, with thatched roof and lit tiki torches, where sculpted men would eye each other coyly over piña coladas. Driving past, however, all I saw was a disappointing old motel with tin foil taped into its windows, barring access to the outside world.

Keith barely spoke the entire car ride, but no one had noticed.   Mom, true to form, rattled off facts and figures about our destination and its illustrious inhabitants, and I was glad for her distracting discourse, which normally would have driven me to the brink.   Lenny listened to her with one ear, while curiously eyeing Keith and me in the back.

With a dejected sigh I realized, as we turned into the familiar Motel 6, that Lenny had partially won the vacation battle.   I'd been campaigning for the Merv Griffin hotel, given its famous patrons and the rumors about its owner.   But cheap son of a bitch that he was, I should've known Lenny would never go for it.   Too "snooty" for him.   The Motel 6 and the nearby Sambo's restaurant were much more his speed.

Entering our room, with its no-frills, charm-free appeal, Keith breathed a long sigh.   "It's wonderful!"

By some fluke, we'd wound up three doors down from my parents, and even as Lenny fumed at the desk clerk about the need for adjoining rooms, I knew that with Spring Break in full swing, they'd never be able to change it.   Besides, even three rooms separation felt like liberty to me, and I knew that was what made Keith so happy.

"Think of it, Gabe," he said, throwing himself onto the

polyester spread, "a week in paradise. Aww—it feels so good to get out!"

I laid down on the bed next to him, careful not to get too close. "Thanks for coming."

"Are you kidding? Your call was like a sign from heaven. An escape plan."

"From what?"

Keith eyed me, with a frown. "My old man," he muttered, as if I should immediately understand.

I nodded, "Go on."

"It's just—he rides me all the time. Like no matter what I do, or how good I am, it's not enough."

"That's it?" I prodded. "Just about every kid I know could say the same."

"Plus," Keith said, head down, "he's been asking about you."

"Me?" I exclaimed. "Whatever for?"

"Because you say things like, 'Whatever for?'"

"He doesn't like me?"

"He doesn't know you, Gabe. He's just curious—wants to know all about you, your interests, what we do together."

"Oh," I said, unsure where this was going. Had my faggotry once again been exposed? "What did you tell him?"

"The truth," he said. "That you are, by far, the coolest guy I know. You're smart, a great writer, and have an excellent and kind of sick, twisted sense of humor. And, basically, that you're my best friend. If he has a problem with it, then he can suck it."

I stared, impressed. He was a chivalrous soul, in an era of Bobby Sherman blandness. Keith had stood up to defend my honor. Something my own father wouldn't even do.

But did he do so as a friend, or...?

Keith rolled off the bed and went into the bathroom to change. I stared at the closed door, wishing I'd been gifted with X-ray vision.

This beautiful, hunky, sweet and kind guy liked me. This was going to be one hell of a vacation.

After an afternoon spent lounging at the pool, we returned to the room to prep for dinner. As Keith showered, my eyes went directly to his striped boxers, tossed leisurely into the corner. As if that were the proper place for them. Gloria had long ago impressed upon me that "presentation counts," and it was in that vein that I crossed the room and picked up the boxers.

Once in my hands, however, other feelings came over me. I longed to smell them, to scour them for any trace of Keith. But I heard the shower stop and, instead, folded the boxers into a proper square before placing them on top of his suitcase.

I wondered why so many boys liked boxers. They bunched up around your ass, stuck out the top of your jeans, let your privates flop about unintended, and did nothing slimming for your figure.

I'd recently switched from plain white briefs to black bikini, which came in a cool three-pack tube. I'd seen a photo of some Italian actor wearing them, and knew they'd look great on me. The briefs fully accentuated my member, making it appear even more intimidating than usual, and while I was puzzled by the odd looks I'd gotten in the school locker room, I'd chalked it up to adolescent jealousy.

Once Keith and I were dressed, my parents gave us cash and dropped us on Palm Canyon so that they could enjoy a "romantic dinner" at the Charthouse. But the idea of Gloria and Lenny looking at each other with goo-goo eyes was enough to rob me of my appetite.

Instead, we wandered through the shops, each filled with the same dusty array of sun-care products and flip-flops. Walking behind him, I loved the way Keith's fresh tan made him glow and the way you could see the white skin just behind his ears, which had been shaded from the sun's glare. He really was the perfect specimen, and yet so utterly unassuming. Either he did not know the impact his beauty had on others, or he'd dismissed it as superficial, which was the more likely scenario. He wanted depth and meaning, and valued those with whom he could share it.

We browsed through a record store, me idling in the show tunes, while Keith explored the more adventurous sections. After a bit, he reappeared, pulling me over to some albums.

"I totally forgot about this!" Keith exclaimed, shoving a

record into my hands. "She's just your thing."

Taking in the stylized cover, so artsy, but with an art deco feel, I looked up at him. "She looks like a sexy Lucille Ball."

"It's Bette Midler, dummy. Haven't you heard of her?"

"They don't play her on 93 KHJ."

"She sings at the baths, stupid," he whispered. "You *know?*"

"What are you talking about?" I was thoroughly confused. "Baths?" I said, much too loudly. "As in bathtub?"

"There was an article on her in *Interview*," he whispered, trying to rein me back in. "She's got this really big following now, but got her start singing in bathhouses."

"She sings to old men in towels?" I squeeked. "Yuck!"

He pulled me closer. "Don't you know anything?" he hissed. "Bathhouses are where homosexualists go to have sex."

"You mean, in showers and stuff? Oh my God... in the open?"

"How should I know? I just thought you might like her," he muttered, placing the record back into the bin. "Forget it."

"Gladly," I huffed as he returned to the Rock aisle. What was he saying about me? Did he know? And why did he know so much about gay stuff?

Later, seeing him happily ensconced in the Tom Waits section, I made my way back over to Bette. The album seemed timeless, somehow, and appealed to my sense of style. But as I had no desire for Keith to win this battle, I refrained from buying it. Instead, I made mental note of her name and vowed to find the album again once safely back in Northridge.

The next morning, we awoke to a knock on the door, and Lenny urging us to hurry and change for breakfast. Before I could gather my thoughts, he turned with a wave, heading downstairs, toward the smell of pancakes.

I must admit that, as a kid, I once shared my dad's love of Sambo's. They had amazing pancakes, and I loved to sit at the counter, away from my parents, and stare up at the brightly lit panels that told the tale of the dark-skinned boy with jeweled headdress, cajoling the prowling tigers.

But as I now knew the history of racism *("Thanks, Mrs.*

Steeby!"), I took issue with patronizing an establishment that wore its hatred so openly on its apron. Lenny pointed out that the name of Sambo's was, in fact, taken from the names of the co-creators of the chain, and that even black people were waiting to get in, which should have shut me up.

But one thing I fully realized, which my family yet did not, was that I, too, belonged to a suspect class. I, their son, would be singled out and discriminated against. The bile which had been spit my way throughout the years, based solely on the *assumption* that I was gay, would soon be crystallized, and I could look forward to a lifetime of fighting, simply to be treated with some measure of respect. And so it was that I chose to defend my Negro brothers.

"They may not be aware of what 'Little Black Sambo' is all about, dad," I argued. "I mean, tigers turning into butter—?"

"What?!?" Gloria exclaimed, ignorantly. "That doesn't even make sense!"

"But that name, *Sambo*, has become a humiliating, derogatory slur used against African Americans. It's not respectful."

Lenny shrugged, muttering, "I don't know. Black, colored, African American, nappy-headed nigger—no matter what you call 'em, it's still the same old shit."

Keith turned away, taking a sudden interest in the Sambo's mural.

"So," I steamed, challenging loudly, "queer, homo, fairy, faggot—all those are alright with you, too?" Gloria gestured for me to keep my voice down, but I persisted, all too aware of the gigantic step I was taking. "All of those are acceptable names for someone to call your son?"

"Gabe—" Lenny started.

"What? A name is just a name, right?" I rushed, my entire body shaking. "So 'fucking little faggot' is entirely okay with you."

"Gabe, can't we drop this?" my mother pleaded, a smile twisted tightly onto her face.

"Words don't matter? A name is just a name? Well, in that case, you're no longer Mom and Dad—okay, Lenny? *Gloria?*" I sneered. "Words don't matter... That's like saying 'love' is just a word. Words do matter, thank you very much."

I could feel all eyes in the restaurant on me, taking in the fey one in their midst.

"Jeez," I turned, waving to my audience. "You heard right, folks. I'm gay. And you're eating racist pancakes. Enjoy."

And so it was that I got my way, and we ended up, instead, eating a silent and inferior breakfast at Denny's.

For the next few days, the topic remained hanging. It was in the arid desert air, swirling around us, but no one was brave enough to address and dismiss it. Instead, Keith and I laughed and played, having the time of our lives.

We'd wake each morning and put on our swimsuits, grabbing a yogurt from our ice chest before heading to the pool. My parents would bring us lunch, then later, after a shower, we'd all have dinner in town.

Shower time was excruciating. Keith would always change in the bathroom, door locked, leaving me to wonder and visualize. When it was my turn, I played all manner of games, walking around in my black bikini briefs; bending over seductively while peering into my suitcase, trying to find some "misplaced" item; stepping from the shower and talking loudly, as I slowly wrapped the towel around myself, giving him ample opportunity to browse the merchandise; making sure that the towel hung low on my hips, revealing as much skin and treasure trail as I modestly could; and every so often, at the risk of overkill, I'd let the towel "slip" off, at which I'd promptly blush like a whore in church. But Keith never took notice.

On our last vacation night, as we lay in our twin beds, I finally broached the topic of Sambo's and all that remained unspoken.

"So, Keith," I started.

"...Yes?"

"About the other day."

"What?"

"At breakfast..."

"Yeah?"

"Sambo's?"

"Uh-huh."

I couldn't believe he was making me say it. "You heard what I said, right?"

"The whole diner heard it, Gabe."

"So, you know I'm gay?"

"Was there ever any doubt?"

Even in the dark, I could tell he was grinning.

"Asshole," I muttered.

"You wish!"

"Don't be so full of yourself, Mr. Gamble. Just because I like guys doesn't mean I like you."

"Yes, you do," he stated, matter-of-factly. "I'm exactly what you want."

"What makes you say that? I mean, you don't know what I like. The type of guys."

"So you're not into me?" He rolled over onto his side, propping himself on his elbow. "Remember, 'words matter.'"

I threw a pillow at him. "You really think you're hot, don't you?"

"I've seen the way you look at me. And, believe me, I'm flattered. Really flattered."

"That's it? Flattered?" I prodded. "I tell you I love you and you're flattered?"

"You didn't say you loved me..."

"But I do," I stated, firmly and with conviction.

He was silent for a moment.

I didn't know if that was the end of the conversation, but suddenly, knowing he was still watching me, I felt naked, exposed. I'd divulged far too much. Under his gaze, I turned away, toward the window, and pulled the covers tightly around my shoulders.

It was all I could do to keep breathing. What was he thinking? Would this be the end of our friendship? Why was he so quiet?

After a few minutes, I heard him rise from his bed. The next thing I knew, he raised my covers, slipping into my bed. My heart raced as his arms encircled me from behind. Was this a dream? Or was this *it*? Had my prayers finally been answered?

He nuzzled his head against my neck and sighed, but made no other move. Was he waiting for me? Did he think I was the more experienced and should take the lead? I thought about rolling over to face him, but didn't dare break this spell. Whatever it was, whatever it meant, I wanted it to last.

He finally spoke. "I've lost a lot in my life, Gabey. I mean, my mom died when I was 10 and it's not—that doesn't make anything easy, you know? Then my dad somehow turned from someone I loved into someone I feared. And while I know he has his reasons, his own demons, I was left with no one. My brothers, they're so much younger. They barely remember her, or what he was like before. They don't understand. And I don't want to be left again, Gabe. I finally have a fucking terrific friend, and I don't want to screw that up."

"We'll always be friends, Keith—you know that."

"If we keep things as they are, yes, I think we will be. But sex changes things. I mean, say we sleep together, and one of us doesn't like it? Or if we're not compatible? Or maybe we have a terrific time, but then, somewhere down the road, we want out? Either way, we end up screwed."

Now I turned to face him. I didn't realize until I saw the moon's reflection glistening on his cheeks that he'd been crying.

I tried a joke, hoping to alleviate his pain. "Well, I for one would rather screw if we're screwed either way."

He remained quiet. I reached up, wiping away his tears, and then his hair from his eyes. "As your dad would say, 'it's time for a haircut'."

"You're not mad at me?"

"Mad? Why would I be mad?" I smiled. "I finally have an amazingly hot guy in my bed. What do I have to be mad about?"

Now he grinned a bit, clearly relieved. "I do love you."

I tousled his hair. "It feels good to hear that... I just wish—"

He sat up and looked at me. "I'm not saying *never*, Gabe. Maybe, at some point, I'll want to take the plunge." My heart began tingling faintly, as a sliver of hope was restored. "But right now," he continued, "I just need to know you'll be there for me."

"I will," I said, giving him a big squeeze. "I will."

We drifted off to sleep, entwined, and in that moment, dusty and dreary Palm Springs turned into my favorite spot in the entire world. There was no place I'd rather be.

My parents and I had not been alone the entire week, leaving my Sambo's tirade, and all it entailed, undiscussed. I knew that Lenny was disapproving; that had been made clear long ago. But Gloria... she was harder to read. For all her faults, I knew she loved me. But would she still love her new take-it-up-the-ass son?

Upon arriving home, with Keith dropped at his dad's, I quickly made myself busy, unpacking and doing laundry, so as not to deal with Lenny and his questions and/or lecture. But my parents seemed reluctant to talk as well, and that was just fine with me. We each went about our chores, carefully keeping distance, until it was time for bed.

In the morning, though, as I sat eating my Special K with skim milk, making certain that my svelte figure remained intact should Keith ever decide to "take the plunge", Lenny walked in. I focused intently on the cereal box, as if it were imparting all-important wisdom, the flow of which could not be interrupted.

"I don't know how you eat that stuff," Lenny groaned, pouring himself a quick cup of coffee. "And with blue milk, to boot."

"It's not blue," I muttered. "It's fat-free."

"Since when are you worried about fat? If anything, you could stand to gain a few," he noted. "In fact, if you want, I could probably hook you up with a gym membership. A buddy manages a club over on Roscoe. You could pump iron any time you wanted."

Given that generosity was not in Lenny's makeup, I immediately looked his gift horse in the mouth. I realized he was offering this as a means to butch me up. As if in adding to my muscle mass, there would be a correlative decrease in my estrogen levels, creating a newer, more masculine, more presentable Gabe. But I accepted the gift, even if undesired, as he was right: I could stand to gain a few. And, more importantly, perhaps the showers there would provide another fun way to burn extra calories.

On his exit, with a backwards wave, Gloria entered, checking her hair in the oven door's reflection.

"I am a mess," she sighed, getting no argument from me. She tried fluffing the side she'd slept on, to no avail. "Oh well, too late to do anything now." Turning, she smiled at me. "Your father gone?"

"Yep."

She glanced to the kitchen door, half expecting him to return. Sensing it was safe, Gloria crossed and sat with me. "That was a great week, huh?"

"The best," I admitted.

"Kind of hate to go back, you know? But I'm sure there is a huge stack waiting for me. You know Janet—she's about as useful as a pitchfork in a snowstorm."

I smiled, knowing it to be true. Looking at the clock, I stood to leave, but she gestured for me to sit.

"You still have a few minutes," she insisted. I could tell she wanted to talk, but I wasn't sure that I was up for it. Still, she so rarely made an actual effort, I felt obliged and sat. "So did Keith have a good time, too?"

"Yeah," I nodded. "I think he needed it."

"We all did," Gloria asserted. "After what you went through—"

"I don't want to talk about it, Mom."

"You must, Gabriel. If not to me, then to someone," she challenged. "Look, what happened—that kind of thing doesn't go away. It can haunt you."

"I know, Gloria."

She shifted her chair even closer, leaning in to make sure she was heard. "You may think you know, honey—but, trust me, you don't. You haven't spent a lifetime trying to escape from ghosts. The decisions you make, the choices—. You run and you run... and yet, if you face things, deal with them, call them out by name—." She looked at me to make sure I was listening. "You have to examine what happened and face it. Life could be so much better if you'd really let it."

The clock warned that I'd be late, but it felt wrong to leave. Gloria was talking about me, but seemed to be talking about herself as well. What had happened to her? Was it one thing, some traumatic event, or a string of bad decisions? Was she admitting that marrying Lenny was a mistake, or was he simply a mistake she had made in attempting to outrun her past?

I thought about telling her everything. What had happened that night. How I'd felt. Who her husband really was. Even telling her other things, better things. About Hy, Keith, my future... Clearly she was opening a door, encouraging me to walk through.

She looked at me, hopefully, waiting for me to speak, but instead I grabbed my pack, giving her a quick peck on the cheek.

"I love you," I said, embarrassed as the words unexpectedly came forth.

Gloria seemed just as surprised as me, her eyes following as I quickly darted out the door.

The end of junior year was a blur, filled as it was with essays, events, and finals. Clare and I wrapped up our various club leadership roles and felt optimistic about senior year. We were clearly poised for future, further greatness. Plus, I had an impossibly hot, quasi-boyfriend in Keith. All of the love, affection, and intellectual exchange I'd sought, minus the sex. Every so often, I would begin to push the boundaries, hoping his willingness would have increased, but he remained frustratingly chaste.

He had such monastic discipline. Whereas I was horny 24/7, with a perpetual totem pole straining my bikini briefs to the ripping point, Keith showed absolutely no interest in sex, that I knew of. He'd ask questions about me and my past experiences, and seemed quite curious. But I was never entirely sure what he was thinking. Gay sex seemed like a possibility for him, but not necessarily the only experience to which he was open. He seemed to appreciate a hot woman as much as a hot guy, which was beyond me.

I'd always found women scary. Not scary in a "Halloween" sense, of course, but scary in an "Eve and the Forbidden Fruit" type of way. In my mind, the female sex was to be appreciated, but always kept at arms' length, for you never could be certain what type of trouble they'd bring. They carried too much emotional baggage, wearing their hearts on their sleeve in the most obvious and calculating way. Merely a few tears, and grown men would cave without hesitation. The power they wielded in their womanhood was staggering, surely that of a thousand kings. And that intoxicating mix of power and manipulation was a combination I knew best to avoid.

Clare, however, was different. While I assumed her to be physically complete, she did not act as if she had a vagina. She'd moon over boys, most assuredly, but not in a scheming, coy sort of way. She just *was*, and I admired her for that natural state of being.

I, on the other hand, seemed to have more than my share of cunt. I could be as vicious and demanding as the most scorned of women, and why I didn't extend more sympathy or understanding to them was puzzling. To me, women were simply a bother. A necessary factor in the evolutionary equation, who luckily knew how to cook.

Gloria was a prime example. She had lived her life subservient to a far inferior man, for what purpose I cannot say. If they had stayed married solely on my account, then that made them even bigger losers. Relationships built on obligation were about as fulfilling as receiving a basket of Hickory Farms cheese for Christmas.

Clearly, much of my discomfort with women came from Gloria. She perplexed me. Her endless chatter drove me insane, and there could be entire weeks which would pass during which she would talk incessantly, and yet barely a word would register.

I wondered what she and Lenny talked about when no one else was around. Or did they, in fact, even talk? It wasn't hard to picture them both going into emotional lockdown mode: eyes half open, mouths firmly shut, moving about, giving clear berth to the other. Well, it was easy to imagine Lenny doing that. Gloria, I feared, never stopped talking. But perhaps that, in itself, was a form of emotional lockdown. How can one penetrate a fortress, when faced with a shield of inconsequential blather?

Surely, I thought, she noticed the lack of substance in her life. And yet her daily life of home-work-home seemed to suit her. While I never saw her express anything resembling actual joy, she seemed to be reasonably content. Even with Lenny. To some degree, she seemed to view her marriage with a measure of pride, while I saw it as entirely negative.

When I marry—well, settle down—I want to be in love. I want to be held, and appreciated, and nurtured. Simply occupying common space is not enough. And for settling so easily, I blamed Gloria. Because her choice—that willingness to live in a love-free environment—directly translated into my low feelings of self-worth.

And while I appreciated her recent efforts to reach out to me, at the one point I truly needed her, Gloria was more concerned about Lenny and what others thought than she ever had been for my well-being. Had she reacted differently in that moment, perhaps everything after could have been altered. And I wouldn't feel quite as fucked as I do.

She'd given me an opportunity to talk. To *share*. But somehow that invitation felt entirely one-sided. I got the feeling that she wanted to hear from me, from the horse's mouth, all of the gory details. Maybe it would have given her comfort, to think that I'd confided in her. But a monologue was not what I needed. And I doubted that Gloria was prepared for the kind of two-way dialogue I envisioned.

Before I knew it, summer had arrived, bringing lots of opportunities to see Keith in his bathing suit. As he stretched out on a chaise, I couldn't fathom how he remained so unaware of his beauty. There was no guile, no self-consciousness. Whereas I prepped endlessly for our forays, with hair perfectly sculpted and every inch of skin dripping with Hawaiian Tropic, Keith would merely emerge from the changing room as if kissed by the sun. He'd dive into the pool, or ocean, or lake, and with a simple shake of mane look as if he'd spent an entire afternoon at Vidal Sassoon's.

I was still up to my old tricks with him. I had bought a very skimpy white bikini on a stealth mission to West Hollywood's All-American Boy. Fully aware of the suit's transparency, I let my accoutrement hang out for all to see.

Clare took one look and said, "Gabey, not sure if this is the look you're going for, but we can all see that your sausage has no casing."

While Keith smirked in agreement, he showed little interest in discovering what actually lay beneath the nylon.

I began encouraging excursions to Will Rogers Beach in Santa Monica, which I quickly learned had earned the moniker "Ginger" Rogers, due to its happily high homo quotient. Clare would eagerly accompany me, pleased to be surrounded by men who valued and enjoyed her company, without expectation. They seemed to view her as some wise and witty shaman, dispensing pearls of wisdom to her adoring masses. But to me, Clare's wisdom looked no deeper than the cheap slip of fortune-cookie paper she'd gleaned it from.

Perhaps my irritation was prompted in some part by jealousy, as she would draw a throng within minutes of our arrival, leaving me unnoticed. But as summer progressed, I'd heard her tired lines repeated so often, I'd begun mouthing along, unconsciously.

Keith was forced by his father into a summer job. "It's time you began thinking of your future as provider," he'd said, though I was uncertain how a menial job in the stock room at JCPenney was supposed to be a springboard to financial stability. A downside to his job was that Clare and I were usually driving to Ginger Rogers alone.

"What do you care?" Clare asked. "It's not like you two are *together*," she insisted. While I knew that to be accurate, I still held out hope that he'd eventually succumb and was doing my best to be patient and chaste. Just *looking* at other men felt like cheating—and that beach overflowed with beautiful men.

While I did attract my share of attention, most of it seemed centered on my youth, as well as the white bikini, the purchase of which I soon began to regret. I'd wanted to look sexy, but all I looked was nubile. I'd wanted to accentuate my bulge, thinking it to be my only asset, but ended up looking vulgar. And while it did bring attention, no one really seemed to want to get to know me. All they wanted was a quick romp with the new kid. They wanted my youth, my cock, my cherry, but not my brain.

While the looks they gave told me that I was, on some level, desired, there was also something in their gaze that reminded me of Joey and Kid. Some measure of malice, of superiority; as if it was clear to all that I was, at best, a play toy. Inconsequential.

Still, I enjoyed the attention. Every appreciative glance, every lecherous stare or overt come-on meant that, regardless of intent or expectation, I'd been noticed. I was not invisible. And that meant something.

One night, hanging out at Keith's after his shift at Penney's, he played me a tune from some weird band called Modern Lovers. I didn't understand it at all, but tried to nod along just the same. Just some guitar and a monotone voice trying to sing. Certainly no artistry involved.

"It's a new band," he said, as the discordant notes proved my point. "Well, not really 'new,' this was recorded a few years back, but just got released."

"Wow," I said, hoping that I'd sounded properly enthused. "This is great!"

Keith smiled, letting his head swing along with the music. "Cool, huh? It's different from anything else out there. Not really rock, not disco—that's for sure. Just, totally new."

"How'd you hear about them?" I queried.

Keith looked away, "Just, uh, a friend." I took note of his sudden hesitancy. "He turned me on to them."

"Who?" I parried, my voice straining to be heard over the awful vocals.

"Huh?"

I reached over, turning down the volume, which I'd never done, given this was Keith's domain. It was his stereo, his room, his bands... but as I felt him holding back, nothing would get between me and the truth.

"You heard about them from a friend, you said? I'm just asking 'who'."

"Ah," he smiled. "Rudy. Not that it matters."

"Who is Rudy?" I pressed. "Not that it matters."

"Just a guy," Keith murmured, his smile telling me more than he'd intended. "He's cool."

I wasn't letting him end the conversation. "He doesn't go to Tiger High, does he? Name doesn't ring a bell..."

"Nah—he's a few years older. He works over at Radio Shack, in the mall," Keith shared. "He knows everything about music, you know? All the latest." Keith turned, flipping through his record albums.

"Is he cute?"

"Cute?" He buried himself in his records.

"You heard me", I persisted. "As in, 'hunky'?"

He finally looked at me, clearly not wanting to have this discussion.

"Don't make me spell it out for you," I implored.

"You're jealous?" Keith laughed. "Here you spend all summer in your skimpy bathing suit, surrounded by studs, and you're jealous of me?"

I let his laughter subside before continuing. "You never answered my question. Is he hot?"

Keith narrowed his eyes. I didn't know if he was focusing himself, or questioning my motives, or gathering courage, but I knew I'd find his answer disappointing. "Yeah, Gabe. He's hot."

"And—?"

I was like a dog with a bone, unwilling to let go. And yet I knew that I'd be better off relenting.

"And I like him," he said, assuredly. I felt as if my entire world were crumbling from underneath.

"And have—? Have you, um—?"

Keith sighed. "Gabe, do you really want all the details?"

"Yes, damn it!" I exploded. "I want the fucking details!"

"Gabe—"

"Do you know how long I've waited, Keith? Ever since Palm Springs?" I averred. "I've waited for you—sucker that I am—thinking, hoping, that somehow you'd find your way to me. I've prayed, even. For you to love me as much as I love you."

"You know I care about you."

"Care?" I practically shouted, "You *care*? Jeez, Keith, this is L.A. Everyone cares. It's all air kisses and handshakes. Of course you *care*."

"That's not what we have, Gabe. Don't demean it."

"But Rudy—what? What does he give you, besides herpes?" Keith gave me a sad look, as if incredulous at my low blow. But that didn't stop me. "He'll never love you, Keith. Not like me."

Keith started to respond, then thought wiser of it. After a moment, when my diatribe appeared to have lost its steam, he queried, "Are you finished?"

"What? You want me to leave?" I asked, eyebrows raised. "Is Rudy gonna be here soon?"

"I'm not talking to you when you're like this. It's not worthy of either of us."

"Not worthy?" I cried. "I'll tell you what's not worthy. You! I don't know why I've waited, Keith. Truly. I mean, I've had offers. Amazing, beautiful men," I asserted, even if it wasn't entirely true. "And these guys aren't hicks from Northridge, either, let me tell you. They are movers and shakers—the best of Hollywood. And they want *me*!" I couldn't stop myself. All that was clear to me was that Keith had rejected me and had to be destroyed. "You really are terrific, Keith. Hanging your hat on a guy from Radio Shack. I could have been yours, you know. I'm a fantastic catch. You'll never know what you're missing!"

On my ending, I'd expected a quick response, but none was forthcoming. After a moment, though, Keith did respond. "Gabe," he stated, softly, "you think I don't know how amazing you are?"

I stared in disbelief. Surely he was joking. Somehow, with me in this much pain, Keith had found a way to laugh at me. "I hate you."

"No, you don't," Keith countered, tenderly.

I could tell tears were coming, but forced them back, unwilling to let him see just how much he'd hurt me. "So, why not me, huh? If I'm so 'amazing'..."

"I have fun with you, Gabe—you know that. We have a lot of laughs. You're my best friend."

"But—?"

"I just—. I need more."

"More what?" I pushed. "You know how much I love you. How I would do anything—whatever it takes—to have you."

Keith looked at me, simply, as if I should somehow understand. "That's it, exactly. You'd do anything. If I said I wanted chocolates from Paris, you'd find a way to get them. If I said, 'I only like red-heads', you'd dye your hair."

"So? I'm a giver."

"That's too much pressure," Keith shook his head. "That's not what love is."

"How would you know, huh?" I countered. "You've never been in love!"

"Not romantically," he granted. "But I've felt it. All I have to do is think about my mom, how she used to look at me, and I feel it. That kind of love is centered. Grounded. It's not something that changes, whatever whim we may feel."

"So you're saying you're in love with your dead mother?" I scoffed. "Very healthy, Keith. That is just sick."

Keith looked at me with what felt like revulsion. "You need to leave, Gabe, before you say anything more. You will not, ever, speak like that about her." He pointed to the door. "Go."

I knew that I had said the unforgiveable, and didn't blame him for hating me. No matter how he'd tried to sugarcoat it, I was clearly a loser. I never did anything right.

But as I drove home, as angry and sad as I was, it hit me that while I could do nothing to change Keith's mind, others did desire me. He'd found another, and so would I. I would become the vaunted person I'd tried to convince him I already was, and have everything I wanted. There was no longer reason to hold back. The world was sitting there, waiting, and I would take it, for all it was worth.

Auntie Mame may have said, "Life is a banquet, and most poor suckers are starving to death," but I knew in that moment that I would do whatever it took, and become the fucking buffet.

The next day, as we headed for the beach, Clare continued the narrative she'd been repeating all morning.

"This is a new beginning," Clare insisted. "You are a blank

slate, sweetie. A canvas awaiting the first brushstroke of paint," Clare continued, enjoying her metaphors. "The world is your oyster. You can be anything, anyone."

"You say that like nothing that came before this moment matters. As if I'm starting out with no baggage. But as we both know, I'm full to the fucking Brim rim with baggage."

"That doesn't matter, hon," she said sweetly, as if I were retarded. "Who you are now is all that counts. Start fresh."

"Without Keith," I stated, finally getting her meaning.

"Yes," Clare affirmed. "Without Keith."

I was silent.

We soon arrived at Ginger Rogers, and as Clare's followers amassed, I took stock of myself. Clare was right—I could be anything or anyone. Looking around at the built bodies, each more stunning than the last, the vision that had emerged last night became more clear and compelling. I would immediately put my new gym membership to use, and by next summer, my soft flesh would be molded into gay gold. I would hone my patter, better choosing my words, to ensure that each bon-mot was devastatingly delivered. I would learn the art of love, and leave a bevy of satiated beauties behind. I would become one of them, and beat them at their own game.

And in the process of becoming this fortified and fabulous new me, Keith would be entirely erased. All memory of him would be banished from my thoughts. For if I could forget what happened with Kid and Joey, forgetting Keith would surely be a piece of cake.

Over a piece of dry-looking coconut cake at Carrows, Gloria eyed me, suspiciously. Ignoring her as best I could, I stared grimly at my slice of pecan pie. The sides of it oozed, so syrupy, as they splayed themselves into a puddle all over the plate, desperate to escape the heavy layers of pecans, bearing down from above. The liquefied mess was so unappealing, I pushed the plate away.

"Passing up dessert? That's a first," Gloria correctly noted.

"Just trying to get in shape, you know—for all of my fans!"

Gloria eyed me, "Everything okay?"

Wondering how to best answer that, I smiled instead. "How's your cake?"

"Not as good as Sara Lee," she admitted, "but at least, here, you get waited on."

"That's true," I murmured, still preferring to be home in my room, alone.

Scooping a spoonful of cake into her overly-lipsticked mouth, she managed, "How's Keith?"

"Fine," I lied, deciding to bite into the pecan soup after all, to avoid the topic. "Busy."

"At the store," she noted. "Right."

I took another bite of the drippy mess they passed off as pie. Just then, she continued, "Do you miss him?"

On that, I looked away, hoping my eyes would not reveal the truth.

I could feel her gaze, unrelenting. "It's okay you know. Natural."

I wasn't sure which part she was referring to, and so chose to remain silent.

"Life is all about connections. Some good, some bad," she noted, sounding a bit too much like Clare for my comfort. I wondered if this little life-nugget was something she'd heard repeated at the post office, but let her continue with her hokum. "We have to honor them, Gabe. Hold onto the good ones. And the bad, well..."

I took that as my cue to change the focus. "Are we talking about Keith? Or Lenny?"

She shook her head, fully aware of where this was headed. "Your father does his best."

"Best what? To be the best 'worst father' in the world? To be a poor, uncommunicative racist?" I faced her, fully. "He is a loser, mom. A fucked-up, miserable loser." Gloria started to stop me, but I couldn't be stopped. "What, exactly, has Lenny ever done good, mom? Huh? Just name one thing."

"He made you."

Even for her, that was a low blow. As if I was or had been something good. And even if once I had been of worth, that had been stamped out by Lenny's own two feet.

"Regardless of what you may think, Lenny loves you," she maintained.

"Ha!" I laughed, head back. "That is really rich, Gloria." I peered at her. "How stupid are you?"

Gloria eyed me evenly, setting down her fork, flakes of coconut and red lipstick still clinging to it.

"You may think I'm ridiculous. Stupid, even. But there is a lot I know. Calling me Gloria does not make you my equal. Whether you choose to believe it or not, other people have valuable knowledge—insight—and if you'd stop being so relentlessly self-involved, it would benefit you to listen to them."

"Did you have a pitcher of martinis at home? Because you're not making any sense."

"I know what you went through, honey." I shook my head, but she continued anyway. "I read the police report. At the time—I don't know what I thought. Boys having fun or—. I had no idea what you'd been through."

I started to rise.

"Hear me out," she commanded, more loudly than intended. Glancing about, I could feel all eyes on me, so sat back down. She played with her fork for a moment, then looked directly at me. "I wish I'd been there for you. A mother's job is to protect their children. And I didn't."

"You weren't even there—"

"Let me finish," she demanded. "I would've done anything for you—to stop that. Do you hear me? That night, when you came home—I don't know what I was thinking, but I didn't act as a mother should."

I nodded, not realizing that tears were coming freely.

"And as far as Lenny—what he did—why—I can't speak to that. I'm not even sure he knows himself. I've asked him to go to counseling, and so far he's refused."

"Do you think that would change anything?"

"Probably not," she stated plainly. "Lenny is many things, but one thing he is not is reflective. He is a man of action. Give him a plan, a task, it'll be done within minutes, expertly. But thinking... being emotional... no."

"He's an asshole," I declared.

"Yes," Gloria admitted. "Len is an asshole." That said, she picked up her fork and speared a piece of my runny pie. As soon as it was in her mouth, it was out again. "Oh—that is terrible!"

"Yep," I agreed. "The pie is terrible. As is Lenny. So why did you marry him?"

Gloria sighed, long and low. "The why is any number of factors. I was getting older; almost 30. In those days, that was ancient."

"It still is."

"Watch it, smart mouth," she smiled. "And I hadn't had a lot of beaus. My parents wanted someone stable. Hardworking. The rest of it—looks, personality, compatibility—didn't mean much, in their eyes. And Lenny, for all his faults, is a hard worker. Reliable. And he was much sweeter in those days. Less rough."

"What happened to him?"

Gloria shrugged. "We all have to face, at a certain point, that some of our dreams just aren't going to come true."

"You're telling me that Lenny actually had dreams? Some big plan for his life?"

"He had dreams. Probably still does. But his were more, I don't know, 'fairytale.' They included a wife free from thought, who would have a homemade dinner ready every night, perfectly timed to be pulled from the oven as his car entered the garage. A wife just like his mom, sitting in a rocker, quietly knitting, darning socks or some such. And a kid who never cried, or messed their pants—"

"Or was gay," I added.

"I don't even think that part bothers him," she disagreed, shaking her head. "It's more that none of this—not one single part of his fantasy—came true. Because life is messy. Nothing is ever perfect. No matter how hard we try. And I did try; we both did. We really made an effort, you know—to be what the other wanted. But you can't magically transform yourself into an entirely different person, just because that is what they want."

Her words struck me as intended for both of us.

"I think that is what I did for Keith," I confessed. "Or tried to. The problem was, I didn't even know what he wanted. But whatever I did, nothing worked. And I finally realized that, whatever it is that he wants, it isn't me."

"Have you tried just being yourself?"

"Myself?" I grunted.

Gloria pushed aside the forgotten dessert plates. "Listen, Gabe. I know that your sense of humor, your cynicism, is a shield—no matter how funny. But I need you to hear me, and realize the value in what I am saying."

"Okay," I said, simply because there was no other option.

"You're listening?" she plied. "Fully?"

I nodded.

"I'm concerned about you."

"Duh."

"Listen to me," Gloria implored. "I'm concerned that you don't seem to see the same value in you that I do."

"You're always telling me that I'm too self-involved." I countered. "Doesn't that mean that I'm plenty full of myself?"

"Braggadocio is very different from appreciation," Gloria pointed out. "Making a laundry list of attributes and touting it from the rooftops, that's what you do. What I'm talking about is belief," she clutched her heart, "in here. Believing that you are an amazing child of God and deserving of all the love and riches the world has to offer."

"Since when did you get religion?"

"You see—that is exactly what I'm talking about. Someone tries to connect with you, and you throw up that wall of sarcasm, hoping to prevent what I'm saying from landing in your heart."

"So, you are saying—?"

"I'm saying that I love you... and, believe it or not, your father does as well." Gloria smiled, despite herself. "Shit that he is."

She must've told Lenny what had happened, what we'd shared, because I noticed an immediate softening. I was surprised, too. Not that he was softening, but that she had even shared with him. That meant that either our moment wasn't sacred to her, or that I was such a hopeless case the situation demanded reinforcements. She was even more pathetic than I'd feared.

And Lenny—Jeez! If you want to say something to me, then fucking say it. Don't hang around my periphery, circling, hoping to be invited in, because my skills at blocking people out are getting more advanced by the day. Say what you have to say, and be gone.

But Lenny, for all his bravado, hadn't a clue how to talk with his own son. It was days before he ventured forth, and did so at the most inopportune moment, when I was getting ready for bed.

Having your dad open the door while you are wearing a sheer black bikini, admiring your new six-pack in the mirror, is not the best way to start a conversation. He must have sensed the awkwardness, but clueless-ass that he was, he just stood there.

"What?" I challenged.

"Those are some underwear. Look kind of—uh—European."

"Did you come to admire them, or is there something specific I can help you with?"

"I was just—. Can I come in?"

I gestured with a shrug. "You pay the mortgage."

He sat, quietly. "You're not going to make this easy for me, are you?"

"I don't even know what you want. Except not to discuss my underwear." Inwardly, I smiled, so pleased with my wit.

He sat for a moment, staring. His gaze was resolute, and it made me uncomfortable. I became acutely aware of my nakedness, so slipped on pajama bottoms. Lenny continued to stare, as if waiting for something. Finally, hoping to move things along more quickly, I sat, which must have been what he'd wanted.

"I've been thinking..." he started, but then stopped. I was really resenting his intrusion. I'd been envisioning a quick wank, but his visit had totally killed my mood.

"Yes...?"

"About what you said in Palm Springs..."

"You mean, three months ago?"

"You asked if I'd be okay with someone calling my son, you, names. Like 'faggot.'"

I eyed him.

"And I wanted you to know that I wouldn't. I would not be okay with that. At all. I want the best for you."

"And so what happened, after school that day—? You were doing the right thing by your son, whom you love so much?" I mocked. "Wow, Dad—thanks so much."

He looked at me, pain and confliction evident on his face.

"Did you think we were playing Barbies, Lenny? Having tea?"

"I didn't—. I'm not perfect, Gabe—"

"How well I know that."

Lenny sat, hands folded. It was a wonder he could even follow the thread of our conversation, idiot that he was.

"Your mother and I—"

"What?"

"We're worried about you."

"You don't like that I'm gay? That I'll have some miserable, lonely life due to this hedonistic path I've 'chosen'?"

"Homosexuals don't own the market on loneliness. Shit— you bein' gay, I've known since you were five. When you set up the kitchen as a diner, made little menus, and told me you'd be my waitress..."

I bet you left a lousy tip, Lenny.

"You were such a happy kid. Always laughing, giggling."

"I can do more giggling, if that'd make you happy."

"Would you fucking listen? Can't you see that I'm trying?"

"Trying what, exactly? To make an ass of yourself?" I stood. "You haven't been there for me for years. I've seen the contempt, Lenny. You can't stand the sight of me."

Lenny stood, angrily, stepping toward me. I instinctively brought my hands up, thinking he was going to hit me. Seeing me, fists raised, his face suddenly changed, and he sank back onto the bed, shaken.

Realizing my instinct had been wrong, I lowered my arms. Lenny sat without speaking, and it felt as if I could hear every creak in the house. *Say something, you asshole.* But he just continued to sit.

Looking about my room, I could see no reason to continue this standoff.

"So..." I managed, "Are we done?"

Hands clasped, staring at the floor, Lenny didn't respond. He just sat. Finally, when he did speak, he never raised his eyes to mine, keeping them firmly glued to the floor. "You think you know what is in peoples' hearts. But if you did, Gabe, if you could see, you'd know that I have never in my life hated you. Myself, maybe. Not you."

I didn't know what to say. "Well, thanks."

Ignoring me, he continued, speaking more to himself than me. "I think of you sometimes as if you're still that little kid. Dancing around the living room, playing with your paints, dressing up—you had such a spark. You would put on shows for us—remember?—and I'd help make the scenery."

I managed to nod, but couldn't understand what had triggered such unwarranted sentimentality.

"In some ways, you'll always be that little boy to me." He sat silently, hands folded and head down, almost as if he were praying.

"What are you trying to say, Lenny? What's your point?"

He slowly looked up at me, finally locking eyes. "That spark? That light? Hang onto it."

And as he headed downstairs, without a backward glance, I laughed, incredulous that this pathetic loser would think I would ever take advice from him. *Hang onto the light, the spark; embrace it, live it, shine it...* Asshole.

As I prepped for bed, I sang a tribute to him at the top of my lungs, for all to hear.

This little light of mine
I'm gonna let it shine.
This little light of mine
I'm gonna let it shine...

Clare had the top down, and while I felt glamorous as we headed down Topanga, sun on my face and wind in my hair, she wouldn't let it go.

"Whose side are you on, Clare?" I huffed.

"Why does there have to be sides? They came on heavy-handed, I'll give you that. But I've never thought of Gloria as mean or hurtful."

"I notice you left Lenny out of your assessment."

"Him?" she declared, "He's a schmuck."

"Agreed."

"But he did try. You gotta give him that. He made an effort."

"To do what, though?"

"Well maybe if you'd kept your big mouth shut and let the man speak, you'd know."

"Jeez, Clare—give it a rest."

"Give it a rest?" she laughed. "You are pissed that your parents 'don't make an effort', or 'don't support you', but when they do, you shut them down. They can't win with you, Gabey."

Clare was right. But there was something so disquieting about how I felt when they made an attempt, any attempt, at intimacy. Everything about it felt wrong. Whether it was the time or the place or them or me, it always felt scary.

"I'm just saying, sweetie, that parents, idiots though they may be, sometimes do have worthwhile things to say. Don't just throw the baby out with the bathwater. After all, any grain of sand can become a pearl."

"This is so not my week," I sighed. "Two crazy parents and one off-the-deep-end friend."

"Oh—but for us, hon, it's such a pleasure, just being in the presence of someone as warm and gracious as yourself," Clare smiled, turning the car onto Pacific Coast Highway. "Is it any wonder you're single?"

Despite the way her sneer left her even more unattractive, Clare did have a point. I needed to add "friendly" to my list of things to become. If nothing else, it would come in handy in landing a man.

As we approached the beach, I exhaled a long, luxurious sigh. "Ah, such a glorious, heavenly day. I see the bright shining orb in the rich blue, and give thanks, oh mighty God, for the warmth and Vitamin C it provides. And those precious flocks of gulls, settling in so nicely next to the dead seal carcass—they lift my heart as they soar, filling me with a bubbling fountain of youthful exuberance!"

"Stop!" she shrieked, as we pulled into the lot. "I give, already. I much prefer the bitter Gabey."

"Thank you," I sighed, relieved. "Being that nice was giving me a headache."

Loading up, we made our way on the beach, choosing a spot filled with eye candy.

"I understand what my folks were trying to say, Clare—really I do. But—look at this as if it were meeting guys."

"Okay," she said. "I don't know where this is going, but I like your analogy."

"Isn't it better," I offered, "to be who you are, fully, than to be someone you're not?"

"I don't think anyone expects you to turn into Richie Cunningham overnight. They just want you to be more—I don't know—pleasant."

"But isn't pleasant the same thing as bland? I mean, think of life as the movies..."

"Another analogy?"

"All those great old movies. *The Women. All About Eve.*"

"Huh?"

"My point is, you never remember the good girl, the ingénue. It's Myrna Loy, with her arched wit. Bette Davis' brass. Or Joan Crawford and her sultry innuendo. Those are the ones who made an impression."

"Okay, darling—you are getting way too gay for me. This line of thought is completely beneath you. Point One: You are not Myrna Loy or Judy Crawford—whoever they are—and you never will be."

"Well, maybe on Halloween," I interjected, thinking myself amusing.

"Point Number Two. Life and movies are two completely different things, not to be confused. Just because I enjoyed *The Towering Inferno* does not mean that I want to be dangling from the ledge of a skyscraper, flames all around me."

"You're already surrounded by flames here," I helpfully

pointed out, taking in all the gay boys.

"And, lastly, Point Three: your parents are right, sweetie. You're turning mean, and you don't even know it. And before you give me any rebuttal, I don't mean 'mean' as in a fun, 'good-girl-gone-bad' kind of way."

"No one understands my sense of humor."

"Do you think we're all stupid, Gabey? You used to balance your wit with some compassion. Some interest in others. You could even be altruistic. But now—you just don't seem to think about anyone but yourself."

I rolled over onto my belly. "You sound like Gloria."

"Is that your way of dismissing me?" she persisted. "Of blocking out what I said?"

I closed my eyes. "That sun feels good."

Hearing her exasperated sigh, I could tell she was rising and stomping away. But I didn't really care. They had it all wrong. It was better to be genuine, to be fully authentic, even if that meant embracing negative qualities. Artifice was the enemy, not truth. And if I didn't have it in me to be nice, so be it. I wouldn't fake it. "Love me or leave me," as Doris Day once sang.

When I opened my eyes again, Clare was further down the beach, happily entrenched with her band of delusional followers. She may have felt that she were some font of wisdom, and that they truly paid heed to the words that poured forth, but I knew they just saw her as an amusing fag hag. Some day, she probably would get just as fat as she imagined, and actually fit the job description.

What a sad disappointment she'd turned out to be. Really, no different from my folks.

I'd wasted half of the summer on this beach, trying to be *pure* for Keith, but all I'd gotten was tan. It was my time, now, to embrace my new self.

Looking about, I spotted a hot young guy, eyeing me from his striped towel. I stood, stretching, and let him take a good, long look. He stood as well, making his way past me toward the restroom. Glancing back over his shoulder, we connected, and I knew what he wanted. I followed him in and found him waiting, holding open the door of a stall.

As soon as it latched, without even a "hello" he had dropped down to his knees. Pulling my package from my bikini, he began licking the shaft, swathing it in spit. Soon, he'd begun attempting to take me in his mouth, as difficult as I imagined that'd be to do. I saw him reach down, pulling out his own cock, which looked puny in comparison. I felt sorry for him, in a way, and mild irritation toward him as his teeth gouged my shaft. He didn't seem to realize what a bad cocksucker he was, but I was so horny, I wasn't about to offer instruction.

Staring down at the top of his head, I realized that, aside from the fact that he had brown hair and owned a pair of blue trunks, I knew absolutely nothing about him. In this gay world, it seemed, introductions were entirely superfluous. And yet, as he sucked, I wondered what his name was and where he lived. Was he a fellow student? Did he have a job?

I envisioned myself surprising him at Gelson's, where he probably worked as a bagger. Upon seeing me, he'd offer a gigantic smile, pleased by my spontaneous appearance. His gruff boss would grin, charmed, and nod for him to take a long break. Wandering the store, he would take me down each aisle, pointing out his favorite products and noting their relevance to his life. His childhood baby food. The brand of toothbrush he preferred, and how often he brushed his teeth. His favorite flavor of ice cream, which just happened to be the same as mine, and which we both just happened to enjoy eating straight from the container! I devoured every morsel he shared, and entwined my arm with his as we continued toward Produce.

But our idyll was interrupted by the loudspeaker overhead calling out, "Clean up on Aisle 9!", and I looked down to see stringy strands of semen hanging from my beloved's chin and his accompanying puddle of spooge on the floor. He grinned at me, licking the cum off his fingers.

While I'd wanted to know everything about him mere seconds ago, even going so far as envisioning our future together, he now looked dirty and diseased. There was no desire or longing left, and all I wanted was to leave.

Oblivious, he rose and gave me a quick kiss, which I could not dodge. "My name's Steve," he said.

"How nice for you," I replied evilly. The look he gave told me that he wasn't sure what to make of me and, quite frankly, neither was I.

"So..." he whispered, as another person could be heard peeing at a urinal. "Can I see you again?"

"Thanks—that is so sweet," I smiled. "But I don't think so."

"No—?" He looked confused. "But we just—"

"If you have expectations, Steve, it's better to introduce yourself before you next suck on someone's tool," I warned, polite smile glued to my face. On that, I gave him my best Barbara Stanwyck stare, then unlatched the door, returning to my towel and a forgiving Clare.

As my paramour walked back to his spot, eyeing me, I pointed him out and giggled, cracking some stupid joke to Clare. That he heard me and was crying inside was clearly evident, but I didn't much care. I would be who I was, no pretense.

I'd wanted to become "one of them," and now, it seemed, I was well on my way.

The rest of the summer was filled with much of the same: quick, nameless fucks and empty conversation. Clare accompanied me less and less, and while she always had an excuse, I began to take it personally. Whether she had, in fact, sided with my parents and thought I was a miserable person, or had suddenly turned anti-gay, it dawned that I no longer had anyone in my life.

While I hadn't talked to Keith, I assumed he was still happily ensconced in the arms of Radio Shack Rudy, and I could picture them listening to bands every night, trying to impress each other with the more obscure find. Lenny and Gloria had evidently decided, jointly, that I could not be saved. Instead, Lenny had relented, and they'd begun twice-weekly couples counseling. I was invited to a family session, "Standing invitation!" Gloria chortled, as if it were an opportunity to lunch with the Queen. And Clare continued to keep her distance, leaving me feeling less and less enthusiastic about our quickly approaching Senior year.

I saw her on Senior photo day, seated in front of the photographer, wearing the powder-blue cowl drape mandated for the girls. She saw me and waved, and while I waved back, I couldn't help but notice how majorly retarded she looked, but kept this fact to myself. Having had so much time on my hands, when not getting blown in the bushes, I'd reflected on my friendless state and had come to the realization that Clare and my parents had actually been correct.

I was far too bitter. Looking around, I saw people laughing and smiling, and it was clear that society favored the buoyant clown over people of substance. Somehow, fake joviality was more treasured than truth. And just as I had done with the gay world, I made a pact. I would be cheerful, tell mindless, pithy stories, and laugh loudly at the lamest of jokes. Basically, to win at the game, I'd become everything I hated. It was my only path to survival.

I quickly patched things up with Clare, wooing her, paying attention to her needs, no matter how pedestrian. And, with the onset of school, Clare as well embraced the wisdom of remaining linked to one of Tiger High's brightest stars.

We once again got involved with campus activities, knowing their importance for our college applications. But as busy as we were, it wasn't quite as exciting as it had been the year prior. Perhaps that was because it was new then. Or that our friendship had been more robust. Or maybe we were so busy with Senior Year obligations that we barely enjoyed anything. Or, for me, perhaps it was because listening to Jerry Saunders rant about school spirit wasn't nearly as satisfying as getting it from both ends from a pair of Latino housepainters. Regardless, things had changed.

Pulling myself from that world I'd briefly stepped into, one of hyper-sexuality, was tough, but I knew it couldn't coexist with Tiger High. Still, as I went from class to event to class, I couldn't help but adopt Keith's refrain as my own. "I can't wait to get out."

It was difficult, seeing him each day. He had few friends, keeping others at arm's length, like me. Did we just not trust others, wanting to keep them away from our secret? Or was the truth deeper and murkier? Perhaps we were too raw, emotionally, and fought to protect our hearts from further devastation. Or maybe we were both just really fucked up.

Every now and then, Keith would nod to me, and I would do the same. Despite my vow to erase him entirely from my mind, I still wondered about him. I couldn't help but feel that he and I would've been amazing together. That, in fact, we *had* been perfect, even as friends. When I was with him, I felt whole.

Why then, in my jealousy, when faced with thwarted aspirations, had I chosen to obliterate my only male friend? As I'd been learning all summer long, sex was just sex—nothing more. A purely physical act that could, in fact, be separated from the emotional. There was no reason I couldn't have remained friends with Keith. But my insecurities had killed any chance of that.

I knew, though, that my friendship with Clare could only go so far. Just as sarcasm was my shield, so too were her pithy sayings; both prevented others from getting too close. Plus, by the various comments she'd made, it was clear she thought me emotionally inferior (though that didn't stop her from riding my coattails at school.) She viewed me as damaged, bitter goods, and I wouldn't necessarily say she was incorrect. Keith, on the other hand—. Well, I had no idea *what* he saw me as.

Did he know of my conquests? And, if so, would I have received lower or higher ranking in his eyes? Did he maintain an image of me as sweet and unspoiled? Or had my parting shot at his mother tainted any affection he might have once held?

Regardless, he'd chosen a different path, one that didn't include me. But just knowing that he'd once seen goodness within made me want to reach out. To somehow tap into that light that only Keith had been able to see. It hit me, though, that he was not the only one who had witnessed it. In fact, Clare, Lenny, and Gloria had all been urging, relentlessly, for me to open my eyes to it. But somehow only Keith seemed safe. Only with him could I open up. And soon, I had the perfect excuse.

The Tiger Spirit Team, which I chaired, was doing a Candy

Cane Fundraiser, in honor of the non-religiously specified Winter Holiday. For just one dollar, students could send a candy cane and message to the person of their choosing, and the Spirit Team would deliver them to the recipient the last day before break—the genius in my plan being that our entire team would miss classes for the day.

Spotting Keith during nutrition, I approached, candy canes in hand. "Hey, Keith," I said, far too jovially.

"Hi," he managed, clearly surprised by my greeting.

I continued as if we had, in fact, spoken every day for the past five months. "How's it going?"

"Good, thanks," he volleyed. "And you?"

"Oh, you know—busy!"

"Selling CandyGrams, huh?" he said, noting my clutched hand.

"Right! For that special someone," I offered. "Wanna buy one?

"Nah," he smiled. "Who would I send one to?"

"I guess Rudy is out, huh?" I replied, trying to be nice and supportive and all of that shit. "I mean, given that he graduated high school."

Keith nodded. "Yep, he's out."

"Are—", I couldn't help myself, "are things good there?"

"You mean, with Rudy?"

I nodded.

Perhaps I shouldn't have asked. I mean, it was none of my business. Still, his reply took hours.

"That didn't work out so well," he admitted, head down.

I was filled with immediate and immeasurable joy. "I'm sorry to hear that," I said, as sincerely as I could.

"No, you're not," he laughed. "You would've killed him in his sleep if you'd known where he lived."

"I still would," I offered, "if he hurt you."

He frowned. "It wasn't like that. We're still friends... He just—." Keith looked into my eyes and simply said, "He wasn't you."

At that very moment, the bell rang, and I cursed the Gods of Tiger High for interrupting what should have been a rapturous reunion.

"I—", I stared at the bell, back to him, and then to the forgotten candy canes in my hand. "I don't know what to—."

"Go to class, Gabe," Keith laughed, pushing me away. "And put your jaw back in your mouth. We'll talk later."

The day flew as I moved with renewed purpose. Keith liked me. Well, okay—he didn't say that, exactly. But still, it all added up: Rudy was out of the picture, I sold all of my CandyGrams, and I got an A on my history paper—what else could it be? It was if Santa had come two weeks early, granting my every wish.

Instead of sharing in my joy, Scrooge Clare again found it necessary to warn me of expectations. From my point of view, given that I'd spent the better part of my summer on my knees, any kind of actual relationship was an earned step up. Even if Keith and I remained platonic friends, that in itself would be victory.

Once home, Gloria noticed the lift in my step immediately. "Well, someone sure is in a good mood."

I just nodded and smiled, helping myself to an apple.

"Care to share?" she urged.

"Nope," I said, taking a bite.

"You know, Gabe—that offer still stands."

"What offer?"

"Dr. Gibson said you're welcome to join us anytime. Good news or bad—you have an open invitation."

"Sounds like fun, Gloria. But I have plans."

On that, Lenny entered, stamping his feet, and catching the tail end of our conversation. "I sure hope those 'plans' include helping me with the Christmas lights," he parried, attempting a jovial tone which sounded creepily like Santa.

"Sorry," I said, moving quickly toward my room. "I'm heading over to Keith's."

Even though my back was turned, I could sense the glance my parents exchanged.

As I dressed, a million questions raced through my head. Was Keith finally interested in me romantically, or was he simply looking for friends? What would he think of my summer escapades, and was it even prudent to tell him? What had happened between him and Rudy? What kind of sex did they have? Do these stripes make me look fat?

I tried on a shirt for every changing thought, but as I left, I knew that I looked much the same as when I'd begun: tight jeans and flannel shirt. My butchest apparel, for what I hoped would be a gay-old time.

Arriving at his home, I was happy to see that his dad's car was nowhere in sight, as just seeing Keith was enough tension for one night. Keith greeted me at the door, wearing faded Levis and a Frank Zappa shirt, whoever he was. With a smile, he ushered me in. His brothers, I happily noted, were focused on an episode of *Match Game '76*. Once up in Keith's room, it felt as if we had the entire house to ourselves.

I wondered if we would have sex. I mean, I hoped we would.

Jeez, was that all I cared about? Wasn't reconnecting with my beloved enough? For most people, it probably would be. But, as I was learning, I wasn't most people.

Keith walked directly over to the turntable and changed the album. Turning it on, he clearly wasn't thinking about sex. Or was he? As the album began, with a slow instrumental groove, he turned to me, holding up the cover. Bette Midler's *The Divine Miss M.*

"Remember?" he prompted.

One of the two Bette albums he'd shown me in Palm Springs. I'd vowed to track them down, but—given the fullness of my summer—never had. After all, how can music possibly compete with cock?

The slow groove gave way to Bette, yearning, playful, hopeful... The music was soulful, heartfelt.

Do you wanna dance?

"She's good," I admitted, surprised at how fully I connected with her voice.

"Told you!" Keith grinned, proudly. He settled in next to me on the bed, but far enough away to make clear nothing amorous would occur. "I knew you'd like her," he sighed.

"Because of the bathhouse thing? Like only gay men like

her?"

"Not at all. It's just—", he searched for the right words. "There's something about her, when she sings, some emotional hunger—"

"Hunger?"

"Kind of a naked honesty," he clarified. "Plus, live, she is so funny. Wickedly so. I knew you'd totally connect with that."

"So you've seen her?"

He nodded yes.

"With Rudy?" I couldn't help but ask.

"Does that bother you?"

"I don't know why it should. But, yeah," I admitted. "I was really jealous. Still am, I guess."

"But you've been with other guys, right?" he reminded me.

I nodded, deducing this was not the optimum time to list my extra-curricular summer conquests. "There is a difference, though."

"Yeah?"

"I didn't love them."

Keith was silent. The song had since changed to the jaunty "Chapel of Love," which was entirely too premature for this point in our reunion.

"I don't think I could ever have sex with someone I didn't love," Keith stated.

There was no way I could reply to that. What else had I been doing all summer? To me, it had been recreation, and a hell of a lot cheaper than a season pass to Disneyland. Still, it seemed that either Keith was entirely too naïve about sex, or, worse, I, at 17, was already too jaded.

Either way, I knew that while he and I varied on how we approached sex, emotionally we were on the same journey with the same intentions. The bottom line for both was that we wanted to be loved. Understanding that, I continued.

"I love you, you know."

Keith looked at me, doubtfully. "We haven't spoken in months, Gabe."

"We don't have to speak every day," I argued. "You and I, we have a connection. A bond. And not seeing each other doesn't make that go away."

He nodded, knowing it to be true.

From the stereo, I heard the familiar strains of the Carpenters' hit, "Superstar," but with a totally different vibe. The song was haunting and spare, and when Bette sang *"Lone-li-ness..."* you could feel her heartache. Her performance was revelatory. We sat in silence, listening, as she brought it to a heartrending close.

As the song ended, the album moving into the unnecessary and vapid "Daytime Hustler," I spoke. "I totally get her. It's almost visceral, you know?"

"True," he nodded

"I'm kind of surprised you like her, though."

"Why?"

"I mean, you like, uh—" I gestured to his t-shirt, "that Zappa guy. Or, what was that band? Velvet Underwear?"

"Under*ground*," he laughed, enjoying my subsequent blush. "You know, it's not so much the style of music that I'm drawn to as much as the artistry. The craftsmanship."

"Huh." I reflected back to some of the off-kilter voices he'd made me listen to.

"Take that song, 'Superstar,'" he said, pointing at the turntable. "Everyone on the planet has heard the Carpenters' version, right?"

"Yeah...?"

"But did you know that Richard Carpenter got the idea for their version from seeing Midler sing it on Johnny Carson?"

"Wow."

"I know, right? He turns a scorching song of desperation into a cup of hot cocoa. Granted, she has a pretty voice and all—"

"Pure."

"Right. But that's not artistry. Hitting notes doesn't make you a singer."

I nodded, unwilling to admit my love for Karen.

On that, there was a knock at the door, and Keith's dad popped his head in.

"Time for dinner," he grunted. "I stopped by Kentucky

Fried Chicken and got those little parfaits you like," he said, as Keith gave him one of those 'Dad, do you have to?' looks and his father finally noticed me. "Oh, hey Gabe." I caught his grimace before his covering grin. "Sorry to cut this short," he grunted, not half as sorry as I, "but dinner'll be cold if we don't get to it."

Here I'd been hoping for some hot sex, or at least a grope, but I was left hanging.

As Keith walked me to the door, he turned. "Hey, what are you doing Saturday?" he asked.

"Um, nothing, after the lawn."

"Good. Mow it first thing, and fast," he winked. "There's some place I want to take you."

I hoped that it would be heaven.

That Saturday, I was up and at the lawn by 7:00 a.m., which provoked sleepy, questioning looks from both Lenny and Gloria. As soon as I was done, I ran to my room and stripped, starting the shower. Given the noise it made, I knew there was no risk of anyone hearing as I ripped open the box and read the directions of *Summer's Eve*. The concept of douching seemed odd, but as I had learned at the beach, there was nothing more apt to kill a hot encounter than the entrance of poop.

While I had no singular vision as to where Keith planned to take me, I had convinced myself that it involved a hotel. That this had materialized as the only option seemed wishful thinking, at best. Keith had given no indication that he was leaning that way, and while we'd talked about love and sex, it was more reflective and contemplative than actual foreshadowing. We were speaking as friends again, not potential lovers.

There was no hidden innuendo. No longing glances. Nothing more physical than his hand on the small of my back, ushering me to the door as we said goodbye. Still, where else on earth could he possibly take me? It seemed our destiny.

Driving away from Northridge on first the 134 freeway then the 210, I realized, as we headed east, my hypothesis was likely wrong. He could have easily found any number of out-of-the-way hotels in the Valley or Hollywood where two 17-year-old boys with cash could get a room, no questions asked. But driving through the dreary nothingness of Duarte, Irwindale, and Rancho Cucamonga, it became clear that either Keith had a skewed version of "romantic", or I'd made an entirely incorrect assumption.

Keith kept me entertained the whole way, though, playing a cassette of all the songs he wanted to share with me. Part of me wondered if he'd actually made the tape for Rudy, but I promptly pushed that question aside. It didn't matter; the important thing was that he was playing them for me.

While some were irritating beyond belief, with their scratchy vocals and sharp guitar howls, others surprised me. I can't say that I appreciated them all, but as we traveled, I began to see the through-line that connected them. As he filled me in on the significance of each song, I kept one ear on the music, and one eye on the scenery, trying to figure out our destination.

At some point past Mt. Vernon, I completely gave up. I had no idea what lay ahead, except ugly topography. Later, as we began to curve up into the mountains, signs indicated Lake Arrowhead and Big Bear ahead, but I couldn't imagine that was where we were headed. While it had been a cold December, it hadn't yet snowed, so I didn't think skiing was in our future. And I hadn't a thing to wear if it was.

Keith just smiled, whenever queried, and I began to hate his cavalier outlook.

As we passed the turnoff for Arrowhead, Keith said, "Just a little further", and I began to search for clues. Was there some quaint little chalet he'd booked for our rendezvous? Or maybe he wanted an outdoor scene, where we'd get it on, raw, in the forest?

But as he signaled left, my eyes went wide at what lay in front of me: *Santa's Village*. The parking lot wasn't even half full, although it was noon and should have been the park's busiest time of year.

"Please tell me you're joking," I laughed, taking in the Bumble Bee monorail and the bright-pink roof of the Welcome Center.

Keith looked crushed. I realized that he'd wanted to share this, just as he had his music. *Santa's Village* plainly meant something to him, even if the overall tackiness struck an entirely different chord in me. Keith was trying to connect, to open up, and here I was laughing. Finally comprehending, I smiled warmly and reached over for his hand.

"This is great," I grinned, giving his hand a squeeze. "A little holiday cheer—just what we need!"

Keith smiled back, his blush telling me I was forgiven. I'd have to rein in my fangs, as this 1950's amusement park clearly held sway with him, and I wouldn't let my sarcasm rob him of this moment.

Strolling through the park, Keith shared his recollections, and I found myself drawn to him as never before. Each year at Christmas, his mother had brought him here, before his brothers were even born, and then later continued the annual pilgrimage with Sam and Steven in tow. Their excursions had never included their father, enshrining these sons-and-mother trips in unblemished hues, filled with the scent of pine and sparkling sunlight, dappled through the trees. In the years since, Keith had continued to pay tribute, following her footsteps on this now-hallowed ground.

I imagined what it must have been like to be a kid in this now-fading maze of bright fantasy. There was Mrs. Claus' Kitchen and the Pixie Flower Stand; Mr. Easter Bunny, walking around the petting zoo; Cinderella's giant Pumpkin Carriage; and the sleigh ride, with Santa himself, pulled by four live reindeer. Could, as a child, anything have been more enchanting?

But not having had such memories on which to reflect, to me, everything looked rather sad. I took in the flaking paint on the gigantic striped and polka-dotted mushrooms, the frayed threads on Jack Pumpkinhead's sleeve, and the irritating smirk in the eyes of the pimple-faced redhead ushering us onto the Bumble Bee Monorail.

Perhaps it was the sadness that made me do it, which seemed pervasive. Or maybe it was the glint in the ride operator's eyes, reminiscent of Kid Dollard's. But all that Keith had imparted resonated within me.   He trusted me enough to share these cherished memories, and I wanted to do the same. I needed to show Keith that I, too, could be vulnerable and honest; that there was reason for my armor, and that I could risk as well, putting my faith in him in return.

Whatever the reason, as we climbed into the giant bees and set off on our slow trek high above the giggling children, it all began to tumble forth.

Details were given, disjointed, and incoherently. How Kid and Joey had toyed with me in the locker room, flashing their dicks.   How I'd responded with jokes, laughing about their diminutive size (though I was privately longing to swallow them.) How later, in science, they'd winked and blown kisses. And then, at the end of the day, how they'd cornered me at my locker, making small talk until everyone else had gone.

I stopped myself.

The look on my face must have alarmed him, as Keith immediately reached for me, cupping my cheeks with his hands. Staring directly into my eyes, he focused me.

"It's alright, Gabe. Breathe. Whatever it is, it'll be okay."

Part of me had been scared, not knowing what any of it meant.   But another part was intrigued.   Having the most popular jocks take an interest in me, even in jest, was somehow validating.

We'd first gone to Joey's, but as his house was crawling with little Italian brats, we moved on to Kid's. While Mrs. Dollard asked all the usual questions you'd ask of someone you had just met in your kitchen, Kid and Joey disappeared. I heard a burst of laughter upstairs and longed to run up, but stayed politely glued on my barstool. Soon, they were galloping back down, and I noticed the pack slung over Kid's shoulder.

Once again, we were on the road, and the sun had started its descent. Something in their mood had shifted. There was an insistent purpose in their step, a measure of anticipation, which was both intriguing, and more than a bit scary.

Watching the backpack swing to and fro, I could hear a muffled jingling noise, but had no clue as to what it was.

Whether the pack held sex toys for some fun-filled fantasy, or a machete with which to hack me to pieces, I didn't know, and didn't much care. It felt as if it were out of my hands. Whatever this was, I had become a willing participant.

We ended up back at Tiger High, now deserted. Walking through the back parking lot, we came to rest at the baseball diamond, where Joey had had so much success. Kid and Joey climbed a few rows up into the bleachers, setting the pack down with a clatter as it hit the metal plank.

I moved to join them, but Joey shook his head. "Nah, Gabey," he muttered, much too familiar for my taste. "You just stand. Right there."

He reached for the pack, unzipping it, and pulled out some beers, throwing one to Kid, who just started guzzling. Popping open another, he stood, handing it to me. On opening his, Joey held up his beer to me, nodding in toast.

I drank greedily, letting the coolness quell any anxiety within. With a grin, Joey nestled back on the bench, handing off the lead to Kid. Letting out a belch, Kid stood, smashing his beer can in his hand before tossing it out to the pitcher's mound. I stood on the grass, before them, watching... waiting for instructions.

"So..." Kid let the single word hang in the air, heavy with expectation. "Is it true?"

"What?"

"That you're a homo?" he sneered. In the twilight, the golden shades tanned Kid's face, making it look smoother, removing his freckles. Just his teeth, shining. Though he definitely needed braces, he was still doable. And in this light, he looked even better than usual.

Not knowing where this was headed, and uncertain they did either, I took over. "Am I a homo?" I pondered. With a laugh, I took a swig of beer, then let my tongue linger on the top of the can, lapping up the remains. Licking my lips, I looked right at Kid. "Does that answer your question?"

"You—uh—," Kid shifted on the bench, "suck dick?"

I bent, setting down the can. Straightening, I stood, feet wide apart, and let my fingers lightly caress my crotch. "Depends whose dick."

Kid squirmed, more than a bit uncomfortable. Whether that was due to his line of questioning or my unexpectedly direct answer, I wasn't sure. Joey, on the other hand, stayed completely focused, eyes trained on me. While Kid had been acting like Big Daddy, all bravado and hot air, this foray had clearly been Joey's idea. Something within was turned on, though he would never admit it.

Kid continued, awkwardly. "We've seen you, you know."

"Yeah?"

"Watching us, in the showers."

"So, you're saying, you saw me watching you, which means that you were watching me, too."

Kid stepped towards me, shaking the bleacher, the backpack clinking in response. "We ain't no homos, Travers."

I remained aloof, not wanting this—whatever this was—to get out of hand. "I never said you were."

Eyeing me, Kid once again sat. Joey finally spoke, somewhat softly. "Take off your clothes."

"Excuse me?" I replied, coyly.

He smiled, more broadly. "You heard me, Gabey." On that, Joey winked, then stretched back out against the bleachers. Once settled, he gave a tug on his crotch. "Give us a show."

I looked at both of them. Kid was clearly uneasy, angry even, while Joey seemed completely comfortable, and more than a little stimulated. Even if I got beaten up by Kid, turning on someone as hot as Joey Tatolla was something I could reflect on for years to come.

My eyes aligning with his, I reached up and slowly unbuttoned my shirt. I let a nipple show, then teasingly let the shirt fall to the ground.

"Now the pants," Joey commanded. Kid glanced questioningly, but Joey ignored him. Maybe this wasn't part of the plan. But Joey was the one to please, so I began unbuttoning my Levis, then pushed them down to my knees. With a nudge to both heels, my shoes were quickly discarded and the jeans fully kicked off, landing at Joey's feet.

"The rest," he ordered, as if checking off a list.

I stood for a moment, wondering if I should comply.

"Don't stop now..." Joey insisted.

I bent down, pulled off my black bikinis, and as I did, my penis sprang forth, hard, slapping against my stomach.

"Enjoying this, huh Gabey?" Joey laughed. I wished he could find some other, less intimate, name to call me. 'Faggot' would have been preferable.

"See, Kid?" he continued. "Now *that* is a boner. Jeez."

Even Kid was impressed. "If you were a girl with a dick like that," he laughed, "you'd have a pussy as big as the Grand Canyon."

Funny, Kid, I noted to myself. *Clumsy, but funny.* Standing there, buck-naked, I wondered if their plan included more than this. Had they just wanted a strip show? Or to actually touch the merchandise?

The sunlight was cresting, and just about gone. I looked around at the empty field, wondering if anyone was watching this. Getting off on us. On me. I looked again at Kid and Joey, who evidently weren't certain of the next move. But since we'd come all this way, and yet not cum, I figured it was my duty to take the lead.

Reaching down, I took my dick in my hand, letting my fingers graze my cockhead. I could feel a bit of pre-cum seeping out, and gently massaged it into my skin. As they watched me in the fading light, I could tell that Joey was stroking himself, almost imperceptibly, through his jeans. Kid alternated between watching me, and looking to Joey for guidance. But Joey, transfixed, never acknowledged him.

I turned profile and encircled my rod with one hand, then the next, showing off just how big it got, fully engorged. Turning again, face forward, I toyed, "Time's a wastin' guys." I sighed, "You like what you see?"

Kid again erupted, "I told you, Travers—we ain't no homos!"

"Then what are we doing here, huh?" I challenged, looking to Joey. "I'm standing here, dick out, and you two have your tongues out like little puppies."

Kid stood, ready for a fight, but Joey just laughed at me. "You think you got this all figured out, huh? Hoping to get into our pants, is that it?"

I held his gaze.

"I'll give you a taste, if that's what you want." I didn't move, unsure if he was kidding. Joey grabbed his crotch, full of swagger, and nodded me toward the bleachers. "Come on."

Kid squinted at Joey, and it was clear he thought Joey had gone too far.

Eyes connected with Joey, I climbed, fully naked, up the benches to just below where he sat. When I reached him, he stood onto the bench, my eyes directly level with his crotch. He looked as if he had a thick steel pipe in there, and I was damn well ready to turn on the faucet.

Grabbing hold of my head, he pulled me roughly into his groin, rubbing my face brutally against the strained denim. As I buried my head into him, trying to work my mouth over his clad shaft and take some part of him into my mouth, I felt Kid's hands gripping me from behind, pulling me off Joey.

"Not so fast, fag," he yelled. "Joey ain't gay."

"You could've fooled me," I spat before feeling a bash as Kid's fist connected with my head. Flung to the side, I crumpled against the metal bleacher, which was cold against my bare skin. Kid remained standing above, shoving his boot onto my shoulder.

"Don't move," he commanded.

I wasn't about to. The game had changed, suddenly, to one I was unprepared to play. Without moving, I assessed myself for injuries, but found nothing wounded, aside from pride.

While Kid pinned me with his foot, Joey moved to the backpack. Unzipping it, he pulled out a glass Mason jar, half-filled with pennies. What the fuck were they doing with Kid's piggybank?

Looking at me, then to Kid, Joey grinned. "Ready, Gabey?"

Kid just laughed. "Do it, Joey! Come on, man!"

I watched as Joey unzipped, pulling out his erect cock. Eyes focused on mine, Joey held the jar with one hand and pushed his dick down with the other, sending forth a steady stream of piss into the waiting jar. Even in the dim light, I could see the urine seeping through the pennies, filling each crevice, until the jar was almost full.

"There," Joey said, slipping his penis back into his pants, as if that was it.

"Good job, Joey," Kid praised, sounding exactly as I imagined he did on the football field after a particularly fine play. Joey approached, handing the jar to Kid.

I looked up at each, and the jar offset by the last rays of twilight. I remember thinking, oddly, that with its amber hue, the glass almost looked like it held honeycomb.

Kid released his boot from my shoulder, then squatted over to me until we were face to face. Without the sun, his face took on bluish hues, making his teeth look more yellow and his freckles more pronounced, like deep craters on the moon. He didn't look pretty anymore.

I tried to think of a way out, a way to escape, or a funny remark, anything to diffuse the situation.

"Please, guys," I insisted, still not sure what they were planning. "Enough is enough, right?"

"Not quite," Kid muttered, holding the jar in front of me. "Drink."

"No way," I gasped.

"You fucking faggot," Kid growled, "I said, drink!" He pushed the jar hard into my firmly clenched mouth, almost chipping a tooth, and I could feel some of the warm spilt piss dripping down my chin. Twisting, I tried to push away before feeling Joey's hands brusquely forcing me into place. I wanted to scream, but all I could feel was bile, surging up in my throat.

"Drink," Kid demanded, roughly shoving it against my mouth. I could feel something dripping from my lips, and realized it wasn't piss, but my own blood. I twisted and writhed as Joey's fingers worked their way around my head, trying to pry open my mouth.

With a grunt, Kid sent a strong knee into my groin, and the pain forced a cry from my mouth, which was soon filled with urine.

I could sense the world swirling around me as my mouth filled with the seedy, primal mix of blood and piss.

But as I sputtered and spit, I remember thinking, "You asked for this, fucker. It really isn't all that different from what you did with Hy. Stop complaining. This is your life now."

Just then, headlights swept across our bodies, as a car pulled into the lot. Kid kneed me once more before grabbing his pack, bolting across the field. Joey hesitated, then picked up the forgotten jar, pouring out the remains and pennies onto my chest. I detected a slight flicker of satisfaction in his eyes before he, too, ran.

The beams again swept over me as the car pulled next to the bleachers. Looking through the slats, my naked body illuminated and exposed in the unremitting glare, I peered out to see my father's face.

I tried to cry out, hoarsely, still spitting the vile brew from my mouth. We locked eyes, and I pleaded, silently begging for help. Tears came, mixing further with the blood and piss. But he just stared. Struggling, I tried to pull myself up, to yell, but before I knew it, Lenny had turned. In a mere instant, he had the car in reverse, gunning it out of the parking lot.

My body wet, sour, and sticking with pennies, I watched as the red tail lights receded into darkness. Forever more would I equate their fierce, steely redness with the beady derision I'd felt, staring into my father's unforgiving eyes.

Somehow Keith and I had ended up on a bench opposite the whirling Christmas Tree ride, whose giant ornaments rose up and down as the tree twirled, taking their occupants to dizzying heights. The rest of the details, the police arrival, my return home, were recited; mere afterthoughts.

Taking in the laughing children, screaming in delight, their innocence struck a chord. Why would God bless a child with naiveté, only to take such capacity away? How could God be so cruel as to punish us so? It was one thing to challenge, to test, but quite another to crush.

I had no answers.

Why pennies? And why the pee? None of it made any sense. A beating would have been easier. But something told me that violence alone would not have been enough. They wanted not just to harm, but to vanquish, obliterate. And they succeeded, perhaps more fully than even they had imagined.

Keith continued to support me in a solicitous manner as we made our way back to the car. He was quiet, but—truly—what was left to say?

Clearly, I'd ruined his visit.   Here he'd wanted to share something cherished, and my outpouring likely killed whatever affection he had held for this place, or for me.

The drive home was quiet, save for Keith's cassette, filled with forlorn and ragged voices, when all I wanted right now was show tunes or Christmas carols.

Pulling into my drive, he put the car in park and I turned to face him. "I'm sorry."

"Sorry?" he asked, clearly surprised. "For what?"

"Everything."

"For being honest? For sharing with me? There's nothing to be sorry about."

"I ruined the trip."

"No, you didn't," Keith shook his head. "Don't even think that. This trip was perfect. You opened up to me in a way you never have. I value that you—felt enough about me to trust me with this. It means a lot."

He leaned over and gave me a big hug. Over his shoulder, I could see Lenny peering out at us through the curtains. I wanted to lift my middle finger to him—both for tonight and that night. *You are heartless*, I say in my head. *You are a heartless, selfish, no-good, mother-fucking father. I hope you rot.*

Keith released me and tried to smile. "You okay now?"

I nodded, then started to open the door.

"Hey Gabe," Keith stopped me.

"Yeah?"

"I'm gonna be pretty busy the next couple weeks—"

"Oh?"

"Penney's, you know. Holiday hours."

"Cool," I shrugged.

"Gotta make a little Christmas cash, right?" he grinned.

"Okay," I concurred, knowing that this was just his way of putting some distance between us.   I'd shared too much, unwisely, in my inexperienced attempt at intimacy.   The friendship was over.

As I stepped from the car, he gave a quick smile, which must've taken every ounce of fortitude. "You take care, Gabe."

I found a smile to return. "You too."

"And happy holidays!" he yelled, much too genially, as he waved and headed off down the street.

I stood watching until he was out of sight. My hopes and dreams were gone, as quickly as that.

Keith once again out of my life, I turned back toward the house. As I did, another image from that day flashed before me—one I'd conveniently forgotten.

It was dark when the policeman had driven me home, but I could sense our neighbors staring from their windows as he escorted me to the door. The blanket around my shoulders did little to quell my shivers, and the stench from the piss turned my stomach. Still, "presentation counts" running through my head, I tried to saunter up the steps, as if there were nothing out of the ordinary about any of this.

As the policeman rang the bell, Gloria appeared, ushering me inside. She thanked the man politely, as if he was a chauffeur, before firmly closing the door.

Inside, I waited for her to rush to me, open arms, and tell me that everything would be okay. I waited, but she faced the door. As she straightened herself, I knew that I would not receive the comfort I sought. Slowly, she turned, looking me up and down with a resigned sigh. "Gabriel Charles, what have you gotten yourself into now?"

For a moment, I thought I'd misheard her. That in the confusion and turmoil, my ears had somehow short-circuited. I stared, waiting for her to respond as a mother should. I heard the screech of the garage door opening, which meant my father had finally come home.

Hearing it as well, Gloria instinctively wiped her hands on her dress, as if she herself was the one covered in urine.

"You'd better shower," she noted crisply, before heading to her room. "You look like hell."

I had two long, empty weeks ahead of me. Winter break held Christmas and New Years, to be sure, but even they promised little satisfaction this year. Having to sit through both with Lenny and Gloria seemed almost too much to bear. Clare cornered me into last-minute Christmas shopping, to which I agreed, though there was nothing I detested more. Still, it was a diversion and got me out of the house.

I made several trips to my favorite bookshop, where I bought every porn magazine they stocked. I'm sure that, amongst themselves, the shopkeepers noted their concern for the well-being of my obviously abused member. Still, I didn't care.

Sometimes I'd sit outside in my car, and watch the people entering, particularly the men. Which were gay? Which were into porn? Which would eventually love me?

Christmas morning arrived with plodding nonchalance; free from surprises or genuine happiness. We suffered through an early dinner, saved by a decent ham, as well as Gloria's characteristic monologue. Later, as I shut my door, I took stock of my life and tried to find something good about it. My life was shit, without a silver lining. *But it's shit of your own choosing, Gabriel,* a voice said. *Make better decisions; correct past mistakes.*

While I perceived the wisdom in the words, I still pushed them away. I deserve better, I thought.

I was about to undress when I heard the doorbell ring and Gloria's high-pitched greeting. After a moment, there was knock on my door.

Opening it, I was taken aback to find Keith standing there, flushed cheeked and grinning, hands held behind him. "Merry Christmas, Gabe!" he sang.

I put on my happy face, which was admittedly happy. "Merry Christmas to you!"

"So how was it, huh? Good holiday?" he entered, careful to keep his body angled so that I couldn't see what he had hidden.

"Oh yeah," I lied. "It was great. Tube socks and pajamas—every gay boy's dream."

He laughed, "Man, I love this time of year, you know? I mean, not just the gifts, but—just hanging out with folks you love." Grinning, he continued, "Which brings me to this!" Pulling out his hands with a flourish, he presented a brightly-wrapped package, complete with bow.

"Wow," I appraised. "Very professional."

"Aw, you know—," he reddened, "one of the perks of working at Penney's. Free gift wrap." He placed the package in my hands. "For you."

Flattered that he'd thought of me, I took it, looking over the perfectly square, 12-inch-by-12-inch package, as flat as a pancake. "Wonder what it could be?" I held it to my ear and shook it.

"You prick," he laughed. "You already know what it is. Now you have to guess what album it is."

"Hmm... Let's see. It's likely to be someone who can't hit a note to save their life," I offered. "Which would include almost any album you've ever played me."

"Nice," he said. "Glad to see how much you've enjoyed my company."

I nudged his foot with mine. "You know I'm kidding, right?"

"No, you're not!" he laughed. "But that's one of the reasons I love you."

Through the smile painted on my face, thoughts flooded my: Did he say *love*? Was he joking? I looked at him quizzically.

"Just open the damn thing." At his prompting, I did just that. "It's Bette Midler," he said as I pulled the album out. "It's her latest one. I figured you didn't have it yet."

"*Songs for the New Depression*," I read.

"It's not as great as her others," he said as I looked the album over. "But it still has some fucking amazing songs."

The cover seemed at odds with the artistic simplicity of her past covers. There was nothing beautiful or refined about it. It showed Bette as a bag lady, walking past a gigantic poster of Bette the star, on which the bag lady had just painted a mustache.

"I don't get it," I admitted, scratching my head.

"She's being ironic. Trying, at least. Pointing out the foibles of fame."

"Huh." I crossed to my stereo and removed the shining black vinyl from its sleeve, placing it carefully onto the turntable.

Keith curled up on my bed and patted the spot next to him. I sat, and as we listened to the music we chatted, getting caught up.

The songs were an odd grab bag, as if someone had, without regard, pulled them from a hat and thrown together the album. Some were okay, some downright strange. But also within lay "Shiver Me Timbers," which would become my all-time favorite. As it faded, replaced by the playful, made-up French of "Samedi et Vendredi", I confessed, "I wasn't sure I'd see you again."

"Me? Why?"

"After Saturday, my confession..."

"You say that as if it's something to be ashamed of."

"Isn't it?"

"A confession is for something *you* have done. But being attacked—there is nothing consensual about that and nothing remotely worth apologizing for."

"I went along."

"But at one point, Gabe, you stopped and said 'no.' And from that moment forward, it was an attack, no matter how you cut it. It was a brutal assault."

"That's not the way the police saw it."

"Fuck the police! This was violence."

"I wish I could believe that," I said, almost in a whisper. "It would be so much easier."

"You have to, Gabe," Keith avowed. "And you need to talk about it. Let it out. Otherwise, it will destroy you. Burn up all that goodness."

I looked down at my feet, thinking not only of that night, but of all my exploits since. "I'm not good."

"Oh, you are, Gabe," he said, taking my hand. "You are good, in so many ways." I started to protest, but he shushed me. "You have such talent—your writing, leadership—hell, everything! You have such passion. And all in one amazingly sexy package."

I blushed, wanting so much to believe him.

He stood, crossing to the stereo, and lifted the arm. Flipping the record to the B side, he moved the needle to the last song.

"Listen to this," he gently instructed. "It's why I bought the album in the first place."

A few introductory notes on the guitar were soon joined by Bette's plaintive vocals. She sang of love, and the desire she felt, so near her beloved, that simply the proximity eased her troubled mind. She wanted nothing more, it seemed, than to just follow behind.

"You hear that?" Keith pointed to the speakers. "That longing? Loving someone so much that just following behind would be enough? That's you, Gabe. That's how I feel about you."

As the music played, I could scarcely believe the words I was hearing. The person I'd longed for and given up all hope of, was beside me, telling me that I was loved.

Bette continued singing as Keith leaned forward, offering a soft, tender kiss. Pulling back slightly, he steadily held my gaze.

This gentle, kind soul sees something good within me. And if he sees it, it must be true.

Perhaps Keith was my prize, a reward, for the pain I'd endured. Perhaps God had a plan all along.

As the record reached the end and the needle began its aimless circling, Keith and I sat, staring into each other's eyes. Everything would be alright.

EPILOGUE

AT TWILIGHT, with the crowds dispersing, pulled inside by white linen tablecloths and untamed streaks of neon, Paris is breathtaking. The wind whips my ears, and I wrap my scarf even tighter. In the distance, Sacré-Coeur beckons, inviting me to explore Montmartre and its many winding streets. It is too strong an offer to pass up.

Perhaps I'll wander the fabric district first. Or I could watch the tourists too cheap to purchase tickets snap pictures of themselves in front of the twirling Moulin Rouge. Better yet, the sex shops could be fun. But as I can no longer join, they might not be the fun they once were.

That's the scary thing about death. I anticipated the tranquility. The slightly-elevated sense of being. But not the longing.

It seems almost too mortal to think about men, and the way they taste, and the way Jon looked as he stepped from the shower, water dripping. Though I can see and hear everything around me, there will never more be reason to smell, touch, taste. To be in this world, with all its wonders, and yet separated, may be more than I can bear. But once you're dead, suicide is pretty much out.

Staring at the city below, I focus on the rows of homes surrounding the tower. In each, families prepare for dinner, enjoying the last hours of the day. And, for a moment, each window seems to hold the face of someone I know. That I have loved. Or killed.

Jon. Gloria. Lenny. Clare. Pastor Sally. Jasper. Charlie. Debi. Keith. And a sea of others, filling each window in view. The faces turn to me, questioning.

I stare, helplessly, unable—or perhaps unwilling—to respond.

Will I ever see them again, these souls I have loved? Will I fly over them, unseen; fluttering about as they continue with their lives, with me as protector and guardian?

Though that would be intriguing, I don't feel as if I've been imbued with any special wisdom or knowledge. And something tells me that I would not be the best candidate for this, given my track record while living.

I stand, staring at the beckoning faces, and wonder what they want.

I wish I knew what my role is to be. Is this some form of purgatory? Am I to atone? To wander? Am I merely a voyeur? I certainly can't sprinkle fairy dust or grant wishes. Instead, I am calm. And, for me, remarkably subdued.

As I focus, staring only into the eyes of Jon, who loved without reservation or demand, unselfishly, I sense that, one by one, red curtains are being drawn on the windows surrounding. I want to stop them; to call out, hysterically, for my friends to stay, even a moment longer. But a slow leaching has begun, drawing my family, my friends, away.

Jon's eyes hold mine, and I know that he, though not religious, is praying. Wishing me Godspeed.

Not breaking his gaze, I nevertheless detect red curtains

enveloping him, bearing my beloved fleur-de-lis, a sign of peace and purity. The drapes shift slightly, and I know that it is time for him to go.

That I should never touch him again, hold him, encircle him in my arms... I touch two fingers to my lips, blowing down a kiss, for him to lock deep within, for the coming days and years in which he will need it.

The scarlet curtains bear down, extinguishing my view. I stand; for how long I am not certain. Until my chest, I notice, is not quite so heavy. Still, I do not move.

Where am I to go? What am I to do?

My moment is broken by the opening of the elevator doors, spewing a more sparse set of tourists out onto the deck. I think of leaving, but am stopped by the sudden sight of a young couple, silhouetted by the setting sun. So caught up in their *joie de vivre* that they notice no one, I am struck by their youth, their innocence. I wish that I was indeed their fairy godmother, so quickly would I wave my wand, willing their buoyant and carefree spirit to be with them always. Instead, I stare as long as I dare, hoping their boundless elation will spill over into my soul, filling it again with life. I pause, checking myself for some inner change. But I remain almost desperately empty.

Shaken, I eventually turn from the couple, stepping into the elevator. As the doors close resolutely, framing the young couple in twilight, I pray that they always hold their joy as sacred, to be remembered even when they can no longer feel it. That they will treasure each other, and treat each other respectfully, for as long as their love shall last. And, finally, I ask God to restore in me a small measure of emotion.

What I wouldn't give to once again experience such brazen, all-embracing delight. To hold Jon in my arms, heart racing, and say nothing. Just to feel a flicker of sunshine, a spark, some reminder, of our love. A love that lingers, now only as memory.

The weight, the truth of it, I am no longer capable of feeling.

And if all feeling is gone, I ask myself, what, then, remains?

With a jolt, the elevator completes its descent, doors opening. The influx of wind sends the sounds and regrets of Paris coursing through me and, pulling my jacket tighter against my throat, I step into the waiting city to begin my life anew.

ACKNOWLEDGEMENTS

THIS OVER 12 YEAR JOURNEY, from inception to completion, has been made easier through the support, ideas, guidance, and feedback of Heidi Arden, Jacy Crawford, Vicki Harper, Robert Michael Morris, Eric Nicoll, Charles Perez, Patrick Tobin, Michael Vaccaro, and Roxane Yballe. Special thanks to Scott Council for his expert photography, with assist by James James, Rebecca Johnson for her copy-writing skills, Russ Noe for his cover design, and to Joan Werblin, for her thorough notes and analysis.

While a work of fiction, *Songs for the New Depression* was inspired by the life and passions of Shane Michael Sawick, who died in 1995, far too young. I would not be the writer, father, or person I am without having known him. He changed my life—and me—for the better, and I am forever grateful.

On a daily basis, I am fed and nurtured through the support of my family, who give me endless joy, encouragement, and laughter. To Russ Noe, and Mason and Marcus Edwards-Stout, you have my heart, and I feel so fortunate to have such a circle of love surrounding me.

Finally, to all those we've lost to AIDS, you live on in the souls of all who remember...

KERGAN EDWARDS-STOUT is an award-winning director, author and screenwriter, and was honored as one of the Human Rights Campaign's 2011 *Fathers of the Year*. *Songs for the New Depression* marks his debut novel, with shorter works appearing in such journals and magazines as *American Short Fiction* and *SexVibe*. Kergan lives in Orange, California, with his partner and their two sons. He is currently at work on a forthcoming memoir, *Never Turn Your Back on the Tide*, and blogs regularly at www.kerganedwards-stout.com.

BOOK CLUB QUESTIONS FOR
SONGS FOR THE NEW DEPRESSION

Songs for the New Depression is a work of literary fiction and the debut novel by Kergan Edwards-Stout. To help generate discussion, the following questions have been created to help guide your book club.

What specific themes did the author emphasize throughout the novel?

How realistic were the characterizations? Can you relate to their predicaments? Do you identify with any of the characters and, if so, how?

What passage from the book stood out to you?

The lead character, Gabe, makes several key moral decisions which greatly impact his future. What are they, and what motivates his choices? Would you have made the same decisions? Why? Why not?

The author chose a non-chronological structure, with three main sections, each covering different phases of Gabe's life. Why do you think he chose to tell the story in such a way? Do you think that was the appropriate way to tell it?

Did any parts of the book make you uncomfortable? If so, why did you feel that way? Did this lead to a new understanding or awareness of some aspect of your life you might not have thought about before?

The author chose certain symbols and imagery to highlight key moments, some of which were repeated throughout the novel. Why images stood out as being symbolically significant? Do the images help to develop the plot, or help to define characters?

In what ways do the events in the books reveal evidence of the author's world view? What do you think he is trying to communicate to the reader?

Overall, would you recommend this book to other readers? To your close friends?

Never Turn Your Back on the Tide

A Memoir by Kergan Edwards-Stout

"If truth be told, and it always should, I was taken in by the view, as so many others, both before and since. For me, it wasn't the sea which proved my downfall, but a pair of eyes. Eyes, specifically, made to drown in."

Imagine thinking you had the ideal life. The perfect partner, on whom you relied and trusted. An infant child, newly adopted. You'd given up your job, to take care of your child, to ensure that he had a terrific life.

Then one day, you wake up, and instead of the life you've been living, you spot an email, not intended for you, with this text, blinking at you from your computer screen: "Rich is so good with my son."

Suddenly, the life you've led is turned upside down. Everything thought true becomes suspect. And you learn, quite quickly, that you can never again trust the person sleeping beside you.

If Kergan Edwards-Stout's life was a *Lifetime* movie, surely he would be played by Valerie Bertinelli, and his husband played by Harry Hamlin or some other charming hunk. But life is far more subtle than that. And the truth even more disturbing—for that email discovery was only the beginning.

Like the wash of the waves, crashing onto the beach, you never know if the tumult will bring glittering riches, highlighted by the sun, or dark, murky residue of questionable origin.

CPSIA information can be obtained at www.ICGtesting.com
Printed in the USA
LVOW07*1521141113

361319LV00019B/139/P